Dena Hunt

Wiseblood Books

Printed in the United States of America

Set in Baskerville Typesetting

Cover Design by L. Maltese

ISBN-13: 978-1-951319-07-6

Fiction / Literary

Wiseblood Books
Belmont, North Carolina
www.wisebloodbooks.com

CONTENTS

The following stories originally appeared in *Dappled Things*:

"Pear Trees," 2008

"The Salvation of Glorianne," 2008

"Bienville," 2009

"The Funeral," 2009

"Lavabo," 2010

"A Train in Germany," 2011, nominated for Pushcart

The following stories originally appeared in *The Pilgrim Journal*:

"Retreat," 2011

"Catherine's Garden," 2011

"Love in Coolidge County," 2013

Acknowledgements

Writing requires the contribution of many people: those who encourage, as well as those who read and provide feedback—both positive and negative. If I were to list all the people who helped to produce *Jazz & Other Stories,* the list would be too long to print. Unique among those who deserve my gratitude is Michael Morow, lawyer, writer, critic, and lover of literature. Michael was an admirer of my first novel, *Treason* (Sophia Institute Press), and wrote a glowing review. It turns out that he'd kept track of other published works, and at a time when I'd ceased to produce anything, mainly because *Jazz* had lain dormant for two years for lack of a reader, he emailed to ask if I had something in the works. I told him about my abandoned novella. Because he read, commented, encouraged, and didn't stop despite his advancing cancer, I finished it. I am grateful I was able to travel to Indiana, where I met him and his wonderful wife, Jewell, about two months before he passed. *Jazz* is dedicated to his memory.

Pear Trees

She had that kind of slightly plump whiteness that needed only bare arms or stockingless legs on a new spring day to look suddenly, even startlingly, naked. Her eyes, round, slightly protruding, a pale blue and rather watery, stared into the shop window at the little black dress, so strangely out of place among the bright pastels. The smooth baby-pink edges of her heels made a little sucking sound against the soles of her backless shoes as she went inside. Why did she want this dress? Why did she want to wear this piece of mourning on this bright spring day? It seemed right. Who—or what—had died?

It was a fit. Slinky, clinging, but very modest, really. A high-necked halter style, no cleavage, but bare-shouldered. It looked rather good. The saleswoman seemed impressed. "Oh, your shoulders look fantastic!" It was only eighty dollars. She'd wear it to dinner that night with Patrick. Gorgeous Patrick, so intelligent, a columnist for the *Atlanta Constitution*, known and admired by everybody. He was a defender of women's rights. His column on abortion was still quoted by Jenn, her roommate. "When those men in those red beanie caps and long dresses around the Vatican have to experience the pain, the agony, of any woman in childbirth, they will have the right to speak about abortion…" Something like that, anyway. To be Patrick's partner, his lover, was cause for self-congratulation. It gave her renown being seen with him, having people know that they slept together, that she was his choice, his woman. *His woman*? What an expression. She surprised herself again.

The little piece of black cowered in the bottom of the hot-pink plastic shopping bag. Yes, it was a mourning dress, even if it was a sexy one. Her own response to spring. Spring always depressed her. Bright green budding leaves, tulips shouting red, rows of singing yellow jonquils, full of exuberance under sprays of pure, blinding-white dogwood, so full of promise, so full of empty promise.

*

"I don't see anything." Dr. Cooper drew his head back, turning on the light above the examining chair. "I don't know what the problem is. When do you see this cloudiness?"

"All the time."

"Not just in the morning when you wake up—or when your eyes are tired?"

"No. Actually, I see more clearly when I first wake up. It's later that this white fogginess seems to creep in from the sides, toward the center."

"Well, I can see no cause, no clinical cause anyway. I could prescribe a moisturizer for your eyes, but you'd do just as well with something over the counter. Try that for a while and see if it improves."

*

That was a week ago. Her vision had not improved; in fact, it was worse. She looked at the Bradford pear trees lining Kay Boulevard as she walked back to her Decatur apartment. *That* was it—the stupid pear trees. They were a hybrid; very popular with landscapers because of their perfectly formed, consistently shaped branches, their white blossoms in spring, and mainly because they bore no messy fruit. They were the problem; with their white clouds of blossoms, they were encroaching on her vision. White cloudiness around the periphery, steadily diminishing her sight, so that she could see only what was directly in front of her, taking away the context for her vision. And every day, on her way to work, shopping, wherever she went, she had to navigate her way through these hybrid, white cloud trees.

*

She twisted her frosted martini glass between her fingers. Patrick was late. He was often late. Was he still angry with her? There wasn't any particular reason she knew of for his being late tonight. Yes, he was probably late because he was still angry. She watched a businessman eating alone at the table in front of her, apparently not so impressed by his dinner as to put aside the folded-up newspaper he was reading. Was he reading Patrick's column? She wondered why she was more curious about what the man was reading than about why Patrick was late. The man shoved his plate aside, removed his glasses and wiped them with a napkin. She could see what he was reading—the stock market pages.

Yes, he was angry—still. She tried to muster some anxiety about that and found that she was unable to, that Patrick's anger had been relegated to the side-clouds, ever receding from her view. For the moment anyway, as she watched this unknown businessman in his gray suit, pale blue shirt, and striped tie, for the moment, she even had some difficulty remembering the scene that had angered Patrick last week:

"I just don't want to."

"But I do it for you."

"Yes, I know but I don't want you to."

"Why not?"

"I don't like it."

"That's ridiculous—you've always liked it."

"No, I haven't. I just knew that you did."

"But you like it when I do it for you."

"No—no, I don't like that. I just knew you did."

Oh, yes, he was angry. Bemused by the striped tie of the businessman, she wondered if Patrick was more angry about the possibility that he'd "read" her wrong than he was about the argument. She guessed it would be irritating to find that after a year of frequent sex, he had not been sending her to the stars after all. Anyway, she tried very hard to bring the subject into her focused thoughts, but it wouldn't go; it stayed on the foggy edges, and the businessman's tie, the frost on the glass, and now the burnt orange cocktail napkin consumed all her attention. Burnt orange with Matisse-style lettering: *Johnny's.* A trendy place, very popular. Lots of noise. It seemed that all "good" restaurants these days were noisy, with waiters yelling at busboys, at cooks—who were, often as not, cooking on an open grill in the dining room—dishes clattering, lots of noisy bustle, customers talking, laughing loudly. She hated eating in a noisy atmosphere. She hated Johnny's, actually. How could that man read in all this noise?

A waiter looked meaningfully at her. They wanted her to order, they wanted this table, and they were wondering if her date had stood her up. She ordered another martini and studied the yellow rose in the center of the tiny black lacquered table, dainty and delicate, looking oddly contained in a sleek stainless steel vase. Patrick had sent her a dozen roses last fall from New Orleans when she'd had the abortion. He was there to write a piece on the racism of the Bush administration being responsible for the deaths of thousands of people. He hoped for a Pulitzer on that one, but there were too many others like it, too much competition. There were a dozen deep red roses. Jenn put them in her bedroom on the dresser, but she moved them out to the living room. They looked like blood, a great blood clot. Just a blood clot, a living one, yes, but just a clot. When Patrick called, she told him about the Women's Clinic, how they told her it would be painless, how excruciatingly painful it was, how there were little cell-like rooms all in a line down a long corridor, each one just big enough to contain a treatment table, a stool for the doctor, and a vacuum apparatus. So many, many little rooms, the doctor rushing down the corridor to spend a few minutes in each little room for the procedure, like an assembly-line operator. She thought Patrick might want to write about it—no one ever did, so he wouldn't have the competition he was having with the Katrina disaster and Bush administration. He wasn't interested, though. The steel vase was like a piston chamber.

Three tables away George Paccheo was drinking with two companions, getting drunk, by the sound of the raucous laughter. George was a friend of Patrick's, gregarious, one would call him, politely.

Twenty minutes. Very late. Why did Johnny's line the walls with mirrors? Did they think everyone wanted to watch themselves eat? On the wall opposite she could see her milk-white bare shoulders on each side of the black halter dress, her light brown curls dipping into the white neck. Then the clouds closed in; she could only see her black dress, the black table-top, and the rose, all the rest was consumed in fog. The businessman between her and the mirrored wall was smiling, reading the comics. The picture of such a serious-looking man reading comics made her smile too.

George was very loud. He'd spotted her, waved, and yelled a greeting. She smiled and waved back. She didn't like George. He was a sports writer at the *Constitution*, and she didn't like sports, so she always thought that was the reason she didn't like him. They simply had nothing in common. She was a copywriter for Houghton-Mifflin, not an exciting job, she knew, but a job. At 33, she should have advanced in the publishing business by now, but she lacked ambition. Her work was adequate, sometimes quite good, but she was always passed over for promotion; worse than that, she didn't mind.

She saw Patrick turning the corner from the entrance alcove. He could see her but he didn't look her way; instead, he stopped and chatted with someone, then moved to George's table, where he stopped and talked for a while. She began to wonder if he'd seen her. Yes, he had, he knew where she was, how long she'd been waiting. Patrick was going to break off with her, she realized suddenly. For a moment, a little pain hit her heart. He was gorgeous, fashionably gorgeous. His black hair was combed behind his ears and met the top of the collar of his gray tweed jacket. He wore a white tee-shirt underneath and faded jeans. His perfect white teeth flashed in the middle of the dark beard-stubble. Why were men doing that now? Why were they not clean-shaven? It was fashionable to have a day or two's growth on their cheeks. Patrick was fashionable. The businessman in front of her was clean-shaven with unfashionably smooth cheeks.

Oh, damn. George was coming to the table with Patrick. Good Lord, he was staggering, really drunk. Why would Patrick bring him to the table in that condition? Damn. She focused on Patrick's face, and the clouds closed in.

Beard-stubble brushed her upturned cheek, a waiter darted to the table to take Patrick's martini order, and then everything stopped.

"My God," Patrick said, "you look fucking gorgeous."

"Hey," said George, "the question is does she look gorgeous fucking?"

Patrick grinned and sat down in the chair next to her. George drew up a chair opposite her—then changed his mind. Water filled her lap as the bud vase overturned. George leaned over the table and his tongue was in her mouth. The table tilted, the martini glass overturned and rolled to the floor. She could no longer see anything at all. She drowned in helpless revulsion. The clouds covered her.

The unexpectedness of violence—not its noise—stilled the air, thinned it, making breathing difficult. Table and chairs were overturned and George was on the floor with a gray-suited knee on his chest, blood gushing from his nose. Patrick was standing a few feet away, his mouth hanging open in dumb surprise. No one moved. The sudden silence seemed to paralyze the room. She sat as she was, looking down at George, at the gray leg. The waiters stood frozen. There was no movement anywhere until the smooth and ruddy cheek turned to look up at her through wire-framed glasses, where she sat, still and silent, waiting. And long afterward, when she tried, she could never explain or even understand how it was that his eyes banished all the clouds from her own, so that she saw everything at once with laser-like clarity—how she knew in an instant that whoever he was, she was; whatever his name was, it would be her own. She belonged to him.

The Salvation of Glorianne

Brother Bob stood behind the pulpit and read the Scripture slowly and sorrowfully: "My God, my God, why hast Thou forsaken me?" The sleeves of his white shirt were rolled up so the golden curls covering his thin arms showed when he raised the open Bible. He had been preaching for over an hour. The shirt was wet almost all over with sweat. His red curly hair was combed back into an oily ducktail with curls on top and a single small corkscrew curl falling down on his forehead. His eyes were light blue, and they could look icy-mean sometimes. That's why Glorianne thought he must be a good preacher. One time when he looked at her—she still remembered it—he scared her. Her own brown eyes were wide with fear now. What did "forsaken" mean? Did it mean throwing away? Did God throw Jesus away?

Anyway, she didn't like to look at the preacher very much and reached down to scratch where the elastic of her panties was stinging and itching. She squirmed to the edge of the painted wooden bench, sticky and wet with sweat, and started to swing her feet back and forth, hoping to make a breeze between her legs. It didn't work. She picked up a fan and studied it. It was made of cardboard with a thin flat wooden stick stapled on for a handle. On one side was a colored picture of little Jesus in the Temple with the Elders and on the other side some Scripture and "MacDonald's Funeral Home, Clintonville, Georgia" printed at the bottom.

"Let your Granny have that fan, Glorie—and don't be playing in church!" her grandmother frowned and whispered.

She handed the fan to her Granny and saw the little backward movement her grandmother always made whenever Glorianne looked at her. Then she would always drop her eyes or look away. She had always done that; it was just part of Glorie's world, just the way things were, like the ground or church or summertime heat. She watched her grandmother make long, slow, peaceful sweeps with the fan: the gray-blonde wisps at her temples were soft wings carrying the blue eyes to Heaven. Granny is a good Christian, she thought, and wondered what Hell would be like for little girls. Probably a lot hotter than church on Sunday night in summertime. She lifted her dark matted hair off her sweat-damp neck and held it there, studying her elbow, and thought about how fast Granny fell asleep at night. Probably because she was going to Heaven.

Glorie hated nighttime, when everybody was asleep but her. She hated being trapped in bed in the dark, especially in summer. She thought that Hell would be all darkness and heat. She'd lie there, or turn over and over to make mosquitoes go away, and wish for Mama to come home, and sometimes she'd still be awake when Mama did come home. The kitchen light would come on and Glorie would creep softly to the door. Mama would give her a big tired smile and whisper, "Hey there, Baby." She'd turn on the radio very low and fix her a cup of coffee and milk. Then she'd light a Chesterfield and sit at the table in her slip to pin her hair up. She'd take the little mirror out of her handbag and prop it up on the bobby-pin box made of cedar. It had her name on the top: Inez. Mama would dip her comb in a glass of water, comb it through her hair, and make neat tight little pin-curls, opening the pins with her teeth and talking to Glorianne at the same time. The hot, dark room, the sweat-sticky sheets, were far away then.

Her grandmother, Evaline, was a widow with heart trouble. For three years now, she and the family had been living off the county welfare and the little money Inez brought home from her job as a waitress. She had many troubles, including asthma. She looked over at her granddaughter's small tanned body, dirty sandaled feet swinging. She wouldn't have minded looking after Glorie while Inez worked; she'd been looking after young ones all her life, her own seven and now three grandchildren. She wouldn't have minded it, but Glorie wasn't her grandchild. She'd been there when Glorie was born, but somehow she never believed it. *Not part of me, of us. The spit right out of her daddy's mouth, just like him, inside and out. Trash.* He'd got Inez pregnant seven years ago and then just took off. It was hard to look after Glorie. She didn't just look different—there wasn't a drop of good in the girl. And sometimes Glorie even made her feel different herself, like she was separate from righteousness, strange, and a little frightening, not the way she always felt with her other grandchildren. She gave out one of her deep quivering sighs and closed her eyes. She thought about the cross and saw herself hanging there.

"Sit still, Glorie!" she whispered.

And Glorianne tried to sit still and listen. She wanted to know what that word meant—forsaken—but Brother Bob didn't mention it again. He was standing down in front of the pulpit now with his hands raised and the Bible in one of them. "Let us sing now, brethren, and pray—pray that somebody here tonight has heard Jesus' call and opened his heart to the Lord." The people stood and sang, "Just as I am, without one plea..."

A man came down the aisle—it was Mrs. Johnson's drunkard husband—with his shoulders hunched over and his head hung low. The singing became a little softer as everyone turned to see who was coming forward: "But that Thy blood was shed for me..."

There were big dark blotches of sweat under Mr. Johnson's arms and on the back of his faded plaid shirt. He spoke to the preacher for a minute while the people kept singing, "And that Thou bidst me come to Thee...," and then he sat down on the front bench, his head still bowed and his shoulders shaking. Brother Bob stood there, looking out at the people like a hungry and beaten puppy looks to his master. The song ended.

"Sing another chorus, brethren. The Holy Spirit is with us tonight—somebody else is here." His eyes slowly swept the people as they sang, "Oh, Lamb of God, I come, I come..." Feet started scuffling softly on the wooden floor, handbags moved from one arm to the other under the weight of his gaze. Nobody came. His face looked like the picture of Jesus praying in Gethsemane over Granny's couch. Mr. Johnson stood next to him then, his hunched shoulders encircled by Brother Bob's arm. His face frightened her; it looked like the picture she had seen one day last spring. She had run up onto the porch to get a drink of water. Granny was there doing the washing.

"Glorie, you been in that mulberry tree?"

"No, ma'am." A lie! Suddenly she was staring into brown and white circles of fear over a mulberry-stained mouth as Granny yanked her up under the arms and hoisted her to the mirror over the washstand. "Then what is that, Glorie? What is that? You just tell me *what that is*!" Glorianne screamed in terror at the mirror. It still gave her bad dreams.

Then Mama was standing there, looking ghost-like through the screen door. "What in the world is all the yelling about?"

"Glorie's been in that mulberry tree again, Inez. I've told her about a hundred times." Granny sighed heavily.

"Well, she's a good climber. I don't think she'll fall."

Granny's eyebrows rose. "No, Lord knows she won't fall." She knew Glorie would never be able to fall out of a tree like other children did, and then cry and want to be held and petted. "But them mulberries are full of worms, Inez, and you know it."

"I wouldn't worry about it so much, Mother. Let me come out there and help you with that wash. Glorianne, go play."

The crickets and frogs were noisy as they walked the dusty road home from church. Granny's broad back was a few yards ahead. Glorie ran from one side of the road to the other, trying to make a breeze, but it didn't work. Were the crickets praying for rain? Had they been forsaken by the rain? She started trying to pray with the crickets by making a chirping noise with her tongue behind her teeth. It didn't work, though—there wasn't any rain.

Later she lay in bed, kicking the heavy sheet off her, then pulling it up again to keep mosquitoes off, trying to breathe the thick air. Hell would be all darkness and heat. Then she heard the sounds of Mama in the kitchen: the striking of the matches, one for the coffeepot, the next one for the cigarette, the radio playing low. Eddy Arnold was singing, "I'll hold you in my heart till I can hold you in my arms..." Then there was the comb dipping into the glass of water and the soft chink of bobby-pins in the little cedar box. Glorianne listened till she fell asleep, and dreamed of cool sunlight splashing among the pale green mulberry leaves high in the tree.

Bienville

Loxie sat at the table stirring her Raisin Bran. There was only a little milk, so it took a while to get the dry flakes moist. She looked at the paper sack of garbage standing under the sink and the empty Pet milk can on top. A roach ran down the side of the sack.

"What you running for?" she said aloud. "You got nothing to be afraid of." She stretched her long thin legs out under the table and studied the fruit basket pattern of the vinyl tablecloth, barely visible on the top, nearly vanished from so many wipes with a dish cloth, but around the edges, it was still vivid. She remembered when Mama bought the tablecloth five years ago, when Loxie was only eight years old. She had long ago observed the placement of the various fruits in the baskets, counted each basket in the pattern; now there was nothing left to figure except maybe how many more wipes would be necessary before the pattern disappeared entirely. She occupied herself with this speculation now as she ate her cereal. It allowed her to dismiss the garbage sack, the roach, and the miserable steaminess of the New Orleans summer morning.

Mama would be home sometime this morning. She worked nearly every night during summer, when there were so many tourists. Loxie had pulled the sheet up on the mattress and smoothed the pillowcase. Mama would sleep all day, and then around seven, get up and wash in the sink before going back to Sal's around eight. Money was pretty good during summer, and she'd probably buy groceries, and more milk, before she came home.

She rinsed the bowl and spoon and left them in the sink, slapped her dirty feet across the linoleum floor and shoved them into rubber flip-flops. She forgot again to turn off the window fan before she left.

Out on the street, she ran into Chang Lee, zipping up his pants as he emerged from the narrow passage between two houses. He showed her his two yellow teeth in a good-morning grin. Chang Lee had a Chinese-sounding name but he was the blackest man Loxie had ever seen, so black his skin had an almost purple undertone to it. As far as she knew, he lived on the street; he was always there when she went out.

She waved across the street to Sonny's Marcine sitting on

the top step of the shotgun house she lived in with Sonny, then decided to run. Her tiny breasts jiggled under her tee-shirt as she ran. Mama wanted to buy her a brassiere but Loxie protested. She knew her twelve-year-old body was changing, but she didn't want it to and pretended it wasn't happening. She turned the corner onto Sauvage, then dipped into a passageway, emerging in a small brick yard, and clambered up the wooden steps to Miss Devereaux's camelback apartment. She could hear the television blaring away. Miss D. was watching "The Price is Right." She had a television and an air conditioner; it wasn't too bad staying with her sometimes—for a while, anyway. Loxie could never stay in one place very long. Wherever she was, she always wanted to be somewhere else. Miss D. was supposed to look after her while Mama slept, but Loxie would never stay if there was nothing good on the TV.

She banged on the door until she heard the key and bolt and chain, and then Miss D. was in the doorway, her hair standing out in carrot-colored wires around her caramel-brown face, her eyes a blurry smear. Damn, Loxie thought, she must have drunk all night long. The stench of whiskey wafted out the doorway, but also the cool air from the air conditioner. She'd stay a while.

"Come on in, girl. You want some coffee?"

"Yeah—with some milk in it, okay?" She plopped on the sofa to watch the television and presently, the old lady came in, her burgundy-colored slippers scuffing the floor, the cups rattling in their saucers. They sipped their coffee and did not speak as Bob Barker yelled and bells clanged and women squealed and cheered. And everybody laughed. It was boring. Loxie looked at the big picture of John-Robert over the television, Miss D.'s son who was killed in the Gulf War. The picture was huge, framed in a wide, curly, carved gold frame. The pictures of Jesus' Sacred Heart on one side and The Blessed Virgin's Immaculate Heart on the other were tiny by comparison with John-Robert's. Before he went in the Army, he'd bought some kind of life insurance, and so Miss D. didn't have to work anymore. "Worst thing that could've happened to her," Mama said. "Got nothing to do now but watch that television and drink herself to death." Every now and then, when Loxie arrived, Miss Devereaux would be slobbering drunk and crying over her dead son. But Loxie knew the old lady needed John-Robert to be dead—so she'd have a reason to drink and so she could afford to. That hadn't been a hard puzzle at all.

She could hear Miss D. slurping her coffee, and the sound was worse than the women squealing on the television. She couldn't take it. She drank the coffee down in a few gulps and said, "Look, Miss D. I got to go see somebody, okay? I'll come back later."

"You not even going to finish your coffee?"

"No. I got to go now." And she was gone. She never stayed long, but she usually tried to stay longer than she did this morning.

Out on the street again, she saw Jimmy, a boy about her age. They had gone to school together until last year, when Jimmy just stopped coming. Loxie wanted to stop too, but Mama wouldn't let her yet. She skipped school all the time, though, at least two days a week, sometimes three. It wasn't bad when the teacher taught math problems, or some other kind of puzzle, but it was mostly just boring, and being in one place all day was something that caused her pain, like she had bugs in her blood, just running crazy through her whole body. Sometimes she would just get up and leave.

"Hey, Lox!" Jimmy was high on something. He was always high on something, but his favorite thing was speed. Jimmy-on-speed was Jimmy-normal. He had a half-eaten hotdog in his hand. "Hey, girl, come on with me. I got something to show you."

"You crazy, Jimmy. I'm not going any place with you."

He was grinning, kind of jumping around, excited. "No, come on. It's funny. Hey, I got some ludes—you want one?" He dug a couple of white pills out of his pocket.

"You know I don't mess with that stuff." But she followed him down to the end of Sauvage to the tree. You could smell the river from there. The tree was the only one in the whole neighborhood: a huge old dead oak tree that marked the boundary between the neighborhood and Bywater. It had always been there. Somebody said one time that gentlemen used to fight duels under it with pistols, and you could still see bullet holes in it. When she was little, she believed the tree was dead because it had been shot to death—maybe that was even true. She was usually right about things even when she was little.

Jimmy started dancing around a few feet from the tree, waving the hot dog, and hollering "Hey, cat! I got something for you. Come on out, cat!" Presently, a small white cat appeared from under a ragged oleander bush. Its face was pinched, and she could see all its ribs. "Watch it, Loxie. Watch it run!" He held out the hot dog as he backed up toward the tree. The cat tried to follow. Its front legs lurched forward, but its back legs were stiff and dragging, and its rectum was red and swollen under its broken tail. Jimmy kept jumping around and hollering at the cat to come on, and the cat kept trying, opening its mouth to meow, but no sound would come out. It looked like some kind of crazy slapstick dance—black boy and white cat, the cat's mouth open but silent, and laughter coming out of Jimmy's mouth, stuffed with the hot dog, red ketchup on his chin.

"Jimmy, you crazy! I got no time for this shit..." She turned and ran off toward the river, then changed her mind, not wanting to go into Bywater, so she turned around again and headed back toward Bienville. She decided to go see Sonny's Marcine if she was still outside. If she wasn't sitting outside, it might mean that Sonny was home and she didn't want to go there if he was there. He was a mean son of a bitch, Sonny was. It wasn't getting close to lunchtime yet, but the dry Raisin Bran was gone already, and Marcine might have something to eat for lunch; if not, she'd have to go back to Miss Devereaux's. Stupid Jimmy. He was going into Bywater, she knew, that edge of it, to get more dope. He wasn't hard to figure at all. A few Quaaludes wouldn't last him long—probably the reason he'd been headed in that direction anyway, not to show her that cat.

Marcine was still sitting on the top doorstep, smoking. "Hey, Loxie. How you doing, girl."

Loxie sat down sideways on the bottom step. "That Jimmy Lugo's crazy, you know that?"

Marcine tried to smile. Loxie saw that her lip was cut on one side and she had a swollen eye. "Yeah, he's crazy. He be dead before long."

"Yeah." Like Miss D., she thought. She studied the cracks in the wooden step, looking for a pattern in them, ran her finger along them to see if there were splinters. Marcine's bare feet were two steps above. Loxie wondered why her ankles were swollen, a question more interesting than splinters in the steps. "Damn hot, huh—you eat yet?"

"Nothing in the house. Sonny get paid today, though. Might get some groceries later on." She drew on the cigarette with the good side of her mouth. Loxie knew that if Sonny was getting paid today, it wasn't likely that Marcine would see any of the money. Wasn't likely that she'd see Sonny either, for that matter.

She looked up at Marcine and finally had to say it out loud—what she'd often wondered. "Why you stay with him, Marcine? Couldn't you have done some better? That man is mean, you know? Real mean." She remembered the time that Sonny had kicked her down those same steps. Marcine had been pregnant. She was in the hospital for almost a week and lost the baby. One of these days, he was going to beat her to death.

Marcine leaned her head back and blew smoke in the air, then smiled in spite of her cut lip. "Oh, Loxie. It ain't so bad. Sonny just love his fun. He a happy man, Sonny is—always laughing. Ain't nothing can keep him down. Besides—you ever notice? He got gold hair." Her eyes were wistful, like she was seeing something far away. "Sometimes, early in the morning, I see his gold head rising over me like the sun rising, like the happy sun rising." Then the smile faded, and the swollen eye fixed on Loxie. "Anyway, girl—something get everybody."

"That's crazy, Marcine. Just crazy!"

"May be. But it don't matter."

"Nothing gets anybody unless they want to be got."

"You got nothing to say about it."

"Well, nothing's going to get me!"

Marcine smiled and said quietly, "It already do."

Loxie took off running up the street, back to the room she shared with her mother. That was stupid. Nothing gets anybody. They just do what they want to do, that's all. That's what people do—what they want to do. And they don't do what they don't want to. Miss D. drinks because she wants to and Chang Lee don't work because he don't want to work. Jimmy dopes because he wants to and the cat—the cat just wants something to eat. The window fan was still running when she reached the door, opening it quietly. Mama was lying asleep on the mattress, softly snoring, her make-up smeared on the pillowcase. A paper sack full of groceries stood on the table. She quietly took items out of it—a box of macaroni and cheese, two cans of milk, a box of roach poison. I guess maybe you do have something to be scared of, she thought, seeing the roach's antennae flicking the air from behind the garbage sack. *"No!"* she whispered aloud, scaring the roach and watching it skitter along the baseboard, *"No, you don't!"* She put the box of roach tablets in the garbage sack and the other items behind the curtain that covered the grocery shelf. Then she took down the box of Raisin

Bran, stuffing handfuls of cereal in the pockets of her baggy shorts, and left as quietly as she came in.

She ran up to the Sauvage corner and down that street to the dead tree. When she reached the oleander bush, she whispered, "Please come out, cat. I won't make you do those tricks. I got some cereal for you. Sorry I don't have any milk." She waited several minutes and whispered again, but the cat did not come out. Loxie peered into the bush. She could see the small cat lying on its side, its face still pinched, its tiny mouth still open. It was dead.

She turned around and looked at the tree. She just stood there for a good long while, in one place, looking at the tree. It had always been there; it always would be there—big, old, bigger and older than anything she knew. Its deep crevices looked like blackened blood oozing forever into the ground. Then she knelt down in front of the oleander bush and parted its ragged branches. She pulled out all the Raisin Bran from her pockets, a handful at a time, and sprinkled it over the cat's body until it was all gone and the small body was mostly covered. Afterwards, she sat back on her heels, smelling the bitter tang of the dusty oleander leaves, and the wet earth smell of the river.

She walked back up the street heading for Miss D.'s, past open doorways and smells of sweet olive and hot grease, people hollering at each other deep in the dark interiors. She looked down at her brown feet in the rubber flip-flops. Her feet were too long and thin to hold the shoes on. She always had to keep her toes scrunched downward to keep from walking out of her shoes. Everything—even keeping her shoes on—was a puzzle to be solved, to be figured out, everything . . . the pattern of dried spit on the sidewalk or where Chang Lee slept at night or why Marcine's ankles swelled up.

Then she knew it was puzzles that had got her. Even the puzzle of figuring out what it was that had got her—just another puzzle. She sat down on the bottom step of St. Philip Neri's, and her busy mind went blank, empty, just nothing. She was staring down at her scrunched toes, at the sidewalk, smeared with ancient stains, but all she could see was the dead tree.

A Train in Germany

Spring, 1979
Ziegelhausen

In Germany, windows open inward. Very practical, thought Elizabeth Petersen, while she sipped her coffee, now tepid from the cold air coming through the open kitchen window. She thought it would be much easier to clean windows from the inside, after all, and remembered all the clean German windows she'd seen, the windowsills filled with plants to catch the winter sunlight, the lintels draped in lace valances. She'd opened the window to look at the walled garden outside. Patches of snow hid under evergreen shrubs in the corners, like little white secrets. Turning the stove on under the kettle, she remembered some cultural commentator on a talk show back in the States making the remark that everyone is either French or German; the host of the talk show had nodded knowingly. It was a wild generalization, of course, but Elizabeth had never forgotten it. The windows of the house where she'd stayed in the suburbs of Paris during her semester abroad had opened outward, and now she remembered, they were dirty. She smiled. What did that mean? That the French didn't care so much about clean windows?

She measured coffee into the white paper cone filter, inhaling the aroma with thoughtful appreciation for the way Germans ground coffee very fine and prepared it in glass drip pots. For coffee lovers like her, it was the best way. She rinsed her cup in the hot tap and placed it under the filter, poured the boiling water slowly into the filter, thinking about Paul's reaction when she told him at breakfast that she'd had another train nightmare. She almost wished she'd said nothing about it; he was taking the dreams too seriously. She could tell he was beginning to worry about them. "Maybe we should get a little help with this," he'd said. For a moment she seriously considered not telling him about the dreams any more. But they'd never kept anything from each other, and she didn't want to start doing that now—but she also didn't want him to worry.

She felt cold and closed the window. The nightmares were happening three or four times a week now. Sometimes she just heard the train whistle, sometimes she could see the train, coming around a curve, as if it were coming out of hiding, heading toward her.

"You're not Jewish," she'd answered him quietly. "That's why you can't understand the terror."

"But that's the point, honey. Neither are you." He kissed her goodbye and left for work.

He's right, she thought, my ears are not Jewish ears—at least, I don't think so, but it wouldn't explain anything even if they were. She took the key to the mailbox by the door, and pulling her thick fleece robe tighter around her, she went outside to the box and withdrew the *Rhein-Neckar Zeitung*. Their neighbor, an old man who lived a few doors down the street from them, was walking his beautiful, black German Shepherd. Once, when they mentioned the dog to their landlord, he told them that there were no mongrels in Germany, and it was true that every dog they saw appeared to be purebred. Elizabeth thought that was a sign that they loved their dogs, but Paul thought it was strange.

She hurried back indoors, not wanting to be seen by the neighbor in her robe. She hadn't told Paul about what was happening now during the daytime—he might really be upset if he knew. And lately it had been more frequent; almost every day now in some way or other, the dreams seemed to be seeping into the daylight, like fog making its way around the edges of a closed door. Seeing the neighbor's dog, for example, brought to her conscious mind a dream scene in which the train was stopped, stationary for once, and there were German soldiers in long black coats holding rifles strapped to their shoulders and dogs restrained on leashes—dogs just like the neighbor's—apparently to catch anyone who might escape from the train. Black figures in white snow.

She slapped the newspaper down on the breakfast table and stared at the German language. For just a moment, the mere sight of it caused her to feel the terror again. But it was becoming familiar, losing its edge as it lost its strangeness. She was not becoming less afraid, but becoming less afraid of *being* afraid. She poured her coffee and sat down to stare at the language she was supposed to learn, to understand, to speak. Elizabeth was unusually good at picking up languages. Fluent in French and Spanish, she could understand Italian, and even knew a smattering of Portuguese. German was easy for her, but this morning her resistance was too strong—maybe because it was too soon after the nightmare. She pushed the newspaper aside.

Paul probably just didn't want to hear anything negative about the country that was his new assignment. He was a public relations expert for Garson-Mews, a company seeking a global market for its technology services. His job was to cultivate a clientele for the company, and he wanted her to learn German, to charm potential German clients, to impress his U.S. bosses. Maybe he simply didn't want to be reminded of Germany's dark past.

She felt alone. This was the first time in her marriage she was not able to share an experience with him. And, she reasoned, she felt alone because she *was* alone after he left for work. Every morning, he went to an office where people spoke English, where almost everybody was American. She felt *abandoned.* But Elizabeth had never felt abandoned before; it wasn't like her. It was not Elizabeth Petersen as she'd always been. She had always absorbed her surroundings, become completely integrated into the community wherever she was like a chameleon, as she'd done when Paul opened the new office in Lima. Within two months she'd improved her Spanish enough to cultivate an active social life with Peruvians and make valuable contacts for Paul. By the time they left a year later, she was almost indistinguishable from any upper-class Peruvian. It was the same way in Brazil after that, though they hadn't been there long enough for her to become fluent in Portuguese. Why was she having a problem now?

Elizabeth knew the problem wasn't idleness or boredom; it wasn't caused by having too much free time or too few interests. She was aware of her unique opportunity to learn other languages and cultures, and she took advantage of it. Nor was it the country itself—Germany. She was actually more at home in Germany than she'd been in Peru or Brazil. She had thought that maybe the strange familiarity of this foreign country was because the culture was more like her own European-descended, American origin. But it wasn't that simple; it wasn't any cultural similarity or lack of it—that had never made any difference in South America. Paradoxical though it was, it was in that very familiarity that the strangeness lay. Sometimes she almost felt as though she'd stumbled into someplace that had always been there but had been invisible until now. And then the dreams came with sounds and images of Nazi death trains.

Anyway, she had a hairdresser's appointment, so she rinsed the breakfast dishes and went upstairs to dress. If she had time before she left, she'd study the newspaper and try to read as much as she could of the front page. Their German teacher had told them to immerse themselves in newspapers, television, radio, films—immersion was the fastest way to learn the language.

*

Driving into Heidelberg, she dutifully listened to the German language radio and avoided the American military station. She had forgotten last night's dream as she mumbled the lyrics to popular German songs, trying to internalize sound and cadence, when she was caught off-guard by the sudden appearance of a road sign that hadn't been there before: "Achtung!" it warned, and she felt a tiny cold stab of fear at the sight and mental sound of the word before she realized that the graphic below it, a shower of small black dots on a cautionary yellow ground, simply indicated snow. How ironic to be frightened by what was only another example of the social responsibility that was so common in Germany, much more so than in other countries she'd visited, including her own. She made a conscious decision to ignore her reaction and to focus instead on the positive evidence of that responsibility. It was everywhere—even to the placement of road signs in early morning to warn motorists of a light overnight snowfall in this late spring.

It reminded her of the first morning after they'd moved into their house. When Paul left for work, he noticed that the sidewalk in front of their house had been shoveled. He looked down the street to find that the sidewalk in front of all the houses had been cleared of the snow that fell during the night. They could only assume that Herr Wyrott, their landlord who lived next door, had shoveled their sidewalk.

"Oh, damn," he whined, coming back inside to tell her. "Now I'm going to have to get up early and shovel the damned walk."

His reaction amused her, and she laughed at him. She had a strong admiration for German social consciousness and said so—which annoyed him. They'd learned some things before their arrival, like never calling people by their first names without formal permission. He could not address his secretary as "Jutta," but must pronounce every syllable of "Fräulein Edelmeyer." He found such obligatory social customs tedious, easy to forget, and he depended on Elizabeth to keep him in observance. She'd adapted easily, almost overnight.

But it was not just the word on the sign that had so affected Elizabeth—it was also the color, the yellow of all the road signs. Each time she saw one, somewhere in the periphery of her mind was an image of a fabric patch in that same hard yellow with the Star of David and the word *Jude* in black letters in the middle, the patch Jews had been forced to sew on all their outer clothing, until, of course, there were no more Jews to wear them. She had seen one of those patches, framed and hanging on the wall over the bed of her college roommate, Judy. Of course, she'd asked about it. It had been a gift from one of Judy's relatives. Judy was only coincidentally Jewish, just as Elizabeth was coincidentally Christian. Neither was really a believer of any kind. The thought crossed her mind now that if God existed, he would probably be less offended by a sincere atheism than he was by their cheerful indifference, their youthful arrogance.

She drove on, wishing she could think about something else, but she remembered instead, about five years ago while she was still in school, asking a German history professor how he accounted for the Holocaust, how he assimilated that reality into his love for his country. Her own love for Germany was growing deeper every day—it would maybe be a good thing to remember what he said now. He said that, first of all, she'd have to admit that anti-Semitism was not unique to Germany, that it existed everywhere. "Then," he said, "you have to acknowledge that it's only German idealism—which everyone has always admired—that made the extremism of the Third Reich possible." He smiled. "The dark side of glory, you might say." Was there an accusation implied there? Chilling to think so, still more chilling to detect an absence of repentance.

Elizabeth parked the Volvo in front of the café on Hauptstrasse. Her appointment with Helga was for ten, and it was only nine-thirty; she had time for a coffee. She loved the little *konditorei* near the hairdresser's salon, the rich Viennese coffee in the little silver pot, the whipped cream in a crystal bowl, the little paper doily under the cup, the snowy white tablecloth and napkin. She loved the polite, reserved formality of the waitress in her black skirt, white blouse and apron, the artfully displayed candies and *küchen* in the glass case. She loved it all. It was as though she knew and acknowledged that this is how a cup of coffee was meant to be. Just—so *right.* It reminded her of some silk pajamas she used to have, in a soft beige color, perfectly tailored, perfectly right. She encountered this *rightness* everywhere in Germany, as something she'd always known but never recognized. Oddly familiar, and almost *private*, like slowly discovering a beautiful secret that had been kept from her.

Then she noticed a middle-aged woman sitting alone at a table a little to her left. She wore a hat, as most German women of that age wore, and a gray-patterned scarf hung around her neck. Every now and then, she reached up to adjust the placement of her scarf, and finally, just as she lowered her hand, Elizabeth saw her bare wrist beneath her sleeve: *it was tattooed with a number.* The entire room seemed to freeze, like an old film about to break, and then move forward in slow, uncertain motion. She placed her cup back down on her doily, slowly and carefully, as though she might drop it, spill it into her lap, make a scene—she felt that she must be very careful not to make a scene. Rigidly, she blotted her mouth with the napkin. She thought, that woman must have been a young girl in the camps. What had happened to her? Oh, God, oh, God! The woman was reading a folded-up newspaper, innocently unaware of her observer in the café, the charming paper-doilied café—which could now never be charming again—except that it was. Everything was different now, most of all because nothing was different at all. Incredibly, all charm remained.

*

"Frau Reinholz called today," she told Paul that evening. "She invited me to go to the ballet with her and Frau Buchman tomorrow night." Frau Reinholz was the daughter of a high-ranking war veteran, a well-respected widow, and president of the socially prestigious Frauenklub. The mayor's wife was a member, and the three generals' wives from the big American Army base in Heidelberg.

"Hey, that's great. You said yes, of course."

"Of course. I'm a good PR wife."

"So," he said emphatically. He was enthusiastic, this was

good news. "So, you think we should have a little wine and cheese beforehand—not cocktails, of course. Are they picking you up at home?"

"No. You don't need to plan anything. I'm supposed to meet them at the Stadthalle."

"Okay. What ballet?" he asked. "Something special?"

"It's a Polish company," she answered. "They're performing *The Firebird*, I think. I'm not into ballet, but Frau Reinholz seems to think it's grand."

"Well, okay. Maybe you'll have time to read up on it." His care about such things as this invitation to the ballet was one reason Paul was good at his job. They made a good team; she understood the importance of small matters like Frau Reinholz's love of ballet. A first step in any assignment was patronage of the arts, and that was Elizabeth's job. The invitation put them in a position to reciprocate with an invitation of their own—and Herr Buchman owned a large electronics firm with branch offices in other West German cities. Because he might be interested in the technical support that Paul's company wanted to provide, the contact could be important.

"There isn't time to read about the ballet now. I think I'll just wing it. At least I'm familiar with the Firebird symphony."

"Okay," he said. "You're a good wing-er."

"Right." He should know, she thought. She knew he watched her sometimes, impressed by her instinctive, seemingly effortless ability to please. Once, after a reception at the residence of a prominent German businessman to welcome the new American firm, he'd said to her, "You know, you almost scare me."

"Why?"

"You can circulate a room seeming to move, but the main reason is that I look at you sometimes and almost see a stranger—a foreigner, a German woman—not my wife."

She laughed at him. "Well, it's kind of like swimming—you just get in the water and let the current move you along. It's easy if you don't put up a resistance. The thing is, most people do resist. They're too stuck in their own identity."

They took a walk that evening after dinner. Their home, leased by the company, was at the base of a mountain, Heiligenberg, or Holy Mountain, so named for a medieval monastery that once existed there. The ruins could still be seen halfway up the mountain. They marveled at the remaining rose-colored sandstone half-walls, the precision of the Gothic archways, the German attention to detail, its orderly beauty. They'd been there before, but not at sunset, when the rose color seemed to glow in a light almost golden. It was so beautiful that Elizabeth felt tears filling her eyes. At the summit of the mountain there were also ruins of a Hitler Youth campsite, but they never walked that far. Paul didn't want to go there, and Elizabeth could understand that. It was impossible to assimilate such ethereal beauty with such unspeakable evil, and he had chosen to see only the beauty. That night, Elizabeth had another train nightmare, a really bad one this time.

When she woke the next morning, while she was making coffee and Paul was in the shower, she thought about the train whistle. American train whistles were low, almost melodious, harmonic, she thought, compared to German train whistles, which were high-pitched, shrill. They sound like a scream, she thought, a long, screeching cry that no one hears. The train last night was louder, closer, and this time she could see its cargo through the slats of its cattle cars: children, children as they were just before they were herded into gas chambers, children with no clothes or shoes, naked, heads shaved, crushed together, an occasional blank and dead face pressed sideways...

She told Paul, but even as she told him, she knew for certain now that she would never tell him about her nightmares again. It wasn't that she had decided to exclude him in any way; it was just that she understood that he couldn't think about it, just as he couldn't go to the mountaintop. But something else, too: the dreams, everything that was happening—it was becoming too personal, too private.

Exasperated, almost as if he wanted to put his fingers in his ears so as not to hear, he said again, "The war's been over for thirty-five years now, Elizabeth. Didn't anybody tell you?"

"Has it?" She remembered a line from a poem and recited it: "Our steps still resound . . . *we* are still here." Even as she said the words, she knew she shouldn't have.

"For God's sake, Beth, you're Christian!"

"No, I'm not. My mother's family was. Anyhow, that's them, not me. Be honest, Paul. Neither one of us is religious. Let's not be hypocritical and claim a religion we don't have."

His head bobbed in a reluctant nod. "The point is you're not Jewish." In a terrifying flash of the moment, it occurred to her for the first time that he was taking it for granted that she identified with the Jews—*and not with the Germans.* He came closer to where she stood at the sink and spoke more softly, frowning a little in concern. "Listen, honey, what about your father? Do you suppose these nightmares might be connected to him somehow, because you don't know him? They might be your own unconscious projection of him—"

She turned to face him and his face changed—as though she'd surprised him, as though he suddenly thought she was a stranger. He'd never understood how she felt about her father. "That's right, I don't know him. And so I don't know that he *wasn't* Jewish." She spoke slowly and firmly, wanting him to understand. "But why do you think it should matter? It doesn't. And the reason it doesn't matter is that *it doesn't matter who he was–period.*"

"Okay, never mind him then. Listen, you know that you're unusually empathic and you think that's a good thing, but maybe it isn't—not always."

"What?"

"I don't know. Just take care of yourself—okay? Remember who you are." He kissed her cheek and left for work, and this time she knew he really was worried about her, not just exasperated with her. She felt guilty for worrying him. Yet somehow everything, everything outside this strange experience—of dreams and daylight—was becoming less important. Everything that mattered so much to her before, little things or big things, including her love for Paul, mattered less now every day, as the dreams increased in frequency and intensity at night, even as her love for Germany deepened in the daytime. And she became less and less frightened by what was happening. But she would not mention any more of it to Paul—she didn't want to worry him. Besides, was anything actually "happening"? Anything *real*, anyway?

Her father's identity had always been a mystery. He was "unknown," according to her birth certificate. When Elizabeth was a child growing up in New Orleans, she made up "hero" stories about him. Her mother, who was a religious woman, always told her that children with no father have God as their father. She was always glad that her mother's family was an old Catholic family, descended from French colonials, and not from some English Protestant culture, where she might have been stigmatized for her illegitimacy. But later, as a teenager, it became a more serious question, always hanging in the air, like some kind of heavy weight on her whole existence. Her mother had died when she was twelve without saying his name; all Elizabeth ever knew was what her grandmother had said: he was no good—whatever that meant. She'd begged her grandmother for his name, but she refused. Finally, when her grandmother died, she'd had to let it go because no one else in the family, neither her uncle nor her aunts, ever knew. Her father would be a mystery forever now. And one can agonize over an unanswerable question only so long. If she hadn't let it go, it would have become an unhealthy obsession.

Elizabeth had long ago stopped thinking about her father at all; not knowing just became a part of her, an irrelevant fact—like the shape of her fingernails or the way she laughed or some other minor detail. It didn't matter now who he was, and even less whether he was Jewish. How should she have answered Paul's emphatic assertion that she wasn't a Jew? "That's true, but it doesn't matter"? No, it wasn't true. No one knew that, not even Elizabeth, certainly not Paul. The truth, which she had long ago acknowledged, was that she wasn't anybody. She had no identity, and she had accepted that reality. She couldn't remember at what point it occurred to her that, being nobody, she could be anybody she wanted to be. Whenever it was, it was probably then that her skill as a chameleon began to develop—probably even her talent for languages. So giving up the quest for her father's identity had been a good thing.

*

"*Guten Abend, Frau Reinholz. Wie geht es Ihnen?*"

"Oh, Mrs. Petersen. Your German is so good. How different from the American women at the Army post. They never even try to learn."

Elizabeth had heard that kind of compliment before and it always irritated her. Did they think she was flattered? She wasn't. Americans weren't indifferent, ignorant or arrogant, as foreigners so often implied. Why did people think they had to put other people down in order to elevate themselves?

"Well, if you think about it, Frau Reinholz, you have to go only twenty or thirty miles from Heidelberg to be in a foreign country. Most American women will not be in a real foreign country even when they travel a thousand miles. After all, Germany is not much larger than the state of Oregon, you know. And, unlike the United States, it doesn't have an ocean bigger than the continents on both sides."

Frau Reinholz's smile froze, and Elizabeth regretted her remark. What she'd said was true, but she shouldn't have said it. It embarrassed Frau Reinholz, and it was wrong to strip away someone's cover and expose them. Sometimes, because she herself had no need for any kind of cover, she forgot that other people did—and that they were dependent on such covers like armor. Without them, they were just little children, helpless and vulnerable.

The Polish ballet was enjoyable enough. Elizabeth had never been to a ballet before, and though it had lovely moments, she thought most of the performance was a running back and forth on the stage to fill in the time between those moments. She decided she liked the symphony more. Intermission came and they went to the lobby to have a glass of wine and try to make conversation in the noisy din that people always feel obliged to create during intermissions. She disconnected briefly from the two ladies, drifting into a familiar detachment, wondering if all those people would have so much to say if they hadn't just been forced into ninety minutes of silence.

Frau Buchman interrupted her thoughts with a loud laugh. Frau Reinholz had made a joke, apparently, and Elizabeth tried to tune in. They were speaking in German, so she didn't know if they'd perhaps meant her not to understand, an assessment she instinctively made. She studied Frau Reinholz's face to decide: the small eyes were made even more obscure by the pale lashes and brows and by the raised and rounded cheeks of her smile. All German women seemed to have rosy cheeks, and women of Frau Reinholz's age and class did not wear make-up. Her face was a white pie-shaped smudge with an unremarkable nose, small square teeth, and large red cheeks. But she was always smiling, and that perpetual smile made her attractive, like a middle-aged Hummel figurine. What were they saying? She couldn't make it out. Whatever it was, it was causing both of them to snicker. If it was something anti-American, they wouldn't want her to understand, but she boldly decided to find out. "What was that?" she asked pleasantly.

"Oh," Frau Buchman said indulgently, as if she were speaking to a child who understood little of grown-up talk, "Frau Reinholz was just telling me that in her father's letters from Warsaw during the war, he said he didn't believe there was a bed in that entire country without lice." She laughed again and raised her eyebrows, expecting Elizabeth to enjoy the joke.

"Oh." She turned away to avoid revealing the little shock of pain. The bell rang; it was time to resume their seats, and Elizabeth was grateful for the distraction. They pushed forward to set their glasses on one of several small tables placed by the auditorium doors. The overhead lights were flashing to hasten the audience back to their seats, the women chattered behind her, she kept her back to them and her eyes lowered. She hadn't expected this—this overt offense. What Frau Reinholz's *Wehrmacht* father had done to Polish Jews in the war—surely she knew—and then to make such a "joke." Anger was rising in her, newborn, strange, and righteous. She slid into her seat and bowed her head over her program.

The stage lights came up, and with her head still lowered over her program, she glanced sideways at the illuminated profiles of the German women. She understood that the joke and the laughter were camouflage to cover anger, but the anger was another cover for something deeper: shame. They were like some white Americans, those whose racist jokes were only an angry cover to hide the shame they had been made to feel of their ancestors who had owned slaves.

She closed her eyes to the dancers on the stage and heard the music of *The Firebird,* and she saw in the darkness, not the story Stravinsky had intended, but its older, deeper source in the ancient myth of the phoenix, Semitic in origin. The bird lives for centuries, then dies in flames, only to be reborn from the ashes—perpetual death and rebirth. But it was not the story of glorious resurrection that some people believed it was. No. The rebirth is the old self, the same identity, repeated forever. An agony of violence and futile struggle, endless holocaust, in a fierce, perpetual, impossible quest for freedom from the horror of what it was, who it was. Pity filled her, welled up behind her closed eyelids, flowed down her cheeks, and fell on the light blue silk of her dress.

There were no train nightmares that night. But the next morning, Elizabeth sensed a stillness not unlike that which happens just before a storm. She went to the mailbox and got the newspaper, but this time she didn't even look at it.

She was in good spirits after reporting to Paul the success of the evening at the ballet. She didn't mention the tasteless joke or her reaction to it, a fact that caused a little sadness in her, as though she were keeping something from him. He was pleased; there was no need to spoil that, and besides, telling him her reaction might worry him somehow.

That day Elizabeth did what she enjoyed most. She went to the market. She put on her lace-up walking shoes, her light spring coat and cloche hat, took her leather shopping bag from its hook by the door, and walked into the village to do her shopping. She walked past trees in budding, blinding bright green, saw crocuses in glorious yellow and scarlet, newly awakened among the lingering patches of snow in gardens that had been well-tended, cleared of winter debris and prepared to welcome them. She resolved to begin cleaning the garden that afternoon.

She was one of several women from their prestigious upper-class neighborhood out for a morning walk. "*Guten Morgen*," they greeted each other in passing. These were women who didn't work because, like her, they didn't have to. They could afford the luxury of tradition. She thought about the way German formality served to connect friendliness with respect for privacy that made everyday life just the way it should be, like the way coffee was served in the shop near Helga's salon.

She went to the *metzgerei,* the *bakerei*, and finally, to the *blumen* shop for fresh flowers. As always, she appreciated the steady industriousness of clerks, their efficiency and deference, which gave them a dignity that American clerks would never know. She negotiated selection, asked questions about availability, aware that she was as competent as any native. No one even knew she was American, if she didn't speak much. Her instinct for mimicry made her speak with almost no accent.

The morning dew had gone from the budding trees and from the grass in the little gardens as she walked home carrying her shopping bag full of fresh-baked brötchen, schnitzel wrapped in brown paper, a bottle of Mosel, and mixed anemones in a cone of white paper. There was a kind of walk, she observed, that was peculiar to German women, best described, perhaps, as *purposeful*, not fast, but steady. She smiled as she found herself walking with that same purpose. She had become aware when she bought the flowers that she was thinking in bits of German. It was all very easy for her.

The treetops moved gently against a morning sky of an amazing blue. She saw herself walking purposefully below it, with her shopping, beside lovely gardens, nodding politely to occasional fellow pedestrians, happy that no encroachment of the dreams had happened to spoil the lovely morning. Maybe it was all over now.

She felt a sudden certainty that it really was over. Maybe the experience at the ballet had ended it somehow. Remembering the ancient story from which Stravinsky's idea of the firebird emerged made her remember the unrepentant German professor, and she saw him now not as frightening, but as a tragic figure, trapped forever in an unrequited love for pagan glory. It was around the same time—her junior year?—that she'd read an essay called "Christ, the Jew" in a humanities class, which claimed that the crucified Christ was the Jewish people, a people whose very identity was *sacrifice.*

She felt very fortunate again not to have the prison of identity. She knew that was what made her unusual adaptability possible. Paul said it was empathy, but why should he be afraid for her? Having nothing to defend made defense unnecessary. She smiled at the newborn leaves of a poplar that rustled gently in a warming breeze as she passed, and she felt her heart surge with love for the tree, for Germany, for its people.

And so, she was completely unprepared when she turned onto the street where they lived and saw the neighbor walking the beautiful, black German Shepherd again. He lifted his hat politely as the dog lifted its head and looked into her eyes. There was no time then to fear. The bottle of wine crashed on the sidewalk; flowers and bread tumbled down as the dog broke from its owner and lunged straight at her throat. She never heard her own scream; all she heard was the dog's growling roar, like a train.

Sh'ma Yisrael
Adonai Eloheinu
Adonai Echad

The Funeral

The car's heater stopped when she turned off the engine, of course, and a chill went up her right arm as soon as she took the key out of the ignition. The car had become warm as toast on the drive from home; it shouldn't get so cold that fast. She decided it was the leaves from the pecan tree swirling around in the parking lot. It *looked* cold, so obviously, she had suddenly felt cold. That was it. That and the silence, of course. Silence just sounds cold.

She flipped down the visor mirror and checked her lipstick. There were small downward lines at the corners of her mouth now, and she always had to check her lipstick. It had a tendency to creep down into those lines. She removed the glove from her cold right hand and ran her forefinger over the lines to remove any wandering Splendid Natural. Maybe she'd look into those injectable wrinkle-fillers, when she could get the time to do a bit of research on them.

The wind was strong enough to make a swishing sound, even in the tightly closed car. The bare limbs of the great pecan tree just in front of her parking place were outlined against the gray stone wall of the church behind it. It looked a bit eerie. She shivered—but she shouldn't be this cold, not in the insulated trench coat, wool muffler and gloves. Well, she was here for a funeral, after all. A chilling enough purpose in itself.

So Mary Louise Watson was dead. It seemed strange. She never would have thought Mary would be the first of them to go. Actually, if anyone had asked her, she would have said that Mary would never die at all—everyone else, maybe, but not her.

She looked at the clock on the dashboard—twenty minutes to go. Why had she come so early? Oh, yes, she knew. It was a bad habit. She was afraid the funeral would take too long and she'd be late for her lunch meeting with Ed. Completely irrational, she knew, but she'd developed a habit long ago of arriving early at any meeting she hoped would not last long, as though her own early arrival would get things moving faster, get them over with. But, twenty minutes! Twenty minutes to sit there and freeze. She thought, this is ridiculous, and started the engine up again, reflecting even as she did, that she could, after all, go inside and wait where it was warm. But no, not in there, not with that coffin there and weeping family members sitting in the front pew. It would be better, maybe even warmer, to wait in the car.

She wished she'd brought some of the mountain of work from her desk with her, or at least the laptop. Ed was likely to talk salary increase, and she wanted to check out what other people were making as assistant deans in her field. Why hadn't she thought to do that before today? Well, she could stall on that topic; that would be the best thing to do in this first meeting, anyway.

So Mary Louise was dead. She was lying inside a coffin in St. Stephen's Catholic Church. How odd. But had she ever had any sort of life, really? Mary never could find a major in college that suited her, so she just followed the General Studies course, and then dropped out a semester before graduation to marry George and have babies. She sighed. It was the closest she could come to grieving, to mourning for her old school friend.

They weren't close, never had been, just two members of a group of five young women who were friends in college. Actually, she hadn't kept up with any of them, and the only reason she was here at Mary's funeral was that she'd run across her obituary last Tuesday, and she lived in the same city, unlike the others, who were—God knows where. She had not seen Mary Louise in six years. She and Leo had returned to Atlanta so that she could take a faculty position at the university. She rang Mary up and invited her and George to dinner. It was very uncomfortable, awkward, really, though Mary and George seemed to enjoy themselves well enough. But she had nothing in common with them. She remembered that they sat there on the couch holding hands, for heaven's sake. How sweet. She'd tried to make teasing nostalgic small-talk, "I see you still love your Georgie, Mary Louise." Mary just looked surprised and said, "Of course." Hard to find a common topic of communication. And there they were, she in her jeans and turtleneck, Mary in her blue crepe dress. She was relieved when the evening was over. Later, when Mary called to invite her and Leo, she'd responded, "We're both just so busy these days." She never saw her again.

So much had happened in those six years—or was it really so little? That thought startled her. Lately, she'd had these sudden little—what should she call it? Flashes? Little light flashes, like blips on a monitor screen. She caught the furrowed brow in the visor mirror. That wasn't new; it was there all the time now. She would get Botox, she'd done the research there and decided it was safe. Fifty years old—fifty, for god's sake.

Leo looked so handsome that night of the dinner. He laughed at her struggle to make thin slices of the roast, wondering why it wouldn't cut until he showed how she was trying to cut against the grain. He was still happy then. The memory of his crooked smile suddenly hurt her heart—caused her stomach to lurch. But no. No, it wasn't that she missed him, it wasn't that at all. Another of those little light flashes: she didn't miss *him*—what she missed was loving him, she missed being touched in that tender spot by that smile. One summer morning about a year after that night, they'd had the inevitable talk, mutually deciding to part, wishing each other well, all the usual good will, no drama or trauma. He'd already become involved with some graduate student. She knew the young woman but not very well. Without untactfully saying so, she suspected that Leo was in a middle-age crisis, and the affair would pass. The truth was, though, the real truth was that she didn't want it to pass. She was done, more than ready to let go. They had lived together for five years, and they were years of great change for both of them. Their paths had begun to diverge, no longer sharing the same opinions, concerns, interests. It was time to move on. Emptiness was painful, but she knew hypocrisy would have been worse.

Now, if she'd been Mary Louise—thank heaven she was not—she'd have been stuck. She remembered the dowdiness of Mary's figure in that blue crepe dress. She had five children—five! She narrowed her eyes, frowning in thought, certain that Mary's love for George, and his for her, had died long before the birth of the third child—maybe even the second. She decided that the hand-holding that night was an intimacy born of shared imprisonment. Now, that would be an interesting topic to explore: the intimacy of shared imprisonment in marriage. Maybe she'd think about that some more.Yes, good title already, too: Bond and Bondage—maybe Bond *or* Bondage? Again she wished she'd at least brought a notebook with her.

She remembered with a start that sitting in a car with the heater on and no ventilation was dangerous and touched the window button to lower the window a couple of inches. Good grief, the wind was cold. A little splash of leaves hit the windshield, the limbs of the pecan tree behind them looked bereft, as though calling after them, but no—the leaves were dead, gone, could never return now. Now there was nothing for them except to decompose. How poetic the wind made her mind. She smiled a little in self-amusement. Morbid, though, dead leaves. Well, it was a funeral, after all.

A car pulled up beside her on the passenger side. A couple got out of the front seats and three people got out of the back—another couple and a portly man with a bald head. She recognized George, and probably the two couples were two of Mary's children, married now. Oh, she definitely didn't want to witness all that grief. No, that was one of the main reasons she'd decided to stay in the car until the last minute. The side windows of her car were tinted and they couldn't see her. She tried to scrunch down in the seat until she realized she couldn't possibly be unnoticeable with the car engine running. George was putting a hat on his head. One of the women hugged herself and shivered, her husband put his arm around her. But—where was the grief? Suddenly, for a moment, she felt outraged. Where were George's tears? He looked sober, kind of solemn, but not grief-stricken, just kind of distracted and serious. Bits of voice came over the wind, something about "Giulio's." My God, she thought, they're talking about where to have lunch afterwards! She felt furious that there was no sobbing, no wailing, there was no grief! She wanted to get out of the car and shake George: "You stupid bastard! She gave up her life for you. Now she's lying in there dead and you're out here worrying about your frigging lunch!"

My goodness, she thought, where did that come from? But they were about to pass by the front of her car with its untinted windshield. They could see her and she did not want George to recognize her, she didn't want to speak to him, to be forced into making sympathetic remarks. She slipped her muffler up over her head just as they passed, turned, and looked straight at her. First she saw the young woman's face. She had to be Mary's daughter. She looked just like Mary; in fact, she looked just like Mary did on the day she heard that her own mother died. Bette and Lauren were there at the time with them, helping her pack, stopping every now and then to put an arm around her, consoling her. But Mary was just like this young woman. She responded with gratitude to the sympathy, but she was not wracked with grief.

How strange. The young woman's eyes looked directly into

her own now as she passed between the car and the pecan tree. And George, walking right behind his daughter, George, who had been careful to cover his bald head in the cold wind, looked at her with the same eyes, then quickly away. Clearly he hadn't recognized her, but the eyes startled her. She blinked, feeling somehow embarrassed, as though she'd inadvertently walked in on someone in the nude. There was sorrow there, so deep it was hurtful to see it. Still, there was no hysteria, not even shock, just an odd calmness—what was it? acceptance? Whatever it was, it made her feel small, as though her anger had been childish, immature. Well, she thought, maybe just a little inappropriate. In any case, it wasn't grief as she understood it.

She looked at the dashboard clock again: fifteen minutes to go. She glanced into the rear-view mirror and saw another car pulling into a parking space behind her. A youngish man, his wife, and three children. Mary's grandchildren, no doubt. She wondered how many grandchildren Mary had and whether she made those silly grandmother remarks, showed pictures, and cooed. Somehow she didn't think so. She couldn't see their faces, but the woman was weeping, or at least she was holding a tissue to her eyes. Now that's a little more like it, she thought. She's your mother, for Christ's sake! Again, she wondered at her anger.

And then she wondered if her own son Ty would come to her funeral when she died. Well, of course he would. Poor Ty would be devastated, she knew very well, not like these ungrateful, emotionless bastards. She was glad she hadn't forced any religion on Ty. She remembered the response she'd made to someone's question about that, one of those answers one remembers because one is especially pleased with one's self for coming up with it: "Oh, I don't have anything against religion; I just don't have anything *for* it."

Still, she thought, she was glad now that they'd all respected Mary's faith—never deliberately shocking her with narratives of their exploits, never making Catholic jokes—probably because Mary had respected their unbelief as well and never tried to convert them. But there was that one night when they had a discussion about it. "Mary," she'd said, "I just don't believe in any God. I'm sorry, I just don't."

"But that means there is no meaning in your life," Mary said, with something almost like pity in her voice.

"Oh, now, that really is crap. We make our own meaning. We can make a difference for good in the world and in our lives if we choose to, without religion. Our salvation is in ourselves."

"No, I know you'll do good. But how can you live without love?"

"What?" She'd almost laughed. "Well, of course, I will love—*that* is the real meaning of life—here and now, in this world, *human* love. Why would you think I wouldn't love? I don't believe there has to be a God for me to love someone! That's crazy."

"But you are mortal—don't you know that?"

What the hell mortality had to do with it she did not understand, and the discussion just ended there. She didn't want to get into any talk about an after-life and she assumed that was what Mary meant by her mortality. Humanity, she knew, was the force for good in the world, not some god, and it was human love that gave life personal meaning—she knew that. Still, it was odd that she should remember the reference to mortality here at Mary's funeral. Well, maybe not. The mind makes logical connections even when we ourselves do not, one of those little light flashes told her. She watched the leaves in little dead whirlwind dances and thought of Ty.

Ty. She saw him in memory and smiled, saw him as he was when she'd adopted him. He was eleven, Vietnamese, and small for his age. She saw his dear little face, so serious, far too serious for a child. He was in college now at Emory, wanting to become a doctor—so smart, and very determined to be successful. She was very proud of him. Her biological clock had started ticking, or anyway, that's what she told people when she adopted him. The idea of a womb wearing a timepiece, though, had always struck her as a silly metaphor. Actually, she'd just come out of a gut-wrenching relationship, and it was not her womb that felt empty, but her heart. Adopting a Vietnamese child was an attractive idea for other reasons; she felt she was doing something good and "right," something to right the wrong her country had done and something right for humanity. Plus it had the added attraction of not increasing overpopulation.

And Ty was just adorable. She could see in her memory that solemn little round face almost worshipping her. Of course, like all working mothers, she never had as much time for him as she'd hoped to have, but she had sincerely tried to be there for him always, and she made sure he had everything he needed. She had even hired a personal tutor to help his English—and he was so smart. He learned English—he learned *everything* so quickly. When had she talked to him last? "Oh, my goodness," she whispered aloud. My goodness, it was two months ago! Instantly, like a reflex, she flipped through the pages of her mental calendar to see if she'd been unavailable to him, if she'd been unable to talk to him when he called. It always concerned her that he should know she was there for him. And it had not been easy to be there sometimes, but she was careful never to let him know that, never to let him see that listening to him, spending time with him, caused any sacrifice on her part. She didn't want him to feel guilty about anything.

Then it occurred to her—it was not Ty who called two months ago, it was she who'd called him. And it was he who didn't have time to talk to her. Why hadn't she remembered that? It didn't matter, of course, she certainly didn't expect him to drop everything when she called, even if she did feel a little stab of nostalgia for the times he'd called her when he first left home. How he had missed her. She was glad that he was involved in his studies and in his life at Emory, busy, building a life of his own and a career. But shouldn't he have called her back later when he had time to talk to her? She watched a leaf, clinging to the windshield in front of her; then it was gone. Odd, his not calling back. How was it that she hadn't noticed that? How was it she hadn't noticed that two months had passed since her call?

She realized suddenly that Ty was gone. He would not come back now. Not really. Perhaps at Christmas for a day or two, perhaps not, but she knew that even when he came home, he would never really *be* there again, never really be her son again. He would have a deep regard for her, respect, admiration, fondness—gratitude, certainly—but not love. That was gone. Taking in a deep breath, she thought, well, okay, so how do I feel about that? After a minute or two, she decided she felt a bit sad, but she was glad she'd had the experience of mothering, glad Ty had been in her life for the ten years she'd had with him. She felt pleased with her answer and leaned her head back on the headrest and closed her eyes to savor it. Then, for no apparent reason, she remembered the dim early light of a dawn some years ago. She and Leo lay in bed, their faces inches apart, their bodies still clinging together, moist and warm. She traced the lines of his face with her finger, encountered a tear, stopped, and looked at him in the dim light.

"You look at me," he whispered, "and I see myself as a fact, real, and the world becomes fact then, too."

"And that makes you feel . . . safe?"

"Terror," he whispered, and he turned his face away from her. Why had he done that? And why had she not asked him what he meant? Suddenly she felt profound sadness. She wanted to cry. Things leave and don't stay, and we don't see them leave; we just see that they're gone. *"But you are mortal. Don't you know that?"* Mary wasn't talking about an after-life.

She raised her head upright to see the bare tree in front of her, the church behind it, and felt a silent detonation somewhere inside her—not a light flash. She knew why she had not asked Leo what he meant. She knew why she had not noticed the passage of two months time. The tears that had welled in her eyes froze there and did not fall.

The clock on the dashboard told her it was time to go inside the church. But she didn't. Instead, she put the car in reverse and backed out of the parking space away from the tree. She drove away quickly. She had time to go back home and get her laptop before her lunch date with Ed. Maybe if she got to the restaurant early, she'd have time to look up some of those figures before he arrived.

Lavábo

Father Joseph Stansel kicked his bedcovers off with one leg and left his knee bent toward the ceiling, the sole of his foot resting on the top of the bedsheet. He opened his eyes halfway and looked at his striped pajama leg in the dim light coming through the closed slats of the blinds; the stripes vertical, the slats horizontal, both in the pale blue of dawn. He ran one hand through his sandy hair, and with the other, reached for the illuminated clock—5:30—he could sleep another half hour. He had to say Mass at 7:00. But if he didn't get up now, he wouldn't be able to have his coffee. Nothing by mouth except water for one hour prior to reception of the Holy Eucharist had always included coffee, as far as he was concerned, though Father Bob told him he was being excessively scrupulous in the matter. He ran his hand over his beard, down his smooth bare chest, and massaged the smooth sheet with the sole of his foot, drowsily closing his eyes again, deciding he'd do without the coffee until later.

But something about the smooth bareness of his chest, the smooth sheet under his foot, and the half-conscious memory of the word "scrupulous" made him open his eyes, fully and suddenly. He lay there for a moment, looking at the dawn through the slats, reciting mentally his Morning Offering, putting off remembering, putting off awakening, the effort having the opposite effect of waking him fully.

He swung his feet over the side of the bed and onto the cool ceramic tile floor, rested his elbows on his knees, and turned his face toward the ceiling. He would have to remember, he would have to think about it, pray about it, do something about it. He knew that. But perhaps Ralph Whatley hadn't recognized him after all, perhaps anything he did now would do more harm than good, perhaps he should just forget about it, face Ralph as if nothing had happened. In fact, perhaps Ralph himself—if he did recognize him—was thinking the same thing. Perhaps, perhaps. It was just *that*: the uncertainty—uncertainty about anything—that was making him crazy. Uncertainty made him unable to decide on a course of action—or inaction. One thing he felt sure of: when he saw Ralph Whatley at Mass on Sunday, he would know. He would be able to tell just by looking at him, he was sure of that. Meanwhile, he had to say 7:00 a.m. Mass today, and Ralph never came to weekday Mass. He stood up quickly and headed for the shower.

With a towel wrapped around his waist, he padded down the hall from the bathroom toward the kitchen, pausing at the open door of Bob's bedroom, listening to his soft snoring, glancing at the nightlight on his dresser—the Blessed Virgin holding the Christ, the soft ivory glow of her face. He wanted to cry.

Coffee seemed a trial, and he regretted that he now had the time for it. He couldn't get the new bag of coffee open, he couldn't find the coffee measure, and he couldn't see the water line on the glass pot. Everything was difficult. He told himself that it was because he'd got in so late last night, he hadn't had enough sleep, he was having trouble mentally transiting back to Tampa after his vacation, and he knew that he was lying.

He poured his coffee, emptying the remainder of the pot into the thermal carafe for Bob when he woke up. He was very fond of the old priest. It wasn't that Bob played any kind of paternal role for him—he was just fond of him. His sarcastic wit, his pragmatic, down-to-earth attitude about everything, literally everything. Forty years as a parish priest would make anybody a realist, he'd often say. He had handled everything at St. Vincent's alone until Joseph arrived last year, fresh out of the seminary, newly ordained, and very willing to help in any way he could—including taking the early Masses so that Father Bob could sleep in. Bob was grateful for the help, and said so, but he had also had to learn to share the rectory with someone almost forty years younger. They had managed together very well, though, and Joseph knew that Bob was now glad of his company. Joseph was very good at making himself liked by everybody; it was probably his greatest asset.

He topped off his cup and went back to his room to dress: black pants, socks, shoes, shirt, and belt. And the collar. He stood for a moment before the mirror, looking not at himself but at the collar. If Joseph Stansel loved anything at all, he loved the priesthood. He always had, ever since he was an altar boy in the seventh grade. He had never wanted anything else in life—nothing, no one, only that collar. He had given up everything for it. No, that wasn't true, but it would be. It had to be.

He walked softly down the hall again past Bob's door to the

back door of the rectory, took the key to the chapel's back door from its hook above the light switch, and closed the door quietly behind him.

About ten o'clock that morning, Ralph and Isabel Whatley went into the church office and asked to speak to Father Bob. The secretary said he was at the hospital to visit the sick, but would return after lunch and they agreed to return then. Joseph overheard this conversation through the open door of his office around the corner from the secretary's desk. Something had to be done. It had to be done before lunch. But Father Bob was at the hospital and probably would eat lunch out before coming back to the office. He couldn't see him until then. If he was going to see him before the Whatleys did, he'd have to go to the hospital now and try to intercept him somehow. But was that the only option? If he did go to the hospital, find him, what would he say to him? He had to think this through, yes, but the problem was that any thinking he did now would have to be decisive. And now there was no time to think it through—he must make a decision now, right now. It came to him: "when in doubt, do nothing." Okay, then. That would have to be it. Ralph Whatley was mistaken. He couldn't have seen Joseph on the veranda of Friday Knights' in Key West. Because Joseph was not there.

He had a habit of going to the gym to work out on Monday afternoons and, deciding he should make no departure from his routine, he went to the gym after lunch. He had a contact there, Jim Rodriguez, who was completely trustworthy, having among his clients the mayor himself; he was also completely dependable for high quality at a steady price. In fact, Joseph had this contact long before he had arrived at St. Vincent's, having known him since seminary. He wished very strongly that his current situation would allow him to speak to Jim. Never had he wanted a hit more than he did this afternoon. But as he ran on the treadmill, then lifting weights, he kept an eye on the clock. He wanted to stay approximately the same period of time as usual, and he needed to use this time to condition his mind as well as his body, so that his innocence would be real and not false, so that his responsive behavior would not be unnatural. He felt fairly certain that Bob would want to speak to him as soon as he returned to the office, so he tried very hard to remain focused.

It was difficult, however. He kept thinking of Kevin, and if he didn't police himself very rigorously, those thoughts became obsessive, keeping him from conditioning his mind as he knew he had to do. Each time Kevin's face came to mind, he forcefully replaced it with Bob's. He reflected that this afternoon was one of the most difficult in his life, but he decided that difficulty was very good for him. He'd never required so much discipline from himself. Involuntary improvement, he thought wryly.

When he reached the office, Bob was there. He wanted so much to ask Betty if Ralph Whatley had returned after lunch, but he didn't dare. There was nothing for it—he'd just have to wait to be summoned. But the summons never came. He had an appointment for confession at four; his appointment arrived, remained in his office about a half hour and left. Still no summons. He checked to see if Bob's office door was open. It was. He was still there. Then he decided that Bob was probably going to wait until this evening and talk to him at the rectory. No, that wouldn't happen; there was a parish council meeting that night. Well, there was nothing to do now but wait—and stay focused on his innocence. He doubted very much that Bob would say anything at dinner when there was so little time before the council meeting at seven and when Mrs. MacDonald would be there. She always remained until after dinner to clean up the kitchen before going home. No, Bob wouldn't say anything to him until tomorrow. He fought against an anxious disappointment; the sooner this was over, the better.

It was then, as he sat at his desk thinking and looking down at his fingernails, that his mild obsession with his hands began. He'd always had a tendency toward obsession, a fact he'd discovered in seminary during one of the many psychological interviews he'd undergone. A year ago, he'd become obsessed with developing and sculpting his thighs during his workouts; he'd very nearly done permanent damage before he was able to let go of it. Actually, he realized that it was probably an obsession with the Mass that led him to become a priest. Had he experienced a "calling" from God? He didn't know, he had never known, he'd only known that he lived for the Mass every day for a period of years before the realization eventually came that he'd fallen in love with it, and that he wanted nothing else in life. That had been his "calling," but he'd never known for certain whether it was just another manifestation of his obsessiveness. In any case, it was still with him: he'd rather be at Mass than anywhere else in the world.

He looked at his fingernails and determined that he very much needed a manicure. Another difficulty: he could go to a nail salon in street clothes but he couldn't be sure that a parishioner wouldn't see him there and disapprove of priests having manicures. It was a risk he was going to take, however, because he really needed a manicure.

Dinner that evening with Father Bob was utterly normal, with the usual running conversation with Mrs. MacDonald about her sons while she served them. Afterwards, Bob left immediately for the council meeting and Joseph decided to watch television for a while. It was possible that Bob would want to talk to him when he got home—which he did usually around 8:30—and so he decided he'd be in bed early that night. This was a confusing decision, however, because he wanted the ordeal over with, so why was he avoiding it? He didn't know, but while he distractedly watched television, he studied his hands. He was fair-skinned, and in the sunny Florida climate, he'd always had a few freckles on his hands. But now the freckles seemed to have disappeared. The contrast with his freckled wrists and forearms was noticeable. How strange, he thought, but then he noticed that his hands were *darker* than his wrists. That made no sense. He turned his palms over—also dark. Could this be some kind of precursor of skin cancer? It didn't seem likely, but maybe he'd better have it checked out with a dermatologist.

At eight o'clock he put on his pajamas and took a book to bed. He had to get up early for Mass, anyway, and he'd just returned from vacation, so he could be expected to be tired. There was really no need to have an excuse for going to bed early, but it bothered him that he'd hardly focused on his innocence at all that evening. That wouldn't do; it must stay in the forefront of his mind until he had the inevitable encounter with Father Bob—which would surely come tomorrow. He remembered that Bob had not once looked at him directly during dinner. He recalled Bob's pink and shiny head showing through his old-fashioned gray crew-cut as he bent over Mrs. MacDonald's beef stew, his horn-rimmed glasses and half-hooded eyes—no, he had not looked at him directly, not even once.

He laid the *Homiletics Review* on his nightstand. He had no intention of reading; he only wanted Bob to see it if he looked in when he came home. He flipped the alarm switch on the clock and raised his hand to the bedside light switch. It looked as if the strange darkness of his hand had increased during the last hour. And it wasn't a tanned kind of darkness—more like gray. Maybe it was a circulation problem; he probably needed a physical instead of just a dermatologist, but he'd start there. He'd make an appointment tomorrow.

How good it was to have the lights turned off! He could think when the lights were out, when he could be assured of no interruption, no distraction. But the first thing that came to mind was not a focus on his innocence, but Kevin. Oh, God, Kevin! He could drown—no, he already had—in those brown eyes, so deep and full of trust! Above that tender mouth, that skin like brown silk. Oh, Kevin. He must never see him again. He would write to him. No. Nothing in writing, *ever.* He remembered Jonathan's wisdom in seminary: Never local, never write, never tell what you do for a living. It was good advice and it had worked very well for him. That James boy, when he served as acolyte, was always flirtatious, and would have been a sore trial had it not been for Kevin—and for Jonathan's good advice of "never local." He hardly noticed him at all during Mass, but in the sacristy before Mass, his little postures, movements at once graceful and sensual, always glancing at him from the side. Oh, God, how many times, Kevin, have I been so grateful for your steadfast love! But this thought brought only anguish.

He had written a check for cash from the priests' discretionary fund to take with him to the homeless shelter and bought a ticket for Kevin to Key West, but he'd been careful to send the ticket by regular mail, not traceable to him. How could he have known Ralph and Isabel Whatley would go fishing in the Keys during his vacation? But, even so. He should have known better than to go to Friday Knights. Stupid, just stupid. And now he had to lose Kevin. His heart was breaking. Tears flowed down his cheeks, past his earlobes, wet the pillow beneath his head. This was what he'd been avoiding, this was what he'd known would kill him. Kevin, sweet Kevin. He wept until he had no tears left.

He was only half asleep when the front door opened and he heard the sounds of Father Bob in the kitchen. But after a few minutes, he saw him standing in silhouette in his doorway. It seemed he stood there a long time, but he couldn't be sure. He was certain, though, before he fell asleep in exhaustion, he was certain that Bob knew everything.

The alarm was painful. His sleep had been restless, repeatedly interrupted by images, dreams—God knows what. He turned on the lamp beside the bed: his hand had darkened even more during the night. He sat up on the side of the bed and held his hands under the lamplight. How could that happen? They looked scaly. He scraped the back of his left hand with his right forefinger. Yes, it was scaly—not a good sign. He must call John Adamson today, see if he could get an appointment just to have him take a look. He reflected, as he had before, that it was good to be a priest when he needed a professional of some kind. It seemed every professional he ever needed was represented among the parishioners. John was a dermatologist with a busy practice, but he was sure he'd squeeze him in sometime today.

After showering, he stopped at Father Bob's door and looked at him, burrowed under the covers, the back of his head barely visible above his broad hunched shoulders. The Mary nightlight stood guard. Suddenly he believed with all his might that Bob knew nothing, he'd not yet been told anything, he was innocent of any knowledge that Whatley might bring. And just as suddenly, he was filled with profound regard—love, even—for this old man. Ralph Whatley became a monster in his imagination, one who would bring hurt and harm to Father Bob, innocent Bob, who'd never hurt anybody. Indignation filled him; he felt like a knight defending the old priest against the dragon of heartbreak that he knew Ralph Whatley would inflict on him. He must do everything in his power to protect him—no matter what it cost. He saw himself as a young Lancelot to Bob's Arthur; he would fight to the death to protect his liege and lord. If Ralph Whatley must be banished from the kingdom—the parish—so be it. He loomed in Joseph's mind as a profound evil.

He went to the kitchen and made coffee but poured none for himself, only filling the thermal carafe for Bob. He felt strong, invincible, and most of all, ready. He would fast until this battle was over. He forgot all about his hands.

In the sacristy, he vested for the feast of the day—St. Dominic—and went into the chapel early to say his morning prayers. He ended with the prayer to St. Michael: "St. Michael, the Archangel, defend us in battle. Be our defense against the wickedness and snares of the devil. May God rebuke him, we humbly pray. . . ." The handful of old ladies who always attended early Mass began to drift into the chapel. He rose from his kneeler in the back pew and processed to the pulpit, kissed the altar, then raised his hands. He was horrified to see that his palms were completely gray. And they looked thin, as though they had begun to wither.

As soon as he got to his phone, he called John Adamson's office. It wasn't open yet. He waited half an hour and called again, but the receptionist said that Dr. Adamson couldn't see him until the next day at the earliest. By the time he called, the color of his hands had normalized to a more even skin tone, and he began to think the whole incident had been in his mind, just a product of this new obsession, perhaps made worse by the flickering candlelight on the altar.

In any case, his strength returned, and when Father Bob came into the office at nine, he smiled and waved to him as he passed his doorway. Bob nodded to him without smiling, but then he seldom smiled anyway, so Joseph was not concerned. However, it was not long after that when he heard him bellow out from his office down the hall, "Joseph! Come in here!"

He was stunned. They never used first names in the office like that, nor had Bob ever called him into his office that way. The soft clacking of Betty's typing suddenly ceased and the silence seemed deafening. This was it. Now was the time. He stood and breathed deeply, strode to his doorway and paused there to cross himself from the holy water font, passed Betty sitting at her desk, looking up at him round-eyed, and went quickly to Bob's office. He was sitting behind his desk, leaning back, and looking at him with his half-hooded eyes, unsmiling. He motioned to the door behind him and Joseph closed the door.

"I want you to hear my confession," he said, moving a lazy finger toward the open closet behind Joseph where vestments were kept. "Suit up."

"What? You want me to do what?" They did not hear each other's confessions—ever. Joseph was thrown off-balance. His invincibility thinned, his face paled, and he felt himself stammer, "Are you serious?"

"Of course I am."

There was nothing for it. He turned to the closet and removed the purple stole. With his back still turned, he whispered his prayer in Latin—he always said the inaudible prayers in Latin. Then he kissed the stole and placed it around his neck.

"Sit down," said Father Bob. Joseph felt the same way he'd felt when he was eight years old and had been called to the principal's office for cheating on a spelling test. His heart was racing, his palms began to perspire, and he could not now, under these circumstances, avoid Father Bob's eyes. This was crazy. What was he doing?

"Bless me, Father, for I have sinned," said Bob. "It has been two weeks since my last confession." There followed a string of venial nonsense—drinking too much at a cocktail party last week, missing evening prayers, frustrations, impatience, etc. He concluded by saying, "Aren't you going to ask me to recite the Act of Contrition? And aren't you going to give me a penance?"

"Yes, of course."

Bob said the prayer, and Joseph absolved him of his confessed sins and told him to make a holy hour—which he knew Bob would do that evening anyway. Then he sat there staring at the elder priest. This was bizarre; was there a point to it?

Bob said, "Thanks. You can go on about your business now. Don't forget we are concelebrating Estelle Maxwell's funeral Mass this afternoon."

Joseph stood up, feeling unsteady on his feet, and hung the stole back on Bob's rack. He turned slowly to walk to the door when Bob stopped him. "You know, Joseph, I could have just told the Lord directly that I'm sorry for my sins. Do you suppose he would have forgiven me?"

"Of course."

"Right. We know we're not the necessary means of the Lord's forgiveness."

"No. But it's a sacrament. Why are you pointing this out?"

"Just thinking and sharing the thought. We're not very important, you know, in ourselves. Estelle's funeral is at two o'clock, don't forget. Do you suppose she'll be less dead for having priests say a Mass for her than she would be if she'd been, say, a Presbyterian?"

Joseph didn't like this conversation. He wanted to get out of there. He was both terrified and confused. What was Bob doing? "No, of course not."

"Right. See you this afternoon."

But Joseph was suddenly angry. "Are you saying that a funeral Mass has no efficacy?"

Bob seemed to have—Joseph wasn't sure—a little smile at the

corners of his mouth. "I didn't say that. I wasn't talking about the Mass. Think about it, Father."

Joseph left. What in God's name was Bob trying to do? Then it occurred to him: Father Bob knew very well how Joseph loved the priesthood. Was he, in some bumbling way trying to disenchant him—so as to soften the loss, to make it seem unimportant? Was he in some awkward way trying to convince him that he wasn't about to *lose* something earth-shakingly important to him? Oh, God, was it that bad? Would he lose the priesthood? Was Bob trying to tell him that? He felt tears fill his eyes as he walked back to his office, feeling Betty's round-eyed stare on him. He closed his office door and sobbed.

A box of tissues was always handy for parishioners on the corner of his desk. He used about half of them before he could stop the sobs long enough to leave his office with some dignity, aware of Betty tactfully avoiding looking at him, and went into the chapel. There he knelt and prayed. He begged and promised until he developed a headache. He didn't know how long he was in there until he heard Bob laughing and talking in the hallway outside with the deacon, George Thompson. Probably going to lunch. They had lunch together quite often. It occurred to him then that he had eaten nothing all day, but as he sat there in the semi-darkness and tried to think of food, he looked down at his hands. They looked as if they'd been rubbed with a piece of charcoal. The nails were ragged and filthy. They were hideous.

The door opened then, and a slant of bright light entered the chapel. Bob asked if he wanted to go to lunch. He tried to think fast. This was a good sign, but no, he couldn't go anywhere in public with his hands like this. And he didn't want Bob to see his swollen eyes, so he only half-turned his head and said, "No, thanks. I'll get something later."

Then Bob said, "You have a wedding on Saturday, don't you? The Gonzalez girl?"

"Yes. Why?"

"Do you suppose they'd be any less married if they weren't married by a priest—if Judy Gonzalez was a Protestant, I mean, which she's not, of course."

My God, Joseph thought. He's still at it. George was standing behind him, waiting. Joseph was praying that neither of them could see his swollen eyes. He didn't answer.

"Well?"

"No, Bob," he said irritably. "What's your point?"

"Judy Gonzalez can be very much married by a Baptist pastor—but that pastor can be married with children—unlike you."

"And your point?"

"The point is that people don't need a priest to be married—not even according to canon law."

His heart sank. It was true. He understood, or thought he did. "Are you trying to tell me that the priesthood shouldn't matter to me so much?" He felt profoundly embarrassed that George Thompson was hearing this conversation.

"No. That's not what I meant. The reverse, in fact. I'll see you later." He closed the door.

What the hell did he mean by that? Was Bob telling him that the priesthood didn't matter or was he expressing contempt for Joseph himself—telling him that he didn't matter, personally? Joseph hadn't eaten, his heart was broken, and now his mind was, too. He was exhausted; he folded his arms on the back of the pew in front of him, laid his head there and fell asleep.

The door opened and someone came in—Bob. He shook Joseph's shoulder. "Hey, wake up, dear boy. You'll have to do the funeral Mass yourself this afternoon. I've got an emergency." Joseph moaned, slowly came to, his shoulders stiff, a kink in his neck. "You'd better get on over to the church. The hearse is already here, and it's 1:30. I've got to go."

He left and Joseph stood, rubbed his eyes, and headed for the bathroom to splash some cold water on his face.

The coffin was already in the vestibule when he arrived. In the sacristy, he saw that he had four servers—the James boy, Anthony, and his two younger brothers. He was thankful that they were already vested. He told Anthony to prepare the censer, vested himself and got ready for procession. Finally, he signaled the pallbearers and organist that all was ready. He prayed no one would notice his hands. He had no anxiety at all about whether he would do everything correctly, as he usually had; in fact, there was no longer any anxiety about anything at all. It had all been spent. He felt destroyed, dead, as though this could be his own funeral. He picked up his funeral Mass book and followed the servers with their candles down the aisle.

Anthony handed him the censer and he incensed the coffin on

the top and all four sides. He had no feeling at all, just a peculiar kind of objectivity about his motions, his words, as though he were an actor in a play and an observer at the same time. There was nothing to be concerned about, except that he remember his lines, and he had no trouble doing that. It was all rote, unconscious memory. He sat in the priest's chair and listened to the readings of Scripture, rose to read the Gospel, delivered his brief homily for the family, and went to the altar to begin the Liturgy of the Eucharist.

He incensed the bread and wine with prayers, then the altar, and when all was incensed, he turned to dip his fingers into the bowl of water provided by Anthony: "Lavábo . . ." He stopped, and Anthony looked up at him quizzically. But he was looking down at his hands, silent, as the water dripped from his fingertips back into the little bowl. They were dark and shrunken, the hands of a dead man. Finally, he continued the prayer, meant to be inaudible: "Lavábo . . . manus meas . . ." and turned to the altar, where the wafer lay on the paten—white and perfectly formed. After prayers on behalf of himself and his congregation, he raised the wafer to God and said, "This is my body!" He willed himself to look up at his hands. They were immaculate, perfect, unspeakably beautiful. The chapel bell chimed softly as he and his people knelt and adored in silence: "My Lord and my God."

The people attending the funeral were touched by the priest's tears as he performed the liturgy that afternoon. They thought he must have been very close to Estelle and grieved for her passing. They couldn't know that Father Stansel had just seen his own nothingness and his priesthood together, face to face, as it were.

Retreat

Peggy stood next to her luggage in the litt door to the parlor, impatiently shifting her heav one arm to the other while she waited for the cc her key. The parlor was cozy and pleasant, but Peg uce her surroundings. Her attention was fixed on the man sitting on the sofa next to the corner table. The first thing she noticed, and what held her attention, was the peaceful expression on the woman's face. Actually, peaceful was not the right word; her face was simply *still.* There was no smile or frown, no look of anxiety or depression, only a very slight attentiveness to the magazine she held—apparently looking at photographs, not reading text, judging by what Peggy could see from a distance of twenty feet or so.

The woman was older—fifty-something, Peggy would guess, about twenty years older than she was. She had a neat salt-and-pepper pageboy haircut and she moved a straying lock of it behind her ear as she turned the pages of the magazine. It seemed important to Peggy to know what the magazine was—to know what would interest this lady. Her right leg, trousered in dark blue Donegal tweed, was crossed over her left knee, and the dark blue loafer, perfectly matching the tweed, moved very slightly—not swinging, just a little reflexive turn, as if to exercise the ankle. Sitting in apparent, perfect comfort, in a slightly slouching position, the woman pushed up the sleeve of her white shaker-knit sweater to see her watch, then glanced at the enormous French clock that stood ticking loudly between two curtained windows. She behaved as though no one stood there in front of her only twenty feet away.

Peggy was captivated, her attention so focused on the woman that she forgot her own restlessness. The woman's crossed leg lifted quickly and the ankle came to rest on her knee. A posture that might have looked ungraceful on someone else was simply elegant on this woman, idly turning pages, unaware of her observer. The sofa adjacent to the corner table was vacant. Peggy wanted to be sitting there, chatting quietly with this lady, as though they were old friends—maybe even sisters.

The concierge, in jeans and a gray sweatshirt, arrived with the key.

in room five. Just go up that short flight of stairs at of the hall there. It's the first room on your right." She ted to the hall that extended on their left. "Dinner is in an hour. The dining room is straight ahead of you." She pointed in that direction.

"You don't have an elevator?"

"No, I'm sorry—but we're just two floors. Here, let me help you with that." She reached for the recessed handle of the rolling suitcase.

"No, no, that's all right. I'll manage." Peggy shifted her handbag to one shoulder and her totebag to the other. The shawl, precariously hanging over one wrist, fell to the floor when she reached down for the suitcase handle. When she leaned forward to pick it up, her handbag fell from her shoulder.

"Please. Let me take that." Without waiting for a reply, the concierge took the suitcase handle and headed down the hallway, Peggy following. The woman in Donegal tweed never looked up at her.

The concierge, who said her name was Jean, carried her suitcase up the stairs and left her at the door. Peggy fumbled through the folds of the shawl to find the key and rolled the suitcase, with a clambering noise, across the metal strip at the threshold to the bedside. She unloaded her shawl, key, handbag, totebag, and finally herself in a kind of plop on the bed, as though she'd aimed her body at the bed, then simply turned herself over to gravity. Everything that was hers, including herself, was on the bed. She fell back across the bed and looked up at the ceiling without seeing it.

"I'm here," she whispered aloud, "and when I leave here, I will be solid, not liquid. I will be stable and sure and strong. I will be able to handle Robert and know how to get the alimony from him that I deserve. I will know for certain that the kids are on my side. How can they not be? I am the one who has nursed them, played and laughed with them, been with them twenty-four-seven. I am the one who has loved them. No. No, I want them to have their father. They need him. But he should not have them, not their love, anyway—he doesn't deserve it." But even as she whispered these words with a kind of determined hiss, her eyes looked up at nothing with the panic of a cornered animal. Then she said aloud, in what passed for prayer, "You *will* do this for me." It was a demand, an assertion of a right she held by all the laws of justice. She was their mother. And she had been a *faithful* wife. She was owed this.

Then she kicked the suitcase to its side on the floor, flicked open the lock, and rummaged through the contents. She wanted to wear something blue to dinner.

She still had not noticed the room, had not moved the towels folded neatly at the foot of the bed, had not seen the small desk under the window with its lamp, its pen and writing paper. Two days later, she still would not have noticed the hardness of the single bed, the Bible on the nightstand. When she left, if anyone had asked her the color of the walls, she would not have known the answer.

*

Fern River Retreat House was a very small establishment on a hillside in the North Carolina mountains. It was run by four monks from a Benedictine monastery farther up the hill on a non-profit basis, a fact which accounted for the austerity of the rooms and the shared bathrooms, but oddly did not account for the rather upscale dining retreatants enjoyed.

There was no charge for retreats, but a "donation" of at least $100 per night was asked, more if possible, to cover the costs the monks incurred in providing room and board, along with free spiritual counseling. Most of its clientele came for this counseling; some came to actually retreat from lives that had become too busy, too noisy, or just too difficult in some way. Retreatants were encouraged to take part in the morning and evening prayers in the little chapel, to visit the room often for private meditation and prayer, and to take long walks along the paths in the surrounding woods. There was a small library next to the front parlor that contained a variety of books. Some were secular in nature, some were religious, but all were intended to provide coping helps of one kind or another, or direction for those who felt lost. The brochures at the front desk instructed those who wanted counseling to sign up at least twenty-four hours in advance for hours specified in the brochure. In the interest of providing everyone with the opportunity for counseling, retreatants were encouraged to let the concierge know if they could not keep their appointments and to adhere to the hour-long time limit for sessions.

This was Diana's third visit to Fern River. She knew well why she had returned. Her life had no hectic schedule, she had no difficulty coping with it, and she had no real need of counseling. What should she say to a counselor? What problem did she have, or what kind of "help" could she seek? No. She returned because, there, it was natural for her—even expected—to be alone.

An hour till dinner meant there was time for another short walk in the woods. She slipped her navy blue wool jacket around her shoulders and went through the front door, out to the small leaf-strewn, stone veranda, where a few wrought iron chairs stood deserted, along with abandoned clay pots that still contained straggling plants, leftovers from summer, their blooms long spent—an atmosphere that seemed sad on this November evening. The woods and their pathways began immediately on both sides of the veranda; only a small space had been cleared, just in front, for parking.

She was always alone among people, but in the woods, she wasn't conscious of it. There, it seemed as though her aloneness were by nature, not by design. It wasn't a choice that she'd made, or that anyone else had made for her. It was simply a natural condition of life—like the shape of her hand, the color of her eyes, just part of who she was. She felt no condemnation there, no awareness of being someone whose company was undesirable, no awareness of being unlovable. She didn't return to Fern River because of anything she gained there, but because of something that was *not* there, that stayed with her constantly everywhere else.

But this time, as she shoved her hands into her pockets and kicked at the dark yellow leaves in the pathway, she didn't hear the birds cawing at one another or the air moving among the dry leaves still clinging to half-skeletal trees, nor feel its breeze on her face. She didn't feel like an integrated part of the life there. This time, her aloneness followed her, and with it, all that it meant.

Peggy sat at a table in the corner where she could watch the entrance to the dining room. The waiter—at least, she guessed he was a waiter—wore jeans and a sweatshirt like everyone else there. He took her order for beef tips and noodles. Actually, it wasn't so much that the waiter had taken her order as it was that Peggy had taken his suggestion, and his recommendation for a glass of Merlot. She sipped the wine now, watching the doorway. The woman in Donegal tweed entered and sat down at a table near the entrance, her back to Peggy, a circumstance that at first disappointed her, but then she was glad, because she would be able to watch the woman without being seen by her.

She was freezing. She was always freezing. That's why she never went anywhere without a sweater or the knitted wool prayer shawl that a woman at St. Patrick's back in Tampa had given her. She wrapped it around her shoulders now, glad that the wine wasn't chilled, and shuddered. Though Peggy herself was unaware of it, the pastel multi-colored shawl looked strange over the dark blue football jersey she'd found in the jumbled contents of her suitcase. She curled her fingertips to the inside of her palms and blew on them, trying to warm them, resisting the reflex to gnaw on the already stubby nails. She wished she hadn't ordered wine. It wasn't chilled, but all wine was cold simply because it wasn't hot. Then she saw the waiter bringing an identical glass to the Donegal woman, so Peggy extended her frozen fingers, brought the glass to her lips again, and sipped—yes, it was good. Had the woman ordered the beef tips too? She would watch and see. The waiter, who had been observing her from the side of the room, came to stoke the embers in the grate of the fireplace just beside her table. Peggy was glad that her room had its own thermostat.

The salad arrived. She ate without noticing the piquant balsamic vinaigrette. When the waiter brought the beef tips, she wanted only to slow down, not to finish her dinner before the woman's food arrived—she wanted to see what she'd ordered. So she ate slowly, without noticing the subtle flavor of rosemary and thyme. Then she saw that the woman had also ordered the beef tips. They'd ordered the same thing—beef tips and Merlot. She was pleased, removed her shawl, feeling warm enough for now, and looked down at the long dark blue sleeves of her football jersey. She felt that she had something in common with the woman in blue tweed.

*

Diana sat in the parlor after dinner, sipping espresso and waiting for Brother Mark to call for her. It was hard not to rehearse what she would say. She knew from long years of professional experience that clients almost always did that. A good part of any initial counseling session was getting past the rehearsed speeches of clients. There was a natural tendency in everyone to control events that affected them, as well as a natural inclination to make the most of limited time by planning, and particularly in clients who had anxiety, an impulse to erect protective barriers to spontaneity. But she had no anxiety; her own rehearsal was more an attempt to rid herself of any kind of concealment that might hinder or delay communication.

Brother Mark appeared, a study in placid comfort, in his flannel shirt and chinos. None of the monks at Fern River wore habits. They felt that retreatants would be more comfortable with them if they dressed in the ordinary clothes of laymen.

"Diana?" he spoke quietly in her direction. "Would you like to come in now? You can bring that with you."

She took her cup and saucer and followed him down the short hallway to his office—if it could be called that. There was no desk, just a small sitting area with warm colors, dim torchiere lamps, two leather armchairs with a coffee table between them on a small Persian-style rug. She settled her espresso cup on the table as Mark settled in the other chair, leaned back, crossed his legs and smiled. "You've been here before," he began directly, "but you've never wanted counseling. What's different now?"

She was grateful for the directness. "Well, first of all, I'm a counselor myself. I guess most of us who are professionals are not so ready to see a need in ourselves."

She hoped he wouldn't say it, but he did: "Ah, yes. 'Physician, heal thyself.'"

She sighed. She'd had small hope for this session, and what little she'd had was already evaporating. Nevertheless, she thought, plunge ahead: "There is no love in my life." And she waited. Sure enough, there it was: a slight, almost imperceptible lift in his upper lip, suppressed disdain for a woman who admittedly had no love for anyone except, obviously, herself—sitting there in expensive clothes with a concern that she was not loved. She thought he was probably aware that the new Lexus parked outside was hers. She knew he thought her to be self-indulgent. Now she waited to see how he would proceed, how he would handle his own negative response to her.

"What about your family?"

"I have no family."

"Friends?"

"What friendships I have are superficial, mostly professional."

There was a long pause then. She knew he was deciding how to proceed, to word his response without sounding judgmental, trying to figure out how to remain compassionate and caring toward someone he disliked. He leaned back a little farther in his chair, tilted his head backward, away from her, and almost like a physical cliché, placed his fingertips together. Here it comes, she thought.

"Well, Diana, let me ask you this. Is there anyone *you* love?"

"Not at this time."

"Love begets love, you know."

"So I'm told."

"Well then, does it occur to you that in order to *be* loved, you must first love?"

She had to hand it to him. He wasn't smiling any more, wasn't mincing around. Though he'd been predictable, he had at least avoided hypocrisy insofar as possible.

"I have," she said bluntly. "I *do* love. And then they go. They reject it and disappear." She would fast-forward to save time: "I do not have *feelings* of abandonment, Brother Mark. I *am* abandoned."

"Hm." There was a sudden sign of slight interest. "Then—you probably already know this, as a psychologist yourself—you may be choosing, unconsciously perhaps, to extend yourself only to those who will reject you. Perhaps you do this in order to *avoid* a loving relationship."

No. She knew better. But she also knew that he'd never believe it. His world was not at all unlike her own practice, a repertoire of rational explanations. Depression caused by loneliness almost always had its origin in a fear of risk, a provocation of conflict—or an avoidance of it—but in all cases it was self-love, though the counselor never named it that. It was a counselor's job to abstain from that kind of judgment and simply to detect the client's avoidance and to reveal it to him. Once his own role in the problem was revealed, the client could accept the illusion, offered as standard fare, that he was really in control after all, that he could solve his own problem.

"In other words, it's my own fault."

"I didn't say that."

Actually, you did. You said exactly that. But aloud, she said, "I see. I hadn't thought of it that way. I'll give it some thought."

"Good," he said cheerfully, leaning forward in her direction. It was a sign that he was done for now, the brief session was over. "Let's talk later, after you've had some time to think about that possibility, okay?"

She left, taking her espresso cup with her. There was no real disappointment in the unusually brief session. It hadn't been as bad as it might have been. He might have struggled to conceal his disapproval—while the struggle itself revealed it. Instead, he'd at least plowed ahead in the script, sparing her the pain of watching his struggle.

There would be no "later talk," of course. She already knew the script, knew what she was supposed to say, what he would reply, what the illusion would be: that she had only to open herself to the risk of rejection, to the possibility of conflict and compromise, and all that. Then there would be the grand philosophical finale: After all, that's what life is really all about, isn't it? Relationships, right? That's how we *grow*. She placed her cup on the serving cart in the hallway outside the dining room and then went through the parlor, heading toward her room. She decided to go to bed early and read a while. She'd take a long walk in the woods tomorrow morning.

*

Peggy looked up sharply. The woman passed through the parlor without stopping. She'd sat there, turning the pages of Better Homes and Gardens, hoping the woman would come back and look at magazines again, but she hadn't. Where had she been? Had she gone for counseling? No. She couldn't possibly need help. Maybe she was one of the counselors—no, they were all monks. Peggy made up her mind to approach her at breakfast. She'd get up early and wait in the parlor till she saw the woman go into the dining room. Then she'd just go up to her and ask to share her table. She'd signed up for counseling at eight, but if necessary, she'd just not show up for the appointment if the woman appeared. After all, she could schedule counseling again some other time.

She sighed in disappointment, tossed the magazine sideways onto the sofa. There were no televisions at the retreat house, no way to find out what was happening on "The Bedington Family," her favorite soap. The only phone was at the concierge's desk and retreatants were discouraged from using it except in emergencies, but fortunately, she had her cell, so she left her coffee cup on the table and went out to the veranda to call her mom's house and check on the kids. After talking an hour or so, she went upstairs to bed.

*

In sleep that had become habitually restless, Diana dreamed of the woods. But the trees had been uprooted and re-planted in a desert. There were no birds or other creatures, just a gray-white sky and mud-brown earth and an endless horizon between them. Here and there one of the trees from the forest stood alone. In her dream, Diana went from one tree to another, but as she approached, each one died for lack of water.

She woke to the slanted shadows of the closed venetian blinds on the ceiling, which was white and otherwise bare. Only slanted shadows, slowly fading in the gray light of morning to complete barrenness. The narrow bed's hardness seemed somehow appropriate, and she lay there on her back, feeling as though it were a coffin, hard, empty except for her, and dark. The illuminated clock on the bedside table read 6:15. She rose, showered, and dressed in jeans and a beige cowl-necked cashmere sweater, slipped on the blue loafers but took the brown suede boots from the closet: she'd come back after breakfast to put them on when she got her jacket. She intended to take a very long walk then. Meanwhile, she'd spend some time in the chapel until the dining room opened at seven.

*

She sat on a bench heavily upholstered in tan velvet. Stained glass panels, in a Frank Lloyd Wright style—all straight lines and angles—were backlit and hung suspended from the ceiling of the windowless room, the bare walls covered in a neutral seagrass paper, ending in a neutral tan carpet to match the neutral upholstery of the benches. The only expression of personality in the room was the contorted, suffering Corpus on the dark wood crucifix that hung behind a small plain altar. She had once attended one of the guided meditations there. Brother Thomas talked about faith, hope, and charity: how trust in each other meant faith in life, how connectedness was the hope of life, and how love is the meaning of life. Hell, he said, was the absence of love.

Brother Mark would not believe, even if she told him, that she had always extended herself to others in complete openness and vulnerability. He wouldn't believe that she didn't choose, consciously or otherwise, persons who would or would not reject her. Because she never rejected *anyone*—period. He wouldn't believe it because it didn't fit any of the theories he used to help people. And therefore he could not believe—if she told him—how it is possible to survive disemboweling, to live through it, and then to extend one's self again—and again.

The dining room was open. She sat down and ordered a bigger breakfast than usual to sustain her for the long walk—fruit compote, an egg, wheat waffles with syrup and butter. She had almost finished when a woman came bustling in and headed toward her table, wearing layered sweaters and a large heavy shawl.

"Oh, hi—good morning," the woman said nervously. "My name is Peggy Rivera. Do you mind if I join you?"

"Not at all. Please do."

Peggy pulled a chair out from the table and began a confused search for a resting place for her large handbag—a dirty paisley-patterned fabric bag that looked more like a diaper bag than a purse. Finally deciding that it needed a chair of its own, she pulled another chair out and plopped it there. Then it became necessary to decide which of its multiple outer pockets should hold her room key. She had just decided on one of them when the waiter poured coffee for her and asked for her order.

"Oh." She looked up at him with an expression that seemed to resent his demand for yet another decision, then said, "Whatever she's having."

"I'm afraid I'm just about done with breakfast." Diana blotted her mouth with a napkin and sipped her remaining coffee. "I'm about to leave. I want to take a long walk in the woods this morning, but I think you'll like the fruit compote. It's mixed berries and melons—very good."

"Oh, no," said Peggy, before she could stop herself. "Oh, do you mind? I'd love to go with you. This is my first time here—and I don't know the paths. I want to go but I'm a little afraid of the woods." She laughed nervously. "I'm always afraid I'll get lost."

Diana heard the anxiety in the false laugh and looked at the woman's large brown eyes, round with a childlike hopefulness. Why was she here? In pursuit of confidence? "No, I don't mind at all. I'd be glad of the company."

She waited with Peggy while she ate breakfast. She ordered more coffee, then she said, "Tell you what. I'll go upstairs and get my jacket and boots while you finish—did you bring boots with you?"

"No, why should I have boots?"

"Well, they protect your feet and legs, and you might get your socks and pants covered with nettles."

"I don't mind," said Peggy, though the thought of nettles bothered her.

When Diana returned, Peggy was enraptured by the brown suede boots and matching suede jacket over the beige cowl-necked sweater—which looked like cashmere. This lady had such good taste. She resolved to do something about her wardrobe as soon as her finances stabilized after the divorce.

Since Diana knew the paths, she led the way along those that were too narrow for them to walk side by side. And Peggy talked without ceasing, oblivious to the forest around them. The talking contributed to her breathlessness, which made frequent stops for rest necessary. She was unaccustomed to such exercise, and she was a bit overweight as well.

By the time they returned to the retreat house, Diana knew that Peggy had been a cheerleader in high school, that she had married when she graduated, that she had devoted the past fifteen years of her life to her husband and three children, that her husband had "walked all over" her during their marriage, and that he had an affair. She understood too that when the scoundrel was confronted with the evidence of his affair, he had *not* begged Peggy's forgiveness (as she'd clearly expected), but asked for a divorce. And it was that fact, not the affair itself—which didn't seem to interest Peggy very much—that had been Peggy's undoing. The absence of contrition would have been insufferable enough, but then he'd actually wanted a divorce. *That* had apparently toppled Peggy's view of reality.

Peggy had spent hours in tears in the office of her priest. The members of her prayer group had prayed for her every day, one of them had knitted a prayer shawl for her, and everyone in the parish knew about it—because Peggy had told them all—and everyone knew the evil that Robert Rivera had done to Peggy. And *still* he had not repented, not changed his mind; *still,* he wanted a divorce.

When she had exhausted herself by sharing all this information, she thought she should show some interest in the companion. Diana was a counselor? What a coincidence—that's exactly the field Peggy wanted to enter. She hadn't worked after she married. She explained that she felt she should be at home with the children, and after they were all in school, she felt she should be there when they came home. She thought briefly of telling Diana that, after all, she was the president of the National Rod Davis Fan Club, the star of "The Bedington Family," but something told her not to mention that accomplishment, achieved only after years of faithful participation in the chat room. Anyway, now she was going to have to go to work. That meant school. Her parents would help, but it was Robert's responsibility, really, not theirs. And she had always wanted to be a counselor, she said, and felt that her experience with rearing children had prepared her. Years of intimate experience with the problems of "The Bedington Family" had also prepared her, she thought, but she didn't mention that. Too bad, she said, that becoming a certified counselor meant years of study, when actually real life experience was so much better.

And Diana listened with a compassion that Peggy would not have understood. She had noted Peggy's long, stringy hair, the old football jersey and filthy athletic shoes. Her appearance bespoke neglect, and her chewed nails revealed anxiety. When Peggy told her about the suffering she'd endured by her husband's demanding nature, Diana knew the suffering was real. Peggy explained that she couldn't clean the house as her husband wanted her to because she thought that raising her children was more important, yet despite all her sacrifice, he complained and criticized. And finally he'd gone too far. He had an affair. She made it sound as if the divorce had been her decision, not Robert's. Oddly, it was never the affair that she cited as the reason for the impending divorce—it was her husband's bullying: "Do this, do that. Why can't you at least cook dinner? The house is filthy and you do nothing all day but watch soap operas."

*

They had lunch together. "The thing is, really, I would have forgiven him…" Peggy continued over the French onion soup, "if he'd only had the humility to ask. That's all."

"But he didn't want your forgiveness?" asked Diana, gently.

"No…" Peggy answered, bemused by the question, her musing interrupted when Jean the concierge came to their table.

"Mrs. Rivera? I think you had an appointment for counseling this morning?"

"Yes. But that's all right. I'll schedule again later."

"That's fine, but if you could, please let us know when you need to cancel or change an appointment. The brothers have a rather tight schedule." She smiled at them.

"Well, of all the nerve…" said Peggy when Jean had left.

*

They had dinner together, and afterwards, sat in the parlor where Peggy talked some more. Having at last exhausted the description of her suffering, she now asked Diana questions—questions that wanted Diana's opinions—about politics, religion, the media, what books or films Diana liked. And each opinion found an identical mate in Peggy's own opinions. Peggy was discovering all the things she thought about everything in Diana's opinions. She dug into her fabric bag and found a small piece of paper and a pencil stub. She wanted Diana's address in Atlanta, her phone number, her email address. When she finally went to bed that night, she slept soundly, peacefully, as though reality was returning, and she began to suspect that she could handle Robert, after all.

*

The next morning Peggy did not meet her for breakfast. Diana looked for her in the chapel, the parlor, even the woodland paths—though Peggy would certainly not have gone there on her own. At lunch, Peggy came breezing into the dining room. She'd gone into the little town at the bottom of the hill and had her hair cut into a pageboy style. She'd also bought some suede boots and a couple of new sweaters.

"I didn't tell you what I was going to do," she said, patting her new hairstyle, eager to know if Diana liked it. "I wanted to surprise you!" she laughed, happy with Diana's enthusiastic approval. She showed her new things to Diana with the excitement of a teenager. "How do you think this green looks on me? I've never worn green. I didn't have the money—but there's always plastic, you know. And Robert is still paying the bills. I thought I should give him a few more to pay before the divorce," she said with happy laughter.

Diana asked if Peggy wanted to go for a walk with her, but Peggy said she was tired from her shopping and wanted to lie down for a while.

So Diana went to the chapel instead. She tried to pray for Peggy. She had often tried to pray for her own clients, but the fact was that she couldn't pray at all. She could only feel her words echo into emptiness, rejected. She stared at the crucifix. It was silent.

Peggy met her for dinner wearing her new green sweater. She talked, but the talk was less animated. The air of desperation seemed to have vanished. Now she talked about the isolation of the retreat, how some people might regard it as healthy, but she herself did not. She thought that involvement with others—with family, with friends—was healthier, and she believed that people who were alone contributed nothing to the lives of others. They were simply selfish.

That night Peggy dreamed of herself as a single woman, confident, a professional of some kind—maybe a counselor. Everyone respected and admired her. Her children were proud of her. Robert begged her to take him back, but she refused. The strong woman in her dreams pitied him and wished him well.

*

Diana didn't see Peggy at breakfast. After reading for a while in the parlor, she asked Jean about her.

"Oh, she checked out early this morning. She's gone back to Tampa. Sure didn't stay long. It's too quiet here for some people."

*

The following February, Diana returned to Fern River. She walked through the woods again, shuffling the dry, dead leaves with the toes of her boots. The undergrowth had died back, the density of the forest was gone, and it was as empty as the desert trees in her dream. All the leaves had gone from the trees; they were stripped bare now, their naked arms stretched outward against the bright cloudless blue of the winter sky, like the small wooden crucifix in the chapel. She lifted her face to the sun and felt its warmth like a kind of love, intimate and knowing, infinitely knowing, and it occurred to her that maybe suffering might be a different kind of beauty, one she knew.

Catherine's Garden

The gray-brown female cardinal perched on the fence, her wings fluttering against her body as though she were having a hot flash. Her beak was slightly open, like parted lips, panting. Her bright red mate pecked on the ground nearby in a leisurely hop, occasionally choosing some morsel he found suitable for her and flying back to her open beak to deposit the food. Then he flew back to the ground again and searched for more until finally the couple departed for another location.

Catherine thought she found some kinship with Lady Cardinal. Some other species might ask why on earth she didn't gather her own food, why wait for her mate—who was taking forever and probably keeping the best bits for himself. Moreover, he was easily distracted, in no hurry to bring food to her, while she waited for him, fluttering and panting. Catherine didn't know why the female didn't get her own food, but she felt that she somehow understood her. It had to do with something besides some answer to *why;* such answers always had to begin with *because.* She had grown weary of *why* long ago.

Watching the birds and squirrels through the kitchen window while she drank her morning coffee had become a ritual in the last few months since Frank died. It was the new ritual replacing the old—when she and Frank had watched the morning news together with their coffee. And that ritual had been new at one time, replacing the one they'd followed before he retired. There had been others—while the kids were still at home, when they were still in school, or when they were small. What would replace the birds and squirrels? Or was this the last morning ritual? Her whole life, including morning rituals, had always been patterned by the activities of those around her. Now that all her family was gone, it was apparently patterned to birds and squirrels.

She rinsed her cup and put it in the dishwasher, puttered around the kitchen, wiping coffee stains from the countertop under the coffeemaker, dumping the grounds, rinsing the pot. What would she do today? She made a mental outline: shower, dress, go to Mass, go to the supermarket. She checked her brief shopping list on the little kitchen desk by the phone: milk, detergent, etc.

Life was not very different now that she was alone, just some variation in its rituals. Everything was the same, really. Sometimes she worried a little about the fact that she was not lonely, or in need of finding some "meaning" in life since the departure of her husband and children. She'd even talked to Father Joe about it once, but he didn't seem to understand her concern; he'd assumed that she was asking what she should "do" now and he gave her suggestions: charity work, adult education classes, the Golden-Agers social group at church, etc. But keeping busy was not what worried her. How does one express concern about the fact that one is not concerned?

In the shower, she thought about what to wear—as she always did—and decided on jeans and the gray sweater, since it was still a little cool in this late April. She dressed, made the bed and opened the blinds.

Her friend, Phyllis, was supposed to call later. She had been widowed too—about six months ago. But her husband died after suffering over a year with pancreatic cancer, a year which had nearly killed Phyllis as well. He didn't go suddenly as Frank had done with a massive heart attack in his sleep. After her husband's death, Phyllis had sold the house, moved into a condo, and started traveling. She came over for drinks one afternoon last week with photos from her trip to Paris with a tour group. Catherine thought she looked tired.

"Are you enjoying yourself, Phyllis?"

"Oh, yes," she answered, "but I wish I hadn't planned this trip to Hawaii next week, so soon after getting back from Europe. But what would I do if I stayed at home?" She laughed a little, and Catherine smiled, but she thought the laugh sounded a little hollow.

They sat on the patio and sipped martinis as Catherine talked about the pink and white tulips along the back fence. "I think I like the pastels better than the bright red and yellow I usually put out," she said, thinking that next year she'd include some blue forget-me-nots as a front border.

"Yes," Phyllis answered slowly. Catherine wondered again whether her friend had been wise in selling her home. The condo didn't even have a balcony where she could have put a few plants, and Phyllis had always enjoyed gardening as much as she did.

She drove the Highlander to Mass. Frank had bought the car

a year ago, but it was too big for her and her small purposes—going to daily Mass, to the supermarket a couple of times a week, and once in a while into Atlanta for shopping. She decided she'd give the car to her son, John. He had a fishing boat it could tow; plus, the rear seat had DVD players for the kids

The Gospel reading at Mass was the part where Thomas doubts: "I will not believe he has risen unless I put my finger inside the wounds," and the Lord appeared to him and told him to do just that—put his finger inside the wound on his side. Then he told him: "You have believed because you have seen. Blessed are they who have not seen and yet believe."

Did she believe? She didn't know, had never really thought about it. She had been raised Catholic, married Catholic, and lived Catholic. Every Sunday, she recited the creed: "I believe..." but she'd never asked herself whether she really did or not. It was a question like the "why" questions, questions that there seemed to be no really truthful answer to—*believe.* She looked up at the crucifix behind the altar as she knelt with the communion wafer dissolving on her tongue. She never chewed it as she'd seen other people do. "Not a bone of him shall be broken," she'd always remembered. *I don't really know what "believe" means.*

She drove to Kroger's market. Her daughter, Mary Anne, had announced when she was sixteen that she didn't believe in God. Frank had been angry with her. "How can you say that? Don't you know you're breaking your mother's heart?" Looking back now, she knew that it wasn't Mary Anne's loss of faith that made her cry. The truth was that she simply didn't understand her daughter. She realized that Mary Anne was gone, her child was gone, and it was her awareness of the irrevocability of the loss, not her daughter's disbelief in God, that made her cry, broke her heart. Her child had vanished.

She was different from her daughter. Odd how it happened sometimes that sons were more like their mothers and daughters more like their fathers. It had been so with her children. Thinking about her now, way off north in Philadelphia, she wondered when she had stopped missing her, had stopped loving her.

She pulled the monster car into a space in the parking lot, gathered her purse and shopping bags, and checked her list again. She hadn't seen her daughter since Frank's funeral, and before that, it had been several years. She was some kind of consultant—

Catherine had never understood what kind—something about video productions for advertising or TV commercials or something, and she'd been living with her lesbian lover for—how long? Catherine didn't know. Mary Anne would not have waited on the fence, but unlike Phyllis, she wouldn't have thought about it first and then decided; she wouldn't even think about it. Catherine could understand Phyllis, but not Mary Anne.

She pulled a shopping cart out from the long line of carts and got her list out from her handbag, poured half a cup of Kroger's complimentary coffee and headed for the bakery section of the store. Frank's anger with his daughter had never really abated since that day when she announced her atheism. Catherine knew—even if Mary Anne did not—that his anger proved that he loved her. She also knew that the absence of her own anger proved that she did not. How can you love someone you don't even know? Instead of anger, she'd grieved in silence and confusion for the loss of her child. But that was twelve years ago, and the grief had subsided.

"Good morning, Mrs. Luccio. What can I get for you today?"

"I need some wheat and some white, George. And half a dozen croissants too, please. How's your family?"

"We're all fine, thanks for asking. Louisa is getting ready to graduate next month."

"Graduating! My goodness, it seems like it was just yesterday when she started school."

George laughed. "I know, I know." He handed her a priced bag of croissants and two loaves of bread. "How did that song go? It was in Fiddler on the Roof. 'Sunrise, sunset'—I can't remember, but that's how it is. You turn around and they're gone." He smiled wistfully.

She pushed her shopping cart on toward the canned goods. Like the male cardinal, Frank had been distracted. More than once. The first time she knew he was having an affair happened when the kids were still small. Frank was an accountant in a large firm just outside Atlanta. All the clientele were local, but suddenly he was having to fly to St. Louis for visits with a client. And there was the laundry on his return. A sudden loss of interest in sex. Daydreaming looks. Once she put denial behind her and let her heart break, she wondered what to do. She didn't want a confrontation—nothing good could come from that. Then, suddenly it was over. Frank became very affectionate—even doting. He looked sad sometimes, and he spent two hours with the priest in Confession.

It happened again a few years later, and it was quite different from the first time. He was irritable, frowned all the time, became short-tempered with the children. That one must have been more intense, less romantic, maybe. It hadn't lasted as long as the first, and he returned. That was when she understood his distractions, really. He didn't actually want what distracted him; he actually wanted someone who was sitting perched on the fence waiting for him.

The last affair happened less than two years before he died, and it was Phyllis. Phyllis was struggling with her dying husband. They'd had no children with whom she could share the physical or the emotional burden. And Phyllis wasn't the kind of woman who could find comfort in the friendship of other women. Catherine was her only close friend. Edgar had been her whole life. Catherine pretended not to notice the "dinner meetings" with clients, the Saturday all-day errands. It ended when Edgar died. Phyllis started traveling, and Frank died not long after Edgar. Phyllis was in Fiji when it happened; she sent Catherine dozens of roses.

She stopped at the butcher counter and bought a package of thinly sliced prosciutto to make the little croissant sandwiches that Phyllis liked so well. At the checkout line, she picked up a Southern Living special gardening issue.

That afternoon, after putting the groceries away, Catherine prayed a rosary while she sat on her patio—trying to meditate on the mysteries and not think about the garden—plans, chores she needed to do. She smiled. "I get distracted too, don't I, Lord? I'm sorry." She thought briefly again about whether she believed. "I don't know, Lord. But I love you. I hope that's enough."

Her prayers were interrupted when she heard the phone ring in the kitchen. She knew it was Phyllis, and she was going to ask her to lunch tomorrow, to have the little croissant sandwiches—and maybe a little wine.

Love in Coolidge County

"I ain't one of your pupils," said Micah Tomlinson through one side of his crinkled, lipless mouth, squinting his eyes at her against the smoke that struggled to rise in the heavy July air. A cigarette hung down from the other side of his mouth. He was looking up at her from the middle step of the porch, though looking upward and being defiant were hard to do together.

"No," Nelda answered, not unaware of her position's superiority. "No, Mr. Tomlinson, indeed you are not." Her gnarled hands grasped the elbows of her skinny arms in a gesture as close as she could come to what she would have called "decisive," and she, too, squinted downward at him in answer to his defiance. "Indeed, now you are not even in my employ. So, if you could just gather up your tools—" She raised her pointed chin in the direction of the tool tray he'd set down behind him on the walkway. She wanted to finish her sentence, but he didn't let her. Dropping his head so that she was talking to the top of a dingy baseball cap, he removed the cigarette from his mouth by pinching it between his thumb and forefinger, hawked loudly, and spat on the step. Then he flicked the cigarette into her petunia bed, turned and went down the steps to pick up the handle of the long metal tool tray and walked away.

She paused for just a moment, a little taken aback by the abruptness of his turning away from her while she was still speaking. Then she went down the steps to close the gate behind him as he threw his tool tray into the back of his pickup with a loud metallic thud. If she didn't close the gate, every stray dog in the county would be in her garden, urinating and defecating and digging holes.

"Those cigarettes will kill you, you know," she said to his departing back.

He didn't turn around, though, didn't even turn his head over his sweat-soaked khaki shoulder to reply, giving the impression that he didn't care whether she heard him or not: "Something going to kill everybody, sooner or later, like it or not. Might just as well like it."

Nelda turned and walked back to the house, her arms hanging down by her sides, and her fingers curled as though they were tempted to make themselves into fists. Micah's truck—a mix of faded blue and rust—started up and took off with an almost deafening guttural noise as she went back up to the porch to get her watering can. She had to fill it three times in order to feel certain she had removed the thick brown sputum from the step. She poured some of the water over the lavender and white petunia bed where Micah had thrown the cigarette, deciding not to remove it from the plants—tobacco was a good pesticide. The screen door slammed behind her. How she'd get the roof fixed now, she didn't know.

Over the kitchen table, the big brown ceiling fan was making a worried noise. The roof had to be fixed. Micah Tomlinson was one of only three handymen in Coolidge County who might have been willing to go up on the roof and replace about five shingles during the heatwave. Fortunately—in a way—the county was also suffering a drought, but the next time it rained, there would definitely be a leak.

Micah had been her last hope after the other two handymen had refused the job. When he had arrived an hour and fifteen minutes later than he said he would, all she'd said was, "Mr. Tomlinson, I expected you at seven o'clock." You wouldn't think that would make someone spit on your porch steps and leave. She had only wanted him to make some kind of excuse, not a real explanation—she didn't even expect that much—so that the difference between his promised and his actual arrival time wouldn't hang there right out in the open as the embarrassing fact that it was. All she wanted was a little help from him to excuse it. After all, she couldn't make up his excuse for him—he had to do that much himself. She sighed: But Micah Tomlinson had a purpose of his own. What he'd really wanted was an excuse not to work at all. And she had unknowingly provided it.

It seemed to happen that way all the time. She could never get anything done if it had to be done by somebody besides her, no matter how nice she was about asking. Why was that? It wasn't as though she were asking for any favors—she was very willing to pay for it.

Standing at the sink and washing the breakfast dishes, she decided that she had no other choice but to go up on the roof and fix it herself. The doctor had told her about her osteoporosis, though. Her bones would break very easily and wouldn't mend like healthy bones. But what else could she do? The roof had to be fixed.

She pulled the plug in the sink to let the dishwater drain out and took up a drying towel, trying to remember where she'd stored the extension ladder. If she had to fix the roof herself, she'd be very careful, and she'd do it first thing in the morning when it was cooler. As long as there was enough light to see, she should be all right if she was careful. But it was a two-storied old farmhouse and the roof had a pretty steep pitch.

Nelda put the clean dishes away and tried to remember where the ladder was. In the last couple of years, she had started to remember things long ago better than she remembered recent things. Things like Rev, for example. She'd thought about Rev all day long yesterday. She had dated Reverdy Johnson in her senior year of high school. That was back when very few girls at Coolidge County High went on to college—and the few who did became teachers, then returned to Coolidge and married doctors or lawyers. The wives of Coolidge's doctors and lawyers were almost always teachers. Teaching was a very ladylike job, like hospital pink-lady volunteers but with a little paycheck that gave them the right to be called "professionals." Teaching wasn't masculine and didn't take time away from home and husband, which was what really mattered. Usually, they'd teach until they got pregnant, then leave their jobs and stay home until their own children were in school. Sometimes they'd return to teaching then. Younger teachers in Coolidge were either fresh out of college or well into their thirties. The custom not only kept young mothers at home where they should be; it also kept the professional branch of the upper middle-class pretty much defined. The upper class was fixed, consisting of about half a dozen families who had their position by birth more than by profession or wealth, though they all owned a lot of land, farms rented out, or timber farms with hired managers. The land had been in their families for more generations than anyone could remember.

When Nelda was a senior in high school, about one-third of the girls in her class were already wearing engagement rings, with plans to be married in June after graduation. She sometimes felt a little bad about not having a ring herself. Not having a ring meant she would get a job instead of a husband, probably as a clerk in a store or as somebody's secretary, if she didn't go to college, and she had no interest in going to college.

That was probably why she'd started dating Rev. He was a nice boy. He didn't try to kiss her on their first date—always a bad sign—but waited until they'd gone out several times, and after they'd dated about three months, he asked her to go steady with him. She said she would, so he gave her his class ring to wear on a chain around her neck. She never got an engagement ring to replace it. When they graduated, Rev went to Vietnam and got killed just two months after he got there. People felt sorry for Nelda even though they'd never got engaged, as though that had just been an oversight somehow—something that would probably happen when he came home on leave. But the truth was that it was never mentioned between them. The truth was that they really didn't have any special feelings for one another at all. Nelda sometimes thought about how they talked, how they acted with each other, holding hands in public, and the perfunctory, dry, good night kiss when he brought her home. It was what they did simply because it was what everybody did, not really meaning anything. When she heard that he'd been killed, what she felt was shock, not grief. Later on, months after his death was old news, she did grieve, silently and privately, when she was alone—though she didn't know why, didn't know what she was grieving for.

She thought about Reverdy all day long yesterday, and sometimes she found herself talking to him—talking to him like maybe she should have done back then and didn't. *I didn't love you, Reverdy. Did you want me to? If you did, you never said so. If you wanted me to, I would have.* And she sat right there in the swing on the front porch with a dishpan full of beans in her lap, picking over them, and found that tears were dropping down onto the beans. *My goodness. You've been dead over half a century. Why am I crying about it now?* She took a Kleenex out of her apron pocket and wiped her eyes. *Because, I guess, because–Reverdy, you were wasted. I don't mean your life was wasted by dying so young. I mean YOU. All that was you and that was supposed to be loved by somebody was wasted.* She remembered him on the basketball court, in the blue and gold rayon shorts and shirt of the Coolidge County Wildcats, the number 19 on his shirt, his black hair stuck to his forehead by sweat. *I wish I had loved you...*

Nelda went to the pantry and cleared a place on the shelf for the beans she'd canned yesterday and tried to remember the last time she'd used the ladder. If she could remember what she'd used it for, she would remember where she'd left it. She was stacking the jars when it suddenly struck her that it didn't really matter about the roof. Here she was, hunting down unwilling handymen, enduring their shiftlessness, and now having to go up there and do it herself anyway—and for what? What did it matter? Because the roof would leak if it ever rained again? *So what?* For a moment the thought frightened her. She'd had such thoughts quite a few times recently, these "so what?" thoughts. It wasn't like her to think that way—not at all. She'd always taken care of things—always. It would never occur to her to just *not* do something that needed doing, whether it was grading papers, cleaning the house, going to Sunday School, canning beans, or fixing the roof, or whatever else needed to be done.

She sat down at the table, reflexively wiping the tablecloth with the dishtowel she still held in her hand; she pushed her glasses back up the bridge of her nose with her finger and just sat there for a moment. *Now why did I wipe this table? Did it need wiping?* No, she decided, it didn't; it was just habit. But—and the answer came like a little ray of light—it was a *good* habit. She had to smile. That little answer was like a little blessing; it was the answer to all the so-what questions she'd asked lately. Because it's habit, that's why, and *because it's a good habit.* When the questions came now—all the why bother? what difference does it make? so what? questions—she'd be ready, she wouldn't be caught off-guard any more. But having an answer now, and a *good* answer, didn't explain why the questions came in the first place. She'd never asked herself such questions before. Just like she'd never thought about loving or not loving Reverdy Johnson before.

*

Nelda had never married. It wasn't some big decision she'd made. It just didn't happen. That fall, after the news about Reverdy's death came, she went off to college to become a teacher. It didn't happen while she was in college and it didn't happen when she returned to Coolidge County to teach fifth grade at the elementary school. It just never happened. She dated sometimes, and sometimes she dated one man almost long enough for people to consider them a couple, but then they either married someone else or moved away. Gradually, people stopped expecting her to marry, and she stopped expecting it herself.

Finally, when she was in her thirties, there was Daniel. He was a coach over at the high school. His wife had divorced him, leaving him and their twelve-year-old boy, and going off to Atlanta to pursue a journalism career. Everyone felt very sorry for Daniel, and when he and Nelda started dating about six months after the divorce, everyone was happy for both of them. The relationship lasted about eight months.

Nelda had always liked Daniel. They were both members of the First Baptist Church, and she'd known him for years. At first, dating seemed awkward to both of them, but after some minor fumbles, they settled into the new roles they played in each other's lives, in the community, at church, and at school functions. They became a real couple. And Nelda had taught Daniel's son, Jimmy; she already had a good relationship with the boy. Marriage seemed inevitable.

But it didn't happen. They'd sat right there on that brown tweed couch in front of the television in Nelda's living room—and decided not to marry. Both of them. And it seemed to surprise both of them, too. Johnny Carson was on the Tonight Show, Daniel had his hand on her bare leg—she was wearing blue shorts—and both of them had their bare feet up on the coffee table.

"Right about now is when I should be proposing, you know," he said, for no apparent reason.

"Yes, I know," Nelda answered. "We should probably be talking about whose house we'll live in, yours or mine, or whether to buy a new one. Things like that."

"Yeah," Daniel drawled the word out slowly, then turned abruptly and asked, "Well, do you want to do it?"

She raised her head from the back of the couch and looked at him. "No."

"I don't either," he answered. And right there on that couch then they made love—the only time they ever did—with Johnny Carson's jokes and the audience's laughter in the background. It was the only time they'd ever felt really close—the way they knew they should feel, and didn't. They didn't see each other much after that. Daniel took a coaching position over in Henry County. He sold his house in Coolidge, and he and Jimmy moved away over the summer.

Nelda knew then that she'd never marry. She was only thirty-four, but it was too late. She was already made, already shaped, formed into the person she would always be, and she knew it. From that point on, there would be no more forming—it was done. Like a loaf of bread taken out of the oven, already baked, it can't be made into a cake or some other thing now. Its nature is to be a loaf of bread, nothing more, nothing other. She would not be a wife. She would never be a mother. She was what she was.

The best years of her life began then. No more restless wondering, no vague anticipation. There was a new peace. And a new sense of presence, of being present in her job with her students, in her house and the garden, its maintenance and comfort, and in her life, a presence she hadn't really had before and didn't know she was missing until it arrived after Daniel left. It freed her. She traveled during the summer months, took group tours to Europe, cruises to the Caribbean, and even went to Hawaii one year. She took up playing Bridge, made friends in distant places, and enjoyed her life, until she retired at sixty-five, ten years ago now.

Several of the women she'd known all her life were already dead now, and those who were still around were great-grandmothers, very much involved in the lives of all their descendants, with their families, and their husbands—those whose husbands were still alive, anyway. Life in old age was not very different for Nelda from the way it had always been: she was alone. From time to time, she thought about that, and sometimes she felt lonely. But not often. Self-pity visited her only rarely and never stayed too long. On the whole, she'd been satisfied with her life—until recently, about the same time the so-what questions started, really.

She grabbed her straw hat from the hook by the back door and went out into the sweltering sunlight to see about the last crop of peppers. They'd be ready to pick in a few days, and then she could think about turning up the soil to plant some greens for the fall. The garden was old, planted back when she was in her forties. The farm—where she'd lived all her life—had been allowed to go fallow, but she kept a kitchen garden for her own use, for things to put up, to give as Christmas presents and as charity for the poor.

When she went to the spigot to turn on the garden hose, she spotted the dirt-encrusted end of the extension ladder sticking out from behind the Lady Banksea roses on the side of the house. "Oh, yes," she mumbled aloud, remembering that the ladder had been used to tie up the roses as they climbed the brick chimney on the side of the house. When was that? Three years ago? She went to the side of the house and stood with her hand shielding her eyes, looking up at the climbing rosebush, green now, but in the early spring, it was a mass of tiny clusters of yellow roses, climbing up the rose-gold chimney, hand-fired brick made from Georgia red clay—how long ago? A hundred years? At least. Every spring it hurt her heart just to look at it with the roses climbing it, making her wonder at the beauty of it.

She trudged toward the front of the house, looking for the other end of the ladder behind the bushes, but she couldn't see it. Was it long enough to reach the roof when it was fully extended? The extension part was hidden behind the bushes; there was only one way to find out, so she returned to the back of the house and pulled it out onto the lawn, struggled with the middle extension, and finally succeeded in leaning the ladder against the roof, just below the spot where new shingles were needed.

"Oh, my," she whispered to herself, pushing against the ladder and feeling it give and bounce a little under the weight of her hand. When it was fully extended, it didn't seem very sturdy; also, the part at the top went beyond the roof line only two feet or so—not much stability there. She stood there a minute, her hands on her hips, thinking, knowing that this was a foolhardy plan, but reluctant to dismiss it. After all, what choice did she have?

*

That evening after supper was over and dishes were done, Nelda sat in the front porch swing with her customary glass of Dubonnet, watching the fireflies, listening to crickets, and thinking about her plans for the next day. It was still so hot that she'd been tempted to put the floor fan behind the screen door, but it would have discouraged the fireflies and crickets—besides, it was just too noisy. She wanted quiet. She had found the shingles in the shed that afternoon, along with a hammer and some roofing nails. She wanted to get up very early, so she could get the roof fixed before the hot morning sun got too high. All afternoon she'd avoided looking up at the roof—how high it was—or at the unsturdy ladder. If it should be done, then she had to do it. There was no point in worrying about it.

But it was not the roof of her house that troubled Nelda now.

During supper, while she was watching the evening news on TV, she suddenly found herself overcome by a heavy sadness, at once both strange and familiar. It swallowed her up for several minutes before she could pull herself out of it and think about it—where it came from, what caused it. It was strange because it hadn't happened to her in recent memory, but it was familiar because she remembered it from her childhood. Her mother had died from pneumonia when Nelda was very small; she had no memory of her mother. And her father never remarried. As a child, sometimes, when she was in bed at night, or playing alone in her room, she was overcome by that sadness—and she recognized it even then as loneliness, a longing for a mother, for brothers and sisters she would never have. She couldn't mention it to her father; it would only make him feel bad, so she kept it to herself. Pushing the wood floor under the swing now with her bare toes, she sipped the sweet drink and murmured, "Ah, yes…that's what it was." It was because of the roof, because there was no son or grandson to take care of this chore for her, and that had made her feel deprived—just as she'd felt deprived of brothers and sisters when she was a child.

She smiled a little as the leaves of the sycamore in the front yard moved gently, and the fireflies seemed to get excited by the movement. The crickets even paused for a moment in their chirping to enjoy the breeze. Her father was such a good and gentle man, kind to her, kind to everyone, really. He'd run the town's newspaper until he died of a heart attack when he was only fifty years old. Nelda missed him now. And she grieved to think again that she had not provided him with heirs, with grandchildren he might have loved before he died. If he had deprived her of a mother, of siblings—of a family—when he did not remarry, she had also deprived him. She sighed and whispered aloud, "I guess we just have to forgive each other, Daddy."

A sudden thought made her stop the swing, the creaking chain was still and silent, and her feet rested on the floor. *Did I not marry and have a family because . . .?* The thought almost shocked her. She remembered reading in a magazine in the waiting room of the doctor's office that people tended to make the decisions as adults that would allow them to continue the lives they'd lived as children, because it was familiar, what they were used to, unconscious of the reasons for their decisions. If they'd come from large families, they tended to have large families, and so on. Even if they'd suffered abuse as children, they tended to marry abusive partners. Had she unconsciously avoided marriage because she was continuing the solitude of her childhood? After a moment, she started the swing again—what difference did it make now? Even if that was true, even if she herself had actually chosen the life she'd lived—instead of it all "just happening" that way—so what? She finished the Dubonnet, went inside and locked the front door—a *good* habit, she reminded herself—before going upstairs to bed.

*

The next morning, she woke before daylight and found to her surprise that the thought of deprivation was still on her mind. *Deprived.* She had been deprived—of what? By whom? She turned on the bedside lamp and threw the covers aside, stretching the muscles in her legs and arms before getting out of bed. Her health was good for someone nearly seventy-six; she still had all her wits—mostly anyway, even all her teeth. She owned her home and had enough money for groceries and bills. How on earth could she feel deprived? She got dressed in dungarees and a loose shirt, brushed her teeth, and then made up her bed, tucking the cotton chenille spread neatly under the folded pillows.

Downstairs frying an egg and buttering toast, she looked at the plastic shopping bag on the table, containing the five shingles, the hammer, and a handful of nails, and wondered again if the habit of taking care of things might not be her undoing, after all. She remembered how weak and wobbly the ladder seemed yesterday when she'd got it fully extended against the roof overhang.

She ate her breakfast without turning on the morning news as she usually did to hear the weather forecast and find out what was happening in the world. The plastic bag awaited her, like packed luggage, and she had a sense of mission, of imminent departure. Pushing her plate aside, she sat sipping coffee, holding the cup with both hands, and thinking about whether she was deprived. Of what? Well, of family, of course—that much was obvious. By whom? By God, maybe. Some choices are given to us, and some aren't, she thought. Not having a mother was not a choice she'd made—not becoming a mother herself was probably her own choice, though—but God had played a big part in that, too. Somehow, though, she knew that it wasn't *family* itself that she was really deprived of. The lack of family was a circumstance, a condition, just something she'd had to make do without, as best she could. It wasn't the deprivation.

She put her plate, cup, cutlery and skillet into the pan of soapy water in the sink, as she usually did, with the intention of washing them later, and looked out the window to see muted turquoise streaks on the horizon. The birds were singing. It was dawn. Time to get to the roof. But she glanced at the bag on the kitchen table and changed her mind: *No, better wash the dishes now, leave them clean.*

The ladder had not gotten any sturdier overnight. But it's aluminum, she thought, not likely to break under my hundred and twenty pounds. She placed one foot, in the old sneakers she used as yard shoes, on the bottom rung and looked up at the sky beyond the ladder's top. A few stars were still visible in the deep indigo overhead. She placed the tied handles of the plastic bag over her shoulder and took a deep breath as though it were a prayer.

The climb wasn't difficult, even if it was long—the roof was high, that was all. But as she reached the top, careful to avoid looking backward or down, what worried her more was the way the ladder seemed to run out; there just wasn't enough of it left beyond the roofline. This, she knew, was the moment of real decision. This was a real choice. If she moved her hands from the sides of the ladder, placed them on the rough red-brown asphalt of the roof, walked them up the roof far enough to move her feet from the top rung of the ladder to the roof—if she did all that, no matter how carefully she did it, there would be no turning back.

And she did it just like that, making a mental note to record in memory her exact position, so that, as she descended backwards once the shingles were replaced, she would be able to feel the rung of the ladder from which she'd moved her feet so carefully, one at a time. And she would have to do that from memory—even the slightest mistake could cause her to kick the ladder out of position and leave her trapped, unable to descend. We have to do things from memory, she thought, all the important things are always done from memory; it's the only way we have.

She crouched on all fours, facing upward toward the broken shingles, and the plastic bag slipped from her shoulder and fell to her wrist. The hammer inside the bag crashed against the back of her hand and she gasped in pain. It was her right hand, the hand she would use to hammer the shingles with. She hoped the hammer had not broken any of the small bones in that hand. If it had, she would just have to endure it, hammer anyway, and get down somehow.

She reached the top, turned around and sat down on the run, about one foot above the broken shingles. She stared down at the shingles in the growing light, afraid to look beyond them, back down toward the top of the ladder, afraid to look outward, afraid to look anywhere except to the task at hand. "Now, Nelda," she whispered to herself, "you just don't need to be looking anywhere except right here, at what you've got to take care of. No point in looking anywhere else."

But she did. And the first thing she saw to her left was the top of the chimney, just at the moment when the sun, rising behind her, made its first morning kiss on the rose-gold brick, bringing a sudden joy to the humble clay. The leaves of the sycamore in the front yard behind her stirred and hummed in a morning breeze, and Nelda swung one leg over the run of the roof to see the treetop, as its great silver-green leaves came alive and sang to the sun.

Her right hand throbbed in pain, and she looked at it to see that it had begun to swell. Yes. She'd probably broken one or more of those small bones on the back of her hand, and she'd have to try to wield the hammer with her left hand—if she was able to wield it at all—and if she could crawl backward down the roof using the underside of her right wrist, she might be able to make it down, deprived as she was of the use of her hand.

Deprived as she was. She sat there straddling the run, holding the bag with her left hand and holding her right hand up to lessen the pain and swelling. Deprived of what? *Deprived of love, of course.* No one loved her. She had lived her life deprived of love. Whether from the pain in her hand, or the pain in her heart, she sat there on the roof of her house and wept.

The fingers of her hand were becoming numb, but she used them to wipe the tears from her eyes and look at the chimney in front of her, glowing like pink amber now in the sunrise. And to her left she could see the horizon, the rooftops of Coolidge, all touched by the coral sunlight, waking, coming to life. Here. Just right here, where she was born, where she'd lived all her life, and where she would die—perhaps today. Every inch, every small plot and portion, was familiar to her—and unspeakably dear. She whispered, "I love you. I have always loved you, every day and hour of my life," and she realized in that moment the blessedness of her life. No, she'd never known a single moment of "deprivation," for no one who loves is ever deprived of love. She sat there until the tears stopped and she could see clearly, then said, "Thank you."

She managed to lie on her stomach and hold the new shingles in place with the elbow of her right arm, nailing them with her left hand, and then began her descent down the path she'd memorized toward the ladder.

Count the Ways

Marcie Ingolls set aside the stack of essays on Elizabeth Barrett Browning and got ready. She folded her hands, then opened her palms to lay them flat on her desk, the Renaissance Rose fingertips interlaced. She leaned her somewhat buxom figure forward a little and put on her most earnest and caring expression—the one with brows raised over rounded eyes, and a slight Mona Lisa smile. It was the expression she always wore when she talked to parents. It said, I care *deeply* about your son's success in school, and I'm *very* concerned about his grades. It did not say what she really thought: Your son doesn't learn anything because he doesn't want to learn anything. It's that simple. And furthermore, I resent the hell out of having to stay late after working hard all day, just to sit here and say crap that isn't true.

"Mrs. Thurmond," she said, looking up and smiling. "Please come in. You wanted to see me about Bick's grade?" She usually started these conferences with a couple of small-talk sentences about the weather, followed by a bit of gush about how glad she was that the parent was taking the time (*her* time) to talk about so-and-so's "difficulties." But this one would be particularly unpleasant. Bick Thurmond was a waste of space, a surly, self-centered bastard who didn't deserve anybody's time. "Have a seat, please," she said, making a slight Renaissance Rose wave toward the chair she'd drawn up to the front of her desk in preparation for the conference. She knew she should stand up, but she was bone-tired.

But as Mrs. Thurmond approached the chair to sit down, Marcie's mood changed, her little smile vanished, and a furrow appeared over the rounded eyes. Oh God, she thought, poor woman. Bick Thurmond's mother was a scrawny little black woman, probably in her late thirties, though she looked fifty, pathetically absurd in the pert little checkered apron and matching shirt-pocket hankie of her Waffle House uniform.

She sat down primly in the chair, clutching a large worn-out black vinyl handbag in her lap. "Thank you so much, ma'am, for taking the time to talk to me about Jimmy. I don't have much time myself, I'm afraid. I only have a half-hour between jobs and so I had to kind of squeeze this in. But I need to find out what I can do to help my Jimmy. You call him Bick, and I guess I should, too—that's what he wants to be called." She made a knowing little smile and said, "I think he thinks it's more grown-up—sort of tough, you know." On the word *tough*, the smile assumed a shared affectionate tolerance for the ways of adolescent boys. "Makes him think he's big."

Marcie saw Bick in her mind's eye—at least six feet and two hundred pounds. But she wasn't interested in Bick. "You have two jobs, Mrs. Thurmond?"

"Yes, ma'am. I do cleaning up until four, and then I work at the Waffle House till about eight or nine—depending on the supper crowd and whether we're short-handed."

Marcie opened her desk drawer and pulled out her gradebook. "Well, we should try to be as quick about this as we can then, shouldn't we. Let me just tell you what the problem is. My policy is that when a student is out on a test day, he has to bring in an excuse in order to be allowed to make up the test. Bick—Jimmy—was out when we had our mid-term exam, and he didn't bring in an excuse. I had no choice but to give him a zero on the exam."

"Out? Oh, my goodness, Mrs. Ingolls, when was he absent? I don't think Jimmy ever misses any school."

"This particular day was Monday of last week." She didn't mention that Jimmy was absent at least two days out of any given week.

"Well, I'll have to speak to him about that, ma'am. But isn't there any chance at all you'd let him make up that test? You know, he's nearly seventeen and if he don't pass this English, he won't go to the eleventh grade. He's failed two grades already, and I know how bad that makes him feel. I'm afraid he'll just give up if he fails again. Isn't there some way we can help him out?"

The woman's face, already wrinkled, was contorted; tears were coming into her eyes. Marcie was helpless. She stood up and extended her hand. "Mrs. Thurmond, don't worry. I'll talk to him tomorrow—and we'll just see what we can do."

"Oh, thank you, ma'am. That's so kind of you. I'll get onto him—I will. I'll make sure he studies hard and does good on that test. Thank you so much." She shoved the big black handbag under one arm and took the teacher's outstretched hand. "He's got the ability—I know he has—he just has to put his mind to it."

Marcie walked her to the door. Bick Thurmond's only known

"ability" was in impregnation. Two girls already that she knew of, maybe more. She saw him in her imagination then, long legs extended into the aisle, daring her to walk past. Giant-sized unlaced shoes that cost at least a hundred dollars—and his mother working two jobs. Bastard.

During a composition exercise in third-period English the next day, Marcie told Bick she wanted to see him for a moment in the hall. He rose from his desk and walked to the door with feigned effort, as if it were difficult to comply with such an unreasonable demand.

"Bick, your mother and I had a conference yesterday about your failing grade, and I've agreed to allow you to make up the mid-term exam." She paused then, by habit. With any other student given that news, there would have followed expressions of relief and even gratitude. Not with Bick.

He leaned his head backward slightly, the more to look down on her from his six-foot height with hooded eyes. "Okay," he mumbled.

"Okay," responded Marcie. "You come this afternoon immediately after school. I'll wait for you until four—and I won't wait a minute longer than that. If you don't show, you don't get another chance. Understood?"

"Yeah."

He made a move toward the classroom door, but Marcie wasn't done. "Bick, I hope you realize how blessed you are to have such a caring mother. Not so many kids do, you know."

His face darkened as he turned the knob on the door.

"Wait a minute," Marcie continued. "Let me make a suggestion to you, Bick. You have no extracurricular activities, no sports—nothing like that. You know, there's no reason you couldn't get an after-school job to help your mother out a little bit." But he had already opened the door and headed back into the classroom.

Marcie wasn't surprised when he didn't show up that afternoon, nor was she surprised the following fall to find out that Bick had dropped out of high school. That was the last she heard of him until shortly before the Christmas break in the teachers' lounge. Bick had been convicted of assault and sentenced to five years in prison. He had beaten a boy nearly to death for making a disparaging remark about his mother. But his mother had pleaded with the judge for clemency and the sentence was reduced to a year in the juvenile offender program. Marcie remembered the little black woman in her Waffle House checkered apron. She remembered the tears that crowded the tired eyes, and she wondered if Mrs. Thurmond had worn that apron and those eyes in the courtroom. If she did, Marcie thought, the judge didn't have a chance.

*

Mrs. Thurmond had not worn that apron; Waffle House had laid her off months before the trial started. Instead, she stood before Federal Court Judge Lionel J. Horton in a dark blue crepe dress that was at least one size too large for her thin frame, and at least twenty years old, judging from the tattered white lace collar at her neck. She stood with her hands clasped firmly in front of her, as if to restrain them from a compulsive wringing.

"Your Honor," she began.

Judge Horton leaned forward in an effort to hear her; her voice was too low. "Could I ask you to speak up, please, Mrs. Thurmond?"

"Yes, sir." She took a deep breath. "My son Jimmy has done a terrible, terrible thing to that boy. He knows that, sir. He does."

The judge glanced at the defendant, James "Bick" Thurmond. He sat impassive and stone-faced, staring straight ahead.

"But I have to ask you, your Honor," she continued, making a visible effort to speak louder, and stopping once or twice to swallow hard. "I have to beg you to consider some things. First, he's just a boy, just turned seventeen. But most of all, your Honor, he's never had a daddy. His daddy left him when he was only four years old—and that's hard, your Honor, it's hard on a boy when he don't have a daddy."

"You've raised him by yourself then, Mrs. Thurmond? Can I ask you what you do for a living?" The woman's poverty was evident, not only in her dress, but in her almost bowed short stature. It was the bearing of a woman inured to poverty.

"I was laid off from the Waffle House a few months ago, and since then, I clean people's houses. And I get assistance from the state."

"How much assistance, Mrs. Thurmond?" He seemed to have forgotten about the defendant.

"Food stamps, sir, and we've got subsidized housing. I could get more assistance, I think the lady said, but I'd have to stop my job cleaning houses." Then she added hesitantly, "I don't feel right not doing anything at all for my keep, sir."

"Does your son help you, ma'am?"

"He can't, your Honor, but he would if he could. He's been trying to find work ever since he had to drop out of high school."

"And why did he have to drop out of school?"

"He was behind, your Honor, and he just never could catch up. It was hard on him ever since he was little, what with the other children all having daddies, and he just got behind. And he just never could get caught back up." As if she saw an opportunity opening, she added quickly, "And that's what I'm trying to say, sir. Jimmy needs *help*, sir. He don't need punishing. He's had enough punishing already."

Judge Horton reduced Bick's sentence from five years in prison to one year in the juvenile offender program. As he pronounced the sentence, Bick stood before him in the bright orange prison jumpsuit, with his head held slightly backward, away from the judge. Even with the judge's elevated bench, Bick managed to give the impression of looking down on him. It may have been that posture that caused the judge to stop and stare at him for a moment, but then he continued:

"I hope you will use this time to learn the discipline you have missed, young man, but more than that—I hope that when you are released from the program, you will find yourself a job and do something for your mother." He nodded in her direction; she was sitting in the front row, just behind her son, weeping tears of obvious gratitude into a shriveled Kleenex. "You can thank her that you have escaped a well-deserved term in prison—*this time*. I don't want to see you in my court again." He already regretted his decision, and it showed in the excessively loud bang of his gavel.

*

But five years later, Judge Horton did see Bick Thurmond again. It must have been in the juvenile offender program that Bick learned about gangs and drugs and how to put the two together to make some money.

Two years after his release, he was gone from home a lot, though he never moved out of the subsidized housing that he shared with his mother, the small two-bedroom apartment on the third floor of a brick building in what the town called "the projects," with its broken windows and halls stained with urine and graffiti obscenities. The little apartment was filled with the latest and most expensive kitchen appliances, stereo and TV equipment, and such huge overstuffed furniture that little space was left to move in the tiny living room.

Mrs. Thurmond's closet was packed with clothes that looked more like what a prostitute would wear than a middle-aged, overworked cleaning woman—though Bick had forced her to quit working. She never wore the clothes because she cleaned the little apartment all day. She tried to read the manuals on all the electronic devices that Bick had bought, but she couldn't understand them. She never drove the Cadillac he'd bought for her because she had never learned to drive.

Bick was always gone, but he would tell her that he had come in at eleven, or twelve, or whenever she was already in bed asleep. So, twice when he was arrested on suspicion of rape, she could say with certainty that he couldn't have been involved because he'd been home with her at that hour. The police had no choice but to take her word for his whereabouts, despite any evidence that said otherwise. Besides, they couldn't get past her tears, as she sat there in the interview room in an old, blue dress, wringing a shriveled Kleenex in her hands.

So, it was five full years after his sentence to the juvenile offender program that Judge Horton saw Bick in his courtroom again. This time, the charge was murder. Bick was convicted and sentenced to death for killing his mother.

*

Marcie Ingolls read the story on the front page of the newspaper. The trial had been brief. The jury had deliberated only thirty minutes. The death sentence was extraordinary, but no recommendation for clemency accompanied the jury's verdict, and the judge said he could find no grounds for it. The defendant had murdered his mother by stabbing her to death with a kitchen knife while she slept in her bed.

Although the prosecution had struggled to establish a motive for the murder, according to a comment from an interviewed juror, it was actually the lack of a really credible motive that worked against a recommendation for clemency. The prosecuting attorney tried to show him as habitually violent, but that claim was difficult to establish because his arrest record had been inadmissible as evidence: The alibis provided by Mrs. Thurmond had made actual booking on any of the rape charges impossible. The newspaper account concluded by theorizing that the case for the defense was weakened by the fact that no witnesses on his behalf could be found.

Marcie remembered Mrs. Thurmond in her checkered apron with her big worn-out handbag, sitting so primly in the chair in front of her desk. She looked at the photo of Bick in the newspaper—he had not changed at all. The full-front photograph, the kind made when a suspect is booked, looked exactly the same as he had looked when he stood outside her classroom, head thrown slightly back, looking down at her with hooded eyes. It was the same Bick, as though all this had already happened then, as though it had all just played out like some kind of script already written.

For some reason, Marcie started crying when she read the story. She cried for Mrs. Thurmond first, but she cried harder for Bick. Nothing could have saved them, no court, no teacher, no program—only the father, the absent father. She cried for at least a quarter of an hour before she put the newspaper in the recycle bin by her desk and continued grading her students' essays.

JAZZ

Chapter One

It's Time

Since the moment he opened his eyes at six o'clock in the morning, Professor William Cauley knew that today was the day to announce his retirement. And since it was a day for endings, it was also the day to tell Joanna goodbye. It was Wednesday, and Lauren, his wife, was coming back from Georgia on Friday night—that would give him at least forty-eight hours to re-stabilize. It was good for Joanna too. She had Monday, Wednesday, and Friday classes, so she would have Thursday at home, and he would have that day without her presence on campus, where they might encounter each other. Yes. It should be today.

All morning long he dreaded it. They had talked about it a month ago. They were both leaving the University. He was retiring and she was going to spend the summer at Oxford before returning home to New England to finish her doctorate. They'd agreed that one of them should simply tell the other that it was time, and after that, there would be no coffee meetings, no phone calls, nothing. He knew she was waiting for him to be the one to say goodbye and end it, formally and forever.

He sat at his desk after his morning seminar trying to concentrate on other things, but it was impossible. After looking at the clock on his bookcase a dozen times or more, he saw that it was twelve-thirty. Joanna's eleven o'clock class would be over and she'd be in her office for the next hour, so he told the secretary he was going upstairs to the dean's office. From there he would go home, he said, in case anybody was looking for him.

He walked down the hall to the English Department and to the little niche where three doors led to three small cubbyhole graduate assistant offices. He entered quietly. She looked up smiling, her sleek blonde hair hanging over her shoulders, hunched over a stack of students' papers on her desk, and held her lovely face up for his customary quick kiss—which didn't happen. Instead, he sat down in the straight chair that students used, facing her desk, and said very softly, "I think it's time. Lauren will come back Friday and I'm telling the dean about retiring today."

She made no response, just dropped her eyes and put her hand over her mouth. Resting her gray-sweatered elbow on the paper-littered desk, she turned her face away from him, closing her eyes. Without facing him, she moved her hand from her mouth and said, "Yes. Okay."

He wanted to tell her that he loved her, not in the way he should, perhaps, and certainly not in the way she thought he did, but from far away, from a great distance over a generation of time. He loved her as he'd loved his daughter Elise when she was about four years old, and one of her cousins had hurt her feelings with a cutting remark about her slightly cleft palate. Elise had averted her face, just as Joanna did now. He had scooped his daughter up into his arms and held her tightly against his chest. He wanted to do that for Joanna now, to get up from the chair and hold her. But he didn't. She didn't move or speak. Finally he stood, moved around the desk, leaned down and kissed the top of her head and left, closing the door quietly behind him.

He and his wife had taken their daughter to a surgeon who specialized in cleft palates. When she cried afterwards from the pain—it lasted for months—Lauren told her that the pain would go away, her mouth would heal, and then she would be able to talk without a lisp, and she would look like other kids. But he couldn't say those things to his daughter. He knew pain never really goes away. It becomes a memory, and nothing remembered ever goes away.

*

The secretary just outside the open door to the dean's office was talking on the phone. Without pausing, she fluttered her fingers and smiled at him, as Dean Donald Penfield waved him in. He sat down heavily in the wine-colored leather chair facing Don's large mahogany desk.

"Well, Don, I've got some news for you. But maybe not. Maybe you've been expecting it. I'm retiring at the end of the semester. The real news is that Lauren and I are leaving New Orleans and moving to Georgia."

There was a long pause while Don stared at him. "*What?* What do you mean *leaving*? You mean you're leaving UNO? Leaving New Orleans?"

"We're moving to Statesboro, Georgia this summer."

"Statesboro, Georgia! Where the hell is Statesboro, Georgia?"

"It's near Elise and the grandkids in Savannah."

"Oh, yes," Don nodded knowingly. "The things we do for our kids, huh?"

William was glad the question was rhetorical. He was feeling the painful void Joanna had left in him, and his mouth was dry. He wanted this conversation to be as short as possible.

"How's Elise doing, anyway—got a good job, doesn't she? Speech therapist?"

"Oh, she's fine, just fine. But being a single mom is tough, you know. Especially with three boys, all under six."

"Yeah, I can imagine. And I'll bet Lauren worries herself sick about her, all on her own now."

He half-shrugged one shoulder. Actually, Lauren didn't worry much about Elise at all, and neither did he. There was no reason to worry. And apart from occasional visits, they probably wouldn't see much of her and the grandchildren. She kept very busy with her work since her husband died in Iraq a year ago, and the children were all in the excellent daycare provided by her office.

"Still. Wow." Don frowned, as though he were having trouble imagining William's absence. "So, you're giving up a chair at the University of New Orleans for—what? What are you going to do in Statesboro, Georgia?"

"Maybe write."

Don ignored his answer, the frown deepening, as the reality of William's departure began to settle. "I mean, good Lord, Will. This is a career you're chucking, you know? Hell of a time to retire. You're too young for that. How long did it take you to make History Chair? Fifteen years? And you're just going to walk away?"

"Oh, come on, Don. You and I both know there may not be a History Department much longer."

Don ignored his remark. William watched his mind working; he was probably already thinking about his replacement—Betty Somers was a likely choice. She'd turned out two major publications in the past year, and her presentations at conferences were videotaped and played in a hundred classrooms across the country. She'd already made full professor, and if they were going to keep her at UNO, they'd have to offer her something more. Honchos like Betty required regular feeding. But Don was a company man; he would always do whatever was best for the university, regardless of Betty's controversial interpretive theory of history—which William thought absurd.

"This is going to shock everybody," Don continued. "Hell, I'm shocked myself. Can't believe it. You've become part of the furniture here, you know? Great reputation. Plus you get along with everybody. You were probably in line for this job right here." He tapped the top of his desk with a forefinger. "I mean, if you were leaving *for* something—like dean, maybe, at some small prestigious liberal arts school, but for *nothing at all*?" His head kept wagging. "When are you turning in your letter?"

"You should get it sometime next week, maybe even Monday."

"Well, what's Lauren is going to do in Statesboro, Georgia, for God's sake? She's got a doctorate now. Will she be able to adjunct there? What's there, anyway—South Georgia U. or something?"

"Yes. It's Georgia Southern University. She's joining the Education faculty. They liked her dissertation on mainstreaming disabled children. And it's tenure-track. That's the whole point of leaving here. She'll tell you all about it next Wednesday—we're still having dinner, right?"

"Well, I'll be damned. Go, Lauren." Don was bemused. "Yeah. Seven. Bayona's."

"Right. See you later."

*

In the elevator going down to the faculty parking lot, William bowed his salt and pepper grizzled head, staring down at the tops of his loafers. He could still smell the sweet clean fragrance of Joanna's hair as he kissed the top of her head. His heart actually ached; every beat was painful, a feeling he'd never experienced before. He raised his head and looked at the top of the elevator doors as they sighed open. *It's done,* he said to himself. *It's done.*

Hands trembling, he fumbled with the key to the door of his old white Volvo. He didn't feel that he could drive with the pain in his chest and his lack of focus, so he sat for a moment and leaned his head against the steering wheel, willing himself to breathe slowly and think about something else. *Lauren.*

When they were both in graduate school at LSU in Baton Rouge, Lauren had dropped out so that she could go with him when he got an instructorship at the University of New Orleans.

After that, she'd stayed home with Elise, then worked with parents of children with disabilities for several years after Elise was settled in school. Finally, when Elise left for college, Lauren commuted to Baton Rouge to finish her graduate program. Since then, she'd taught part-time at Tulane until last year when she started applying for full-time teaching posts. Despite her age, this small university in Georgia had offered her what she would have had, perhaps *should* have had, decades ago, before there was a William or an Elise. And she'd never complained, never felt deprived. *Yes*, he said to himself. *It's Lauren's turn.*

He started the car and backed out of his parking space, marked on the gray concrete curb in front of him in faded, barely legible stenciled letters: Dr. Wm. Cauley. The engine was knocking, as it had been for some time now. He knew he needed a new car, but he was attached to his twelve-year-old Volvo. It had driven him to campus all these years, and to his mother's cottage on the Gulf in Bay St. Louis, to Savannah for Elise's wedding and her husband's funeral. The car was part of his life; he didn't want to let it go—just as he didn't want to let his job go, even though the History Department itself was dying. Falling enrollment for the past eight or nine years and even lower projected figures for the coming fall was a death knell, however distant or muffled it may seem on this beautiful April day.

As he drove off campus, he was thinking of Joanna, in spite of his weak effort to avoid it. She had been the bright star in his darkening world for the past nine months. And she was gone from his life. The only good thing about this day was that his betrayal of his beloved Lauren had ended.

He turned south onto Elysian Fields, heading home. "Okay," he whispered aloud to himself, "let's file it." He was over fifty. It was, he decided, the infamous mid-life crisis when an aging man is supposed to have an affair with a much younger woman. "So, okay," he said. "That's it. It's done." But he knew it was not that soap-opera simple, and he was not at all "done" with it. He decided to get a Chinese take-out on the way home, and then find some way to deal with it, to *understand* it, to understand why he'd been unfaithful to his wife, whom he loved dearly. Unlike most people in his acquaintance, he'd never been unfaithful before. He had to understand it so that he could let it go. And if he failed in that attempt—well, with some help from a little bourbon, he'd make it through the afternoon somehow till five, when he knew Lauren would call from Georgia.

*

William put the Chinese take-out on the kitchen counter, kicked the loafers off his sockless feet, and poured two fingers of Jack Daniels bourbon, dropped an ice cube in the glass and a small wedge of lime. He took his drink to the brick-floored patio off the back of the breakfast room and sat down in the wrought iron chair to watch the birdfeeder in the center of the courtyard and try to understand why he'd had an affair with a woman younger than his daughter. It wasn't sex; in fact, there had been very little of that. It wasn't lust; it was actually love. But what kind of love?

Long ago he'd discovered that there are people who love and people who are to *be* loved. Joanna was in the latter category. She thought she loved William, but it wasn't really him. She loved academic life, Victorian English literature, teaching, the things that gave her identity and purpose. Her vulnerability, her unconscious *need,* was the universal trait of the beloved, and she was innocent of any awareness of it. He understood her very well. He did not understand himself.

He knew that the affair had not been a consequence of any problem in his marriage. If there was a problem there at all, it was that he and Lauren were alike. Neither of them was very good at being loved. That similarity cemented them, making them more kin than marriage itself did. And it had suited them both very well. He was not so naïve as to believe that it was impossible to love two women. Of course, it was possible. Joanna had simply appeared as an English graduate assistant last year, a brilliant young scholar, so fresh with her keen intelligence and dedication. He noticed then—and not for the first time—that any attempts to understand himself seemed to end in thoughts of her.

He rolled the cool glass across his cheeks and along his forehead, feeling flushed, and stared unseeing at the wrens congregated at the feeder. *Why was it necessary to understand himself?* Maybe he couldn't. It was just that—he struggled to articulate in his own mind *what* he needed to understand; and then he discovered that his face was flushed because his eyes were full of tears.

He put his drink down on the glass-topped table, leaned his

head back on the chair and closed his eyes. Somewhere in the darkness behind his closed eyes, he knew that there was more to his sorrow than Joanna, more than he chose to see, but his mind was fevered and weary, and he allowed himself to doze until he heard his phone buzz on the kitchen counter behind him where he'd left it with the Chinese take-out. Lauren. He glanced at the clock standing in the corner of the breakfast room as he padded across the lacquered brick floor on bare feet—five o'clock.

"You're so predictable, my love," he said, smiling into the phone.

"No, Will. *You* are. You and Jack watching the birds together?"

"I miss you."

"Well, I'll be home day after tomorrow. I got some apartment information we should look at. You know, we have to talk about closing the townhouse, Will."

"Yes, I know," he said with a little twinge of annoyance. He hadn't thought about leaving their home, and he didn't want to think about it. "How did it go?" he asked, forcing himself back to her trip.

"Oh, great. The chair had a lunch for me with the rest of the Special Ed. faculty. They seem okay, I guess. At least, I didn't get any negative vibes from anybody. Marilyn Wallace—remember, I told you about her? She seemed extra friendly, sort of—apparently, she's in a kind of mentoring role."

"Well, are you pleased about that?"

"Yes. I think so. She's very well informed, up to speed on what's happening in the field, plus she's been there for eight years and knows all the departmental things I need to know. They're kind of big on student evaluations here, by the way. Makes me a little nervous."

"Oh, you'll do fine."

"Well, I'll see you Friday night. Tell you more about everything then. Love you."

"Wait. I want to tell you—I told Don today. Guess what he asked."

"I can't imagine. Right, okay. He got down on his knees and begged you to stay?"

"No. What's Lauren going to do, he asks."

She laughed. "Seriously, was he shocked about your retirement?"

"Oh yeah. Sure."

"I'll see you Friday. Love you."

"Love you too."

He closed the French doors to the patio, put the Chinese take-out in the microwave, and turned on the kitchen television to watch the evening news. He'd never felt so lonely in his life.

Chapter Two

Timing is Everything

William sat at the counter the next morning buttering an English muffin and turning the pages of *The Times-Picayune* without reading it. The radio was playing soft jazz piano and he felt comforted by the music. Music had always had the power to smooth any troubled waters he was navigating. The phone buzzed beside him on the countertop. It was Charlie Taliaferro.

"Hey, Charlie. What's up?"

"Just want to know if poker is still on this weekend. Isn't Lauren supposed to get back from Georgia?"

"Yes, but she's coming back Friday evening."

"Right. Okay, so we're still on for Saturday?"

"Yes. Seven-thirty."

"Well, look, there's something I want to talk to you about. Can you have coffee sometime today?"

"Maybe." William answered. "You can't talk on the phone?"

"Well, I'd rather not. How about sometime after lunch? I'd take you to lunch, but I've got a client. Tell you what—I'll buy you a drink after work."

"Charlie, this wouldn't have anything to do with real estate, would it?" William was pretty sure Charlie wanted him to share an investment someplace in the city. There were still a few hidden pockets of post-Katrina investing going on in New Orleans for people who knew where to find it, people like Charlie. Low-interest loans from the federal government made these investments very attractive.

"Well, I'd rather tell you about it in person. So, is five o'clock okay? Patty's?"

"Yeah, sure. See you then."

He took his muffin to the patio doorway, opened one of the doors and leaned against the frame. *Real estate.* Lauren had mentioned closing the townhouse. He didn't know if she meant just closing it, renting it, or selling it. He didn't want to do any of those things, but of course they'd have to close it. He didn't want to rent it out to strangers, but he certainly didn't want to sell it. It was *home.* He glanced at his little herb garden with the sundial he'd carefully positioned so that it told the time of day accurately whenever the sun was shining.

He tried to think about leaving the city where he was born, where he'd spent his whole life. He tried to think about selling the townhouse, going away to some foreign country called Georgia, but it was the wrong time of year to think about leaving New Orleans. It wasn't good to think about leaving when the fragrance of tea-olives was everywhere, not good to contemplate leaving the billowing, bright pink bougainvillea that was climbing the courtyard wall. Not good to think about closing the house now, to leave. Not now...

He thought about closing his mother's house in Bay St. Louis after she died. He'd come across old eight-track tapes, and he played them while he went through her dining room, wrapping china and crystal in white paper, preparing to send it to storage for safekeeping, for Elise to use someday. He could hear the music now: "I'm leavin' on a jet plane... Don't know if I'll be back again..." Elise would never use Limoges or Baccarat, but he didn't know what else to do with it.

William's wandering thoughts were not a consequence of approaching age; he'd always done it—followed a thought to a memory, a memory to a speculation, or maybe some unanswered question, then back to memory, possibly the thought patterns of someone whose life work had been reading, writing, and teaching history—though in the last several years, his "meandering mind," as Lauren called it, had a more personal and less scholarly character. In either case, what he always meandered *through* was time—the past, specifically Europe's past, and lately, his own past. His mother's china and crystal and silver were all still wrapped in the white paper and stored in the attic of the family home on St. Charles, undamaged by Katrina. Elise had never even thought of taking it when she married. It was "stuff," stuff no one wanted now. Yet, like bones in a tomb, it was still there, stored in time.

Leaving. It made him remember leaving New Orleans for his year abroad when he was a student, and the party his friends had for him the night before his departure. Paul Cunningham's rumination—how long ago now? Thirty years? He was an undergraduate at Tulane then.

"Do you suppose," Paul waved a Styrofoam cup of wine as he spoke, "do you suppose that the Romans—or, for that matter, the

Greeks—sat around a table and said stuff like this?" Paul smiled, self-amused, as though he were imagining a scene: men—women wouldn't have been present, of course—in sandals and togas, holding cups of wine, lying around on cushions and mats, having the same kind of conversation they were having.

Jocelyn had laughed. "And how would that go?" She looked at William across the low coffee table with wine-blurred eyes. "Ah, Williamicus—what do you think? How long will these hairy barbarians be able to hold sway over the Roman people? I mean, all they have are axes and bloodlust—they have no art, no literacy or learning—not even civilized manners."

"I must remind you, Jocelynimus," William answered. "Neither did we Romans." He smirked, raising his cup and his brows teasingly in her direction.

But it was an odd moment. In their smart-alecky drunkenness, they'd stumbled on a kind of unwelcome truth. Time moves. Things pass. All things pass and become past. And all of them chased the past, building their future on the past. Jocelyn was an art history major, Paul studied baroque music, Jason was writing a thesis on Immanuel Kant, and William was a medievalist. They were all Romans. They perpetuated, by their studies, and by their endless talk, talk, talk—which was a kind of embalming—a dead culture, in much the same way Romans might have done as that civilization crumbled around them. There wasn't a single healthy barbarian among them, not one computer programmer, not one systems analyst, not one business or finance major, economist—not even a pre-med or pre-law. And, indeed, if there had been, that conversation wouldn't have been happening. Amidst candlelight and marijuana smoke, the room darkened, as though a spirit, thin and wide, had entered the room like a pall, and, unnoticed during all their talking, drinking, and laughing, it had enclosed them. They were silent for a long moment as they absorbed an image of themselves, an image not unlike patricians enclosed within a palace under siege by invading hordes of proletarian vandals.

Jason gave it voice: "We are dying," he said slowly, looking down into his cup, a weak smile making an attempt to avoid the serious reflection. They glanced at him, eyes narrowing a little in unwelcome sobriety.

"No," said Jocelyn. "We're not dying. We're already dead."

It was 1980. It was Jocelyn's little one-room studio apartment above a garage in the Garden District. It was after William's farewell party, and only the four of them remained, sitting on the floor around Jocelyn's coffee table among the litter of wine bottles, Styrofoam cups, ashtrays and cigarette butts. William was leaving the next morning for Paris, for a year's study abroad, leaving to learn western civilization first-hand from its Gothic remnants, as a dead man who sets out to examine the tomb that contains him.

Leaving. We are always leaving, he thought. We are always dying. He looked at the sundial again. Everything was already in the past. We've already left, he thought. We are already gone. Time is like that…

He didn't care about Charlie's "investment opportunities" and didn't want to be bothered with hearing about this one. He had money—or at least, his accountant said he did. He didn't know exactly how much because he didn't care enough to know. He'd always had money, ever since he could remember. His mother's family was part of the wealthy old Creole aristocracy, and his Irish father made another fortune drilling for oil in the Gulf. And Lauren had come from a wealthy family in Mississippi. Money, he decided, was like love: it only mattered if you didn't have it. And Joanna had probably never thought about love—just as he never thought about money. Because she'd never been unloved. We can only want what we don't have… isn't that what *want* means? To *lack* something? He didn't want money.

*

Like the city that surrounded it, Patty's Bar gave the impression of not giving a damn about what people think. It was filthy almost by design, from the spit-stained floor to the unwashed lacquered mahogany bar. It was located, like many New Orleans bars and restaurants, in the middle of a neighborhood. On a corner of Esplanade, surrounded by expensive apartment houses that had once been Edwardian homes, it wasn't far from the UNO campus. William was not a fan of grime, nor of Patty's, but Charlie was. In fact, he conducted a good deal of his business there, on a smartphone.

Charlie was sitting at one of the small tables lined up against the wall opposite the bar, talking into his phone, twirling a glass of gin in which an olive moved among ice cubes. He looked up and smiled at William, waving a pudgy little finger in greeting as he continued his phone conversation. William went to the bar to get a drink before sitting down at Charlie's table.

"How you doing?" said Charlie, slipping the phone into the pocket of his blue-striped seersucker jacket.

"I'm okay. Can't take too long with this though. I've got to pick up some groceries. Lauren'll be back around six tomorrow and there's nothing in the house to eat."

"Batching days are over, huh?" Charlie had the illusion, as a middle-aged man still single, that married men had lives alien to his own. It didn't occur to him that he, too, bought groceries, and he, too, sometimes had to live around someone else's schedule. He'd had live-in girlfriends before, but they never lasted long. William knew that he found long-term relationships like marriage somewhat mysterious.

"She's only been gone four days, Charlie. It's not like I just got married."

"You know I think it's cool that you guys have been together for—what is it?—twenty-five, thirty years? Wow."

"Yeah, wow. What is it you wanted to talk about?"

Charlie made a little production of it—leaning forward and slightly lowering his voice, putting on his confidential face, taking time to sip his drink before answering. "Well. You know that warehouse in Bywater—big old thing—used to be Wainwright's Storage?"

"Yes. Katrina almost leveled it. What about it?" Here it comes, thought William. He wants me to buy that old warehouse with him.

"Well, it's going on the market *next week*."

"So?" Make him work for it, William thought, feeling mischievous.

"So, Will, listen. Listen carefully. I happen to know somebody in Dallas who would be very interested—*very*.

"So what, Charlie? Everybody owns a piece of this city. It's still cheap. Didn't you tell me somebody in China bought two whole blocks of the ninth ward?"

"Yes, but listen, Will. Nobody *knows* Wainwright's is going on the market. That's the point. The owner is this old lady in Hattiesburg who doesn't think it's worth anything now. But that place is half a block off the river. It's a gold mine for somebody who knows what to do with it—and this guy in Dallas does know. Only he doesn't know it's going up for sale—and I do." He paused for effect. "And now—*you* know it, too."

"Sorry, not interested." He listened to Charlie sigh, rattle the ice in his glass and lift it toward the bartender, while he fingered the plastic stirrer in his own drink. After a moment, during which he knew Charlie was waiting for him to mull it over, he asked, "How do you know Hattiesburg wants to sell?"

Charlie didn't even look at him. "She's ninety, Will. Her lawyer's already sold everything else she owned. Only the warehouse is left."

"That doesn't answer the question. *How do you know*?"

Charlie drummed the table with his well-manicured fingertips. "Never mind, okay? I know."

Yes, thought William, he probably does know. Aloud, he said, "Well, how do you know Dallas would buy?"

Charlie's drink arrived and he raised the glass and his eyebrows toward William. The bartender waited for an answer. William shook his head.

Charlie resumed: "Look, Will, going by what the old lady got for the rest, that falling-down warehouse will be a giveaway. Even if Dallas turns out to be a dead-end, there's no way to lose here! I mean, Christ, look where it *is!*"

William had to admit that it was prime investment property in the remnant of the feeding frenzy that pervaded the city after Katrina, like blood in the water. "Let me think about it."

"No, Will. I can't do that. You've got to let me know before the game on Saturday. It's going up next week. I have to make an offer by Monday morning, latest." His phone made an assertive whine in his pocket. "Got to get this text. Hold on a minute." He punched keys while William studied the dirty black and white chicken-wire pattern of the tile floor. Charlie slipped the phone back in his jacket. "You'd be three, Will. Five could do it cheaper, but there's not enough time to scout. It's got to be an odd number, you know, in case there's disagreement when we sell."

"I get it. I do," Will answered. "But why do I have to answer before the game?"

"Well, just because I don't want to talk about it when Hans and Freddie are there."

"Oh, right. Okay. I'll let you know. I'll call you before Saturday night. But you haven't mentioned a share price, you know."

"I'll have that information when I get the stakeholders in place—three, or five. I should know by tonight. I'll call you then."

"Okay. Thanks for the drink. I have to think about this." As he left, Charlie was retrieving his phone from his pocket again and punching numbers.

*

William got into the rattling old Volvo smiling, thinking about how simple life was for Charlie and for all the hunter-gatherers like him. It was false to believe that Charlie's life was empty or lacking in any way just because he had no wife and children. He didn't have a family because he didn't want a family. It was that simple, and Charlie never confused himself about it. Life was getting money, making a good deal, and he enjoyed living that life. He turned onto Barrone Street enjoying the idea of Charlie hustling to get more stakeholders in the Wainwright deal.

He and Lauren had made a decision early in their marriage not to live in the city. They had both gone to Tulane and then to LSU in Baton Rouge for graduate work. Lauren was from Mississippi, but she had spent a good deal of time in the city because she had relatives there. They were both New Orleanians. But after renting an apartment near the campus for about a year after their return from Baton Rouge, they bought a small house in Mandeville and left the city. By then, Lauren was pregnant, and William thought the long drive, twenty-four miles across Lake Pontchartrain was worth it. Mandeville was safer, quieter, and it was a better place to raise a child and to have a garden. But the inconvenience got to be too much for both of them, so when Elise started school in the city, they returned. "So much for small-town life," Lauren remarked when they bought the townhouse on Prytania.

Ever since then, they'd bought groceries in the same stores. He headed that way now, deciding to wait until Saturday morning to hit the farmers' market with Lauren; for now, there was no fresh bread at home and not much food in the freezer or the pantry.

By the time he pulled into a parking space in front of the bakery, his good humor over Charlie's deal-making had dissipated. When he got out of the car, he glanced up the street and saw Immaculate Conception. He hadn't been in the old urban church, squeezed between tall buildings, in many years, but he remembered its cool darkness, its silent vastness, and something he'd thought of once as its "timelessness." He decided to go in and sit for a few minutes before getting the bread.

He went through the great carved doors to the echoing new marble tile floor—the old floor had been destroyed by Katrina. Except for the light on the distant altar and the gold reredos, the church was dark. He sat down on the back pew on the right side of the aisle. On the left side, a drunk was sleeping, sprawled on his back with his arm crooked over his forehead and eyes. After a while, he checked his watch, surprised to find that he'd been sitting there almost an hour, and his mind had been quiet, wonderfully mute.

*

William pushed a shopping cart around Bon Marche thinking about what Lauren would say to Charlie's warehouse deal. She'd be in favor of it. He rolled the idea around in his head as he loaded the cart with rice and beans, cereal and milk, remembering to pick up pretzels, beer, and peanuts for poker Saturday night. Lauren knew they didn't need the money, but unlike William, she was too practical to turn down a relatively small investment for a quick profit. He'd often wondered how their different personalities worked so well together; all he'd ever been able to think of was that she somehow set the rhythm of his life and provided the grounding he needed. He had no idea at all what he provided for her, except possibly some amusement. Whatever it was, he could not imagine life without her, and he'd never tried.

As he loaded the groceries in the trunk of the car, the streetlights came on; somewhere in the distance somebody was practicing a trumpet, long, slow mournful notes—blues. He stood there several minutes listening in the growing dark. The affect was like velvet on his arid, aching soul. He had some difficulty in pulling away from it to get in the car.

He drove home thinking about why Charlie approached him in the first place. Over the years, he'd made some money with a few of Charlie's plans, but he usually declined. His friendship with Charlie Taliaferro went back to childhood when they'd both attended St. Vincent's, but they'd never been close friends.

Charlie came from an Italian neighborhood that wasn't close to his own—and they'd gone to different high schools. Then there was the interruption of college for William and military service for Charlie. William knew some members of Charlie's large and extended family; he'd even dated one of Charlie's sisters when they were in high school, but although they shared some history, a Catholic school education, and a few other interests, it wasn't until they both became poker players at a regularly scheduled game that any real friendship emerged.

He'd never been completely sure of how Charlie made his living. He thought it was mostly real estate, but not exclusively. The Taliaferro family had involvements all over the city—law, real estate, local politics, even a few stores and restaurants. And like many other large New Orleans families, there was the ubiquitous smudge of corruption. Charlie's father had even had a couple of indictments handed down by the courts, but nothing ever actually stuck. William couldn't remember the cause—something to do with the racetrack. It was nothing as glamorous as organized crime, just the typical ongoing flirtation with corruption that was as much a part of New Orleans culture as jazz.

He pulled into the narrow drive to the carport behind the townhouse and unloaded the shopping bags from the trunk. Lauren called while he was putting the groceries away. "Hi," he answered. "You're late. How come?"

"Well, I'm in Savannah staying with the boys tonight, and I just forgot about calling you till now. Elise is out on a date. You believe that?"

"When did she start dating? Tell me about it." Elise's Marine husband had been killed in Iraq a little more than a year ago. William was glad to hear that she was dating. He'd begun to wonder recently if her grief might not be going on for too long.

"This is the second or third time she's gone out with this guy, I think. But don't read anything into it. He's not 'the one.' I think she's just sort of testing the water, that's all. For one thing, he's not into the kids."

"Well, I know that wouldn't sit well with her." Elise was a devoted mother, almost *too* devoted in William's opinion, since the death of her husband. He wanted her to have a life outside her children and her job. "I bought some groceries, by the way. We'll have something in the house to eat when you get back tomorrow."

"Good. Do you want to speak with the boys? Joey's old enough to make some sense on the phone."

"No, not unless they asked to speak to Grandpa—and my guess is that they didn't."

"They're watching a Disney movie."

"So give them a kiss."

"Right."

"And one for you, too."

"Love you. See you tomorrow."

He turned on the radio and listened to some light classical while he put the remaining groceries away. His cellphone rang again. Charlie.

"Okay, Will. Good and bad news—you're one of five. That means lower investment, but also lower return."

"So how much?"

"Can you commit to eighty thousand?"

"Does that mean you're going to offer four hundred thousand?"

"No—hell, no. I'm going to offer two-fifty, but I need to know how much wiggle room I have."

"What do you expect from Dallas?"

"You should be able to double your investment within, say, two weeks."

"I'll let you know."

"Soon, Will, soon. Delay is deadly here. Timing is everything."

"I understand, Charlie. I got it. Within thirty-six hours." He hung up.

Why did he feel vaguely troubled about this? There was nothing immoral about the deal, not even borderline unethical. It was simply a buy and sell arrangement for profit. It was sensible. It was the kind of thing Charlie did for a living, and Charlie was not a criminal. A very old woman in Hattiesburg was apparently settling her affairs and divesting herself of several properties. She was going to want a quick sale, and Charlie was going to oblige. What was wrong with that? Nothing.

Yet it made him frown to ponder his own participation in it. It felt dishonorable; he didn't like it. He told himself he didn't have the axes and bloodlust drive that Charlie had. Charlie did not have a business he could actually name, like an honest merchant—no office or store, no staff to support, no rent to pay, no "overhead" as he might have called it. Nothing that would allow him to claim an outrageous profit as something he had to pursue in order to support others who depended on him. Charlie owned a smartphone, and he had an office in his million-dollar condo. He also had a Mercedes, and probably at least one woman to keep entertained. He did all this by using that smartphone and his own predatory instinct. There was nothing wrong with that. Why did it bother William?

Because that's not enough. His frown deepened. *Not enough for whom? For Charlie, or for me?* In his distraction, he dropped a bag of rice and it burst on the kitchen floor; the noise seemed deafening, like a crash drowning out Mozart on the radio. It was an accident that at any other time in his life might have made him curse but he didn't. He just stood there, looking down at the scattered grains for what seemed like several minutes before going to the broom closet to get a broom and dustpan and clean up the mess.

Yes, he felt disgusted by Charlie, for the selfishness of his life, but then he was equally disgusted by himself, for his own hypocritical aristocratic disapproval. Weary, suddenly overwhelmed with a fatigue that fell over him like a suffocating blanket, he ceased his aimless pondering. He skipped dinner, and went upstairs to bed early, taking a drink, instead of a book, to bed with him. He lay in bed, propped up against the headboard and sipping bourbon in the dark. Whose lack of virtue annoyed him, Charlie's or his own? But he knew it wasn't a matter of virtue. And the knowledge gave him, not recrimination or shame, but sorrow. For he also knew that his real problem with Charlie was that Charlie had something he cared about. But he'd lived for History, for love of it, and belief in it—belief in its value, its transcending value above all human endeavors, its immortality. And History was dying. Maybe it was money—the real gold of human endeavor—maybe it was money that was immortal after all. He realized that what he actually felt was petty jealousy.

Chapter Three

Improvising Time

It was raining. William stood at the window of his office overlooking the student parking lot, wet asphalt splattered everywhere by raindrops. Not many cars on Fridays. Beyond the parking lot, he could see Lake Pontchartrain in the rain-hazed distance, stretching out like a vast sea. He saw a young woman with a blonde ponytail, drenched by the rain, running toward the parking lot, and for a moment, his heart stopped. She got into a blue Toyota. It wasn't her. He turned from the window, feeling at once relieved and disappointed.

There wasn't much to do on Friday mornings. For the past few years, not much of his work was his own. He had no heavy enrollment to deal with, no administrative workload, and lately Don had passed some of his own work down to him, even reviews of departmental budgets other than his own. Usually, students avoided Friday appointments, and that had always worked in his favor in the past. Except for graduate seminars, it had always left Fridays free to deal with his administrative tasks. But there wasn't much of that anymore.

Lauren was coming home that night. That thought gave him a kind of relief, but it was troubling also. It had become difficult to hide his sadness from her; he was sure she'd noticed his increasing withdrawal, but she said nothing. She wouldn't. It would never be like her to mention it if she was concerned about him. Neither had ever focused attention on the other, but on something or someone else in their lives—primarily Elise, of course, but also on Lauren's work with the families of the disabled, William's scholarly work—other things, other persons, not each other. Now in middle age, Lauren had a new academic career to attend. Ostensibly, he was going to write his magnum opus on Charlemagne, but he had no energy for it, no enthusiasm, no desire. Years ago, if he'd been able to take a sabbatical to write this book, if he'd been able to block out the attention space it would require, he would have jumped at the chance. Now, it seemed an arduous task, tedious labor, and he'd begun to suspect that he'd never do it. William was one of perhaps five or six living persons who knew most about Charlemagne, but that knowledge had become irrelevant to the point of extinction. That fact alone would not have been enough to disengage him, but the real problem was worse: it had become irrelevant to him, too.

Don called around three and asked him not to turn in his letter of resignation just yet.

"Why not? What's the problem?"

"Oh, Christ, Will. There's more involved now than you think. Things are changing next fall."

"What kind of change—and why should my resignation make any difference to changes in the History Department?"

"You won't be replaced."

"What? Why not?"

"Because," Don whined, "it's not certain that there will be a History Department for anybody to chair."

He was quiet for a moment. This had been mentioned before, like a rumor or an idea is talked about, but it had never been a real possibility, never seemed like something that would actually happen. "Oh? So that decision has been made, has it?"

"History will be subsumed under Humanities."

"Well, I'll be damned," he said. The wall had been breached. The barbarians were inside the gates.

Late that afternoon, around five, William turned the key in his office door. The secretary had already left, and the hallway was deserted. Offices closed on Fridays at three; no classes were scheduled after that hour, and so the emptiness of the building was not unusual. But in light of what he now knew, there was an eerie palpability to the emptiness, and he had again that sensation of being a dead man, groping along the walls of his tomb. He nodded to one of the janitorial staff on his way to the elevator, and then, as he descended to the faculty lot, he felt a despair that was overwhelming. It's not the end of history, but worse—the end of the importance of it, he told himself. Perhaps there had never really been an importance at all.

History of Western Civilization I and II had been a two-semester requirement for all majors for so many years, then it became required for only arts and humanities, and finally it had become a mere elective. Enrollment had declined rapidly in the past several years. Faculty had been cut, and double major graduates and adjuncts hired to replace departing faculty. History had been in a death agony for some time. Now it would be subsumed, buried, under Humanities, like philosophy, art appreciation, and other such courses for liberal arts students.

He drove home slowly, wondering if Lauren was home yet. Lauren, whose field was Education, an area of academics very much alive and growing. He swallowed the bitter irony that education was dying even as Education thrived. The college of Education had exploded in the past few decades and now contained within itself all sorts of threads—sociology, psychology, and the now-ubiquitous "administration" areas. All these and more were further divided demographically, by age, geography, or urban versus rural, and then Lauren's area of disabilities, physical, intellectual, and so on. Universities now grounded themselves completely in professional functionality, not in knowledge, still less in the idea that knowledge could, if the ground were fertile, inspire wisdom. The thought returned to him again: It's Lauren's turn...

*

She was home. Her green Subaru was parked on the bricked pad next to the covered carport, left empty for his aging Volvo. The dryer vent made a soft clattering sound next to the French doors of the patio as he entered and went through the breakfast room to the kitchen. She wasn't there, but probably in the laundry room next to the kitchen. "Hello, my love!" he called out, heading for the liquor cabinet.

"Well, that's a fine thing," said his wife, coming up behind him and putting her arms around his waist. "I'm gone nearly a week, and my husband heads for the bourbon before he heads for me."

"Ha!" he said, turning and grabbing her in mock-passion. "I only needed to fortify myself for the joy of your return! Join me?"

"Yes," she said, turning away from him and heading toward her suitcase, lying open on the breakfast table. "Go ahead. I'm going to get the pictures."

A tendril of hair fell down her neck from the large clamp on the back of her head. It fell over the blue sweatshirt in a mix of auburn and silver, a wonderful color. In her youth, Lauren's hair had been a glorious vivid auburn; he was glad she chose not to cover the gray as it crept in, year by year, and softened the striking color. Like the curves the years had added to her figure, it only made her more appealing.

"I've got pictures of everything—the kids, Elise, the campus, the town. Will, I think you're going to love it!"

She took her iPad to the patio, and he followed her with the drinks, pushing the door closed with his foot. A little cluster of wrens scattered from the feeder as the chairs scraped the brick floor, then made a tentative return as they settled in to look at the photos of what would become their new hometown of Statesboro, Georgia, their new life in a new place. She had, of course, visited nearby Savannah, where Elise and the grandchildren lived. Lauren—immune to any charms that lovely city might have had to offer—had no pictures of Savannah, but many photos and videos of Elise, her home, the children. The grandchildren had grown, Elise had gained weight—they all appeared healthy and happy. The town of Statesboro, however, was appalling, like a Wal-Mart suburb attempting a Disneyworld veneer. But he asked questions, feigned interest, and tried to absorb his wife's enthusiasm.

Lauren grilled some salmon and William made a salad. They spent the evening talking about Elise, the grandchildren, and about Lauren's new position at Georgia Southern and Statesboro. William told her about Charlie's real estate scheme.

"If it works," he said, "it wouldn't just pay all the expenses of moving but also pay our rent for a long time—a couple of years and maybe more."

"Why rent so long?" Lauren asked, surprised. "Are you thinking we shouldn't buy? Will, are you thinking I won't make tenure?"

"No, no, of course not. Of course, you'll make tenure—if you want to. But, you know, we may not like it there. You may not like it there. Of course, they're going to love you—but will you love them? Will you love Statesboro, Georgia?"

"Hm. Will you love it? That's the question, Will."

"Where you go, I go." He smiled at her, a smile that said, This isn't just banter, my love. I'm dead serious. "Anyway, I thought we'd take a look at the Wainwright property when we go to the market in the morning..."

"Why should we even delay long enough to look at it? For heaven's sake, you know it's a wreck—none of that property over there has been touched since Katrina. What it looks like doesn't matter. My goodness, Will, it's the location."

"I know, I know," he said. He'd forgotten that Lauren was a

pragmatist, like a good barbarian should be. "Eighty thousand…"

"Oh, come on. You know we can handle that. We could get an equity advance on this place if you'd like that better. I know we haven't checked on selling the townhouse yet—we should ask Charlie about it—but I imagine it should bring at least two-fifty, probably more, don't you?"

"I hadn't thought about selling so quickly."

"Why on earth not?"

*

Why on earth not? He lay in bed late that night asking himself that question. Why not? He thought it was odd that he hadn't even flinched at the eighty-thousand investment, but the possibility of selling the house made him pause. Rather like closing down history, he thought, perhaps one should pause. Yes, he knew it would come to pass—eventually—but so soon? So off-handedly? He watched through the window of the upstairs bedroom a full moon moving slowly behind an oak tree, hiding its transit from him. Time moves, he thought, his arm behind his head, listening to Lauren's occasional soft, snuffling snore. No—it's not moving—we are. We are what's moving… Where? *Why?*

We are dying, said Jason. No. We are dead, said Jocelyn. He turned his gaze away from the moon and looked instead at its light where it fell on the back of Lauren's bare shoulder. "What on earth are you going to do in Statesboro, Georgia?" Don had asked him. A coldness seized his chest. "Maybe write," he'd answered. He didn't want to write. What would he write? History? That would be pouring water into the ocean.

She's leaving… No, she's already gone, he thought, turning back to the window. Joanna was not unhappy to be leaving New Orleans, however she might feel about leaving him. Certainly the city had not impressed her. He'd thought once that if her area of concentration had been American literature instead of British, particularly American southern writers, she might have had an easier time. But the truth was, as literature students discovered sometimes to their disappointment, words are not the language of New Orleans, but music—specifically, jazz. For tourists, that's a sound, but for New Orleanians, it's more like a pulsebeat, and notably absent from the rhythms of jazz is any sort of work ethic, a trait that caused Joanna constant irritation. He tried to explain to her that it didn't mean New Orleanians didn't work, just that they think of getting up in the morning and going to work not as a matter of discipline, which would be an alien concept, but as a personal existential choice. Otherwise, it's doubtful anyone would actually do it. The same was true for planning anything; there must always remain room for improvisation, so while plans are made, actual follow-through on those plans is not a given. New Orleanians improvise everything, including time. Joanna frequently complained about her students, and about New Orleans in general, saying she could never actually count on anyone keeping a promise, a schedule, an appointment. She didn't like the city or its citizens.

But it wasn't just the laissez-faire way of life that gave her problems with the city; it was also a matter of what really did impress her—intellectual achievement—and that was something New Orleanians, regardless of their own achievement or lack of it, found pretty much uninteresting, an attitude that left her with no point of contact with the city. She found the heat and humidity unbearable, the food inedible. Most of all, she despised jazz. "Sounds like rhythmic sloth," she'd once said. William made no attempt to defend the city of his birth, but he did think sometimes that beautiful Joanna, slender, fair, clear-skinned, had a purity that narrowed her and made her fragile. He would laugh at her irritation with affection even as he felt vague concern for her. There was no room for improvisation in Joanna. She would be safer back in her native northern country.

Chapter Four

The Past is Present

"Oh, look. There's Paul." Lauren nudged William's shoulder to get his attention as they wandered through the market Saturday morning, carrying plastic bags of shrimp in crushed ice, green onions, tomatoes and corn. "Let's go talk to him."

"No," William answered. He stepped backward a bit to get a better look at the tall, slender man in jeans and sweatshirt a few stalls away, his head bent over some fish. "If we talk to him, we might get hung up. We want to go by Wainwright's and we need to get the shrimp home."

"Well, it's on ice. Besides, I want to get some snapper, and it's right where he's standng. Doesn't he *ever* wear his clerical garb? Come on. Let's go ahead and speak—I need the fish."

But the bespectacled man with wavy gray hair turned and headed toward the parking lot. "Doesn't matter anyway," said William. "He's gone. Let's get the fish and go to Wainwright's."

They bought fish and a couple of crabs, then headed for the car. "Do you suppose Paul wears a collar in his classroom?" Lauren asked. "Does he ever wear one at all, you think?"

"No idea. Never been in his classroom." William drove the Subaru toward Bywater. "You should ask him, not me." Lauren had had an entanglement of some kind with Paul back when they were all students at Tulane, before he and Lauren became a couple. Paul was a year ahead of them, and after graduation, he went in seminary. He knew the affair was brief, but he also knew it was rather intense. She had never talked about it. "Was it you who drove him into the priesthood?" He was teasing, but when he glanced sideways at Lauren's face, she wasn't smiling.

"That's not funny."

"Hey. I was kidding. But now I'm wondering. Well, was it? Was it you? He went in seminary right after you guys broke up." He'd never thought about it before, mainly because it happened several months before he and Lauren became a couple. "Seriously. What happened there? I never asked, but you never said, either."

There was a long pause before Lauren heaved a sigh. "Oh, not much. I'll tell you about it sometime."

William negotiated the heavy traffic around construction sites toward the Bywater neighborhood. "Raise your window," he said. "Dust alert." The silence inside the car became audible. Was there something about Lauren he didn't know? What happened there? Paul was a trumpet performance major at Tulane with a love for Baroque music. He'd planned to do concert tours, pursuing a career as a professional on the symphony circuit. There was this thing then, with Lauren, an Education major from Mississippi. William knew her only slightly at the time. She wasn't a member of the little group of "dead Romans." As he drove, he tried to remember, to unscramble the close chronology of events. He'd met Lauren when she was with Paul, and—come to think of it—it seemed obvious to everyone then, including William, that Paul was very much in love…

"Were you in love with him, Lauren? Was it really all that serious?"

"Oh, Will. For Christ's sake!" She turned toward the passenger window and pushed the power button to lower the window again, letting street noise smother the conversation. "That was ages ago."

Well, thought William, yes, it was—but that didn't answer his question. All he remembered about Lauren in those days was her glorious hair. She was with Paul, and then she simply wasn't. He tried to remember why, what he'd heard at the time, but all he could remember was that his friend Jason said they'd broken up, and for a while, Paul seemed really down. A few months later, William and Lauren dated a few times, and then he went to Europe for a year's study abroad. She wrote him letters, he sent her postcards, and when he returned, they picked up where they'd left off. After a few months, he moved into the room she had in her aunt's house not far from the campus, and a year later, they were married. By then, Paul had completed the seminary. He became a Jesuit priest and taught music theory now at Loyola. From time to time, William ran into him. They would renew broken promises to have lunch, then vanish from each other's lives again.

William realized that he'd always assumed Paul was gay. Why? Because he was a priest? He recognized the absurdity of the assumption. When he ran into Paul, he always felt a little uncomfortable. Was that because he thought Paul was gay or was it because he was a priest? He had never asked himself why Paul made him uncomfortable. He glanced sideways at Lauren behind her sunglasses. She was never going to tell him about Paul. If she were, she would have done it already—years ago. He would never know now; he only knew that the past always remains present.

"Good grief," said Lauren with a little start. "Will, look at that!"

"I don't believe it," he replied, slowing the car to a crawl. "My God. They're rebuilding that dump."

They both craned their necks to the right, where *Wainwright's Moving and Storage* appeared in faded red letters on the side of a dilapidated structure that looked as if it would fall at any moment. A small crew of workers in hardhats walked around a scaffolding. From the driver's seat, William ducked his head down past Lauren's shoulder to see better.

"What on earth…?" he breathed. "That's insane." He reached for his cellphone where it rested on the console between them, punched the keypad and spoke into Charlie's voicemail: "Charlie, I'm at Wainwright's. You got some bad information. Call me. You need to back out of anything you've got yourself into here." He put the phone down. "You know," he said to Lauren, "this is the first time I've ever known Charlie to lose a deal."

They drove home slowly, ponderously. "I don't get it," said Lauren. "It's not just that Charlie got it wrong. Obviously, it's already sold, yes, but the really weird thing is—who would want to *restore* that old thing? That makes no sense."

"I don't know. Maybe Charlie will find out."

He drove home, listening to Lauren complain. She was disappointed, but William was conscious of a vague feeling of reprieve, though he said nothing about it. He felt like someone who'd just been spared, by some accident or other, from putting his life savings on a roulette wheel.

They took the bags in, put the shrimp in the refrigerator and the fish in the freezer, waiting for Charlie to return William's call and explain away their confusion. He was on the patio cleaning white corn and getting it ready to roast when it came to him: He'd been aware that he didn't want to move to Statesboro, Georgia, he didn't want to resign his position—he hadn't really wanted to end the affair with Joanna. Everything he was doing was what he did not want. He knew it was all for Lauren, but that wasn't all there was to it. All that he did not want wasn't due to his want of something else, something other—like remaining in the townhouse in New Orleans, continuing in a job that was disappearing, or clinging to a doomed affair. No. No—he didn't want those things either. The fact was he simply didn't want *anything.* To leave, to stay, to work, to write—even to love. He wanted nothing.

It felt like a shock, but a strangely soft, cool shock, without pain. He did not examine it. He dared not. It was not like the cold stillness he sometimes felt in his chest, a sensation that was now familiar. It was not like the intellectual discoveries that sometimes occurred to him in his meandering thoughts, nor was it a discovery about Lauren or Joanna, Elise or anyone else—or about any relationship at all. On the contrary, it was the most acutely personal awareness he'd ever experienced. It was like stumbling on a huge abyss he didn't know was there.

While he pulled husks from the white kernels on a planet far away from her, he could hear Lauren chattering to somebody on the phone in the kitchen behind him about her trip to Statesboro. She sounded so intense, so involved in her future there. She had her phone propped between her shoulder and her cheek while she washed romaine lettuce in the sink, naming the several committees on which she'd have to serve in the fall, those she looked forward to, those she dreaded. He could hear the naïve self-importance seeping into the tone of her voice, and it made him smile, as one might smile at the airs of a little girl playing dress-up, but then the smile vanished, dissolved into lonely awareness of how far away he was from her and how impossible it was to go back where she was.

Still holding her phone between shoulder and chin, Lauren brought him his own buzzing phone; Charlie's name was on the screen. He dropped an ear of corn in the pan and took the phone: "Charlie! Hey, guess what Lauren and I just saw at Wainwright's." Lauren ended her own conversation and stood by as he put the phone on speaker.

"You saw a construction crew, right?" Charlie seemed almost amused.

"Yes, right! How did you know? What's going on?"

"It's gone, Will. We missed it."

"*What?* How'd that happen? We were all revved up and raring to go," he said, for Lauren's benefit. He didn't care about the investment.

"Well," Charlie drawled, somehow making William feel that the deal had been lost because he'd been slow to invest—though he knew that wasn't true. "I called Hattiesburg to make an offer and they said they closed last week. Never even put it on the market. Timing, Will. Time is *always* of the essence. Hey, get this—they closed for one seventy-five."

"Really? Why so little?"

"Who knows? What's really weird is the buyer is rebuilding Wainwright's, only they're changing it into one of those self-storage places, you know? Got to be somebody foreign. Any American fool would know the value of that real estate—hell of a lot better return could have been made."

"Oh, well. I'll see you in about four hours. We're still on for seven-thirty. You want to come early and eat with us? We're making shrimp etouffee."

"Sure. I'll bring the wine. Might as well drown our grief."

Lauren, obviously angry, walked heavily back inside. "Well, so much for that!" she pronounced, as though a promise had been made to her, and then broken with no excuse.

*

Charlie came to dinner. They ate shrimp, corn, artichokes, and they drank Charlie's Chardonnay. Lauren had some difficulty finding her peace with their guest. First, she blamed him entirely for the loss of Wainwright's, then she blamed William for not buying in on the spot, and then, finally acknowledging with some bitterness that the deal was already gone by the time Charlie spoke to William about it, she threw a half-eaten ear of corn down on the parchment paper in which it had been roasted, and announced, "Well, shit!"

Charlie laughed. "Exactly, Lauren. That's the stuff that sometimes happens."

The table was cleared and made ready for poker. Cards were brought out, bowls of pretzels, popcorn, and peanuts appeared. Lauren disappeared into the kitchen with a rattle and clatter of dishes, and Charlie and William took espresso to the patio.

"Sorry, Will." Charlie leaned against the wrought iron post of the patio and sipped his coffee. "I don't know what happened, but I can tell you it's not worth finding out."

"That's okay. Who wants to make a quarter-million in a week, anyway," he answered with satiric good nature, conscious that he really didn't care. Back inside, they could hear the dishwasher hum in tempo with Jimmy Stokes' slow trombone on the kitchen radio, an old New Orleans jazz tune, "If I Could Shimmy Like My Sister Kate."

"You're going to miss this city, Will."

There was only a short pause before he answered, "No, I won't. Might miss Jimmy Stokes, though. But it's not a bad trade. We'll get fireflies. Lauren says there are fireflies in Georgia. Remember those?"

"Yes. We killed them off with mosquito spray. Christ, Will, you're such a damned romantic. I'd rather have Jimmy Stokes than a bunch of bugs." He laughed softly.

The doorbell rang then, and they could hear Lauren talking with Hans inside, cooing over his Pekingese, which he took everywhere with him.

"Hansi's here—and his little lady friend," said William. Charlie once told him that their gay friend Hans Mueller was no more gay than his dog, Cecily. "He's just scared to death of women, like most of them, you know. All that gay crap is camouflage."

"What's he scared of?" William had asked.

"Well, you know. He's afraid of getting smothered, trapped. He sees all those pretty little playthings on the outside as a way to trap you inside—where you get suffocated, don't you know, and you *die*." Charlie chuckled. "Scared to death of women—that's how 'gay' Hansi is. There's a reason he keeps a female under his control, even if she's a dog."

William smiled, thinking that Charlie had just revealed nothing at all about their friend Hans, but maybe a great deal about himself. They went inside, greeted Cecily the Pekingese, then lapsed into banter about Hans' overtly gay appearance. "But fuchsia is just so passé now, Hansi," Charlie said, in a mocking sneer at Hans' blinding sequined tee-shirt. "Oh, how are you, darling Cecily—love those blue-polished nails, dear!" He held one of the dog's paws in his hand. She acknowledged the compliment with a slurp of his palm. Lauren took the dog from Hans' arms and went to answer the doorbell and let Freddie in. Then she passed them still holding Cecily and heading for the courtyard, muttering something about femme fatales having bladders. She disapproved of their ridicule of Hans' sexual preference, even though Hans himself didn't mind it; he even seemed to enjoy it. Lauren regarded gay people as a persecuted minority and therefore deserving of deference.

*

The poker game went well. William was grateful for the distraction, but as he lay in bed later that night, he was also aware that the idea of "distraction" begged the question: *distraction from what?* At first he thought that he'd been distracted from thinking about Joanna. But, painful as such thoughts were, that wasn't what accounted for his feeling of distance from the game, the camaraderie, and even—he tracked back to certain points earlier in the evening—from Lauren. When did it start? He'd felt that distance for some time; only now, when the end of everything was imminent, he felt as though he were dying—alone.

He got out of bed and headed downstairs to the patio, his bare feet padding the wooden floor of the hallway, remembering to turn off the alarm before opening the outside door. Strange, he thought, how he did ordinary things without pause, without thinking about it, as though things were ordinary. He turned off the courtyard lights and sat in the darkness, leaning back, with his fingers laced across his tee-shirted stomach over the top of his pajama pants. He felt less lonely now he was alone.

He thought of Lauren sleeping upstairs and was flooded with tenderness. He pictured her pink fingertips, pink palms and soles of her feet, her skin, milky white, splattered with faint freckles—which she hated with an odd passion. He wanted her always to be happy, always to be healthy, to be fulfilled in every way. He looked skyward and wished the city lights did not kill the stars. He tried to remember a night sky filled with stars, but he couldn't. Worse than an absence of stars, he thought, was the absence of any memory of starlight. There was only empty darkness.

Somehow he had to get through this. He did not try to understand it. He was past that. It was Joanna. It was more than Joanna. He had to get through this for Lauren's sake. He felt a moment of gratitude that something mattered to him. *Lauren.*

Chapter Five

Time Stops

It was Wednesday evening and Lauren was fretting in the kitchen about her figure. She ended with a long, drawn-out sigh. "Will, I want to lose fifteen pounds before the fall semester starts."

"Well, you better get started then." He sat at the counter reading *The Times-Picayune* "Guess what," he said, looking up at her over his reading glasses. "Buddy DiMateo's been indicted for fraud. Isn't he Charlie's cousin?"

"I don't know—never heard of him. But if he's Charlie's cousin, he'll probably get off. Listen, I think if I lose four pounds a month, I can do it. What do you think about Weight Watchers? I could set short-range goals and work towards each goal one month at a time. Isn't that how they do it?"

He dropped the newspaper and looked at her. The extra roundness of her bare shoulders in the halter dress only added to her beauty. He murmured, "My God, woman, you're irresistible." He made a low growling sound in his throat.

"Ha!" she scoffed. "You're just trying to break my resolve!" But he could tell she was pleased. One of the things he loved about his wife was her ill-concealed vanity. It was a part of her femininity that he found especially charming. There were other parts, less frivolous, that sometimes created in him a sense of awe, like the time he watched her nurse Elise in the dim early-morning lamplight of their bedroom in that house in Mandeville. No Madonna was ever more beautiful. It left an indelible imprint in his memory he wanted never to lose.

William loved his wife, sometimes with an intensity that almost frightened him when he thought about it, so he'd learned not to think about it too much. Years ago, on some late-night talk show, a guest—he could not remember who it was—answered the question, "How do you account for your happy marriage?" by saying that he believed he had a happy marriage because he and his wife had never had a single in-depth conversation. Perhaps that was true of his own marriage, perhaps he and Lauren had drawn a line somewhere that neither ever chose to cross, and perhaps they had stumbled on that little formula for success very early on.

If so, it had been a blessing, a happy accident. He had stabilized somewhat since her return—as he'd hoped he would. They'd gone to a concert in City Park on Sunday, and he'd enjoyed it. He began to feel hopeful that he'd get past the sadness that still came at unexpected moments and threatened to swallow him.

She slapped the newspaper down on the counter. "It's six-thirty already. We're going to be late if we don't leave right now." That wasn't really true. They weren't due at the restaurant until seven, but the remark did serve to make him pay attention to the time, stand up, sort and stack the newspapers. They were having dinner with Don and his wife Ellen, part social, part political, both parts obligatory.

At Don's request, William had postponed submitting his resignation until the fate of the History Department was firmly determined. Don said he thought that any announcement of a major change only muddied the water, but William knew Don had some kind of idea that if he resigned, it would encourage the decision in favor of closing the Department, but if he remained, if everything seemed "normal," the Department might also remain—which was nonsense, of course. The decision would be based entirely on enrollment figures and budgetary constraints, but as the days passed, and no news came down from the chancellor, William began to harbor a faint hope that the Department might get a reprieve, at least for the coming year, a "stay of execution," as he called it when he talked about it with Lauren.

When he told her what he'd heard from Don about the History Department's terminal condition, she said, "Well, what I don't understand is why you should care." He just stared at her. He must have looked somewhat stricken by the comment, because she added quickly, "I mean, I know, honey, that the History Department means a lot to you—but after all, you *are* leaving, you know." She rambled on, coming up with whatever mollifying remarks she could think of. He felt sorry for her, struggling for spontaneous amelioration, not understanding that he did not confuse the demise of the Department as a personal assessment of his performance. "I wonder what they'll do for you when they find out you're leaving," she went on. "I mean, as much as you've done for the university, and for the liberal arts college . . . . They'll have to do something really special," she concluded with an indulgent smile, and after a moment, she asked, "How's the book coming along?"

"Oh, fine," he said, letting her off the guilt hook, "Great, in fact." But the truth was he'd written at most only forty pages or so, and that was just a rough draft of an outline. Just what the world is waiting for, he thought, a detailed analysis of the influence of Charlemagne on the formation of western civilization. Despite his habitual sarcasm, there was no bitterness in the thought; he knew that only a dwindling few cared about the things he cared about. If he ever finished the book, those few would buy it and read it, they'd correspond with him about it; his publisher would arrange a lecture tour, and if he wanted to go, he would; if not, he wouldn't. No one would care much either way. He'd written six books altogether on medieval European history since finishing his dissertation on Charlemagne. A few of them still produced royalties, only because at some small liberal arts colleges around the country and in Europe, Dr. William Cauley was still required reading. His books had been translated into French and German—Spain and Italy had never bothered with translations, though he knew he was read there in English. Sales in the UK, where no translation was required, were not as good as in France and Germany. There were two reasons for that: England had a suspicious attitude toward history in the first place—having invented so much of their own—and secondly, European history was interesting to the British only insofar as it affected Britain. There prevailed to this day at Cambridge an attitude toward European history of *And what is that to us?* It had to be about them.

"Come on, fat woman, let's go," he said, patting her behind.

"Smart ass," she murmured.

*

Don and Ellen were already seated in the courtyard at Bayona's on Dauphine Street when they arrived. Ellen Penfield's wheelchair was placed on the far side of the table with the back to the wall, a position that permitted no side view of her chair and allowed her full view of the other diners. Whether she was aware of it or not, it was also a position that allowed others full appreciation of her beauty. It framed her fair complexion and almost white-blonde hair against the dark green of the ivy-covered wall of the courtyard. In the candlelight flickering on the table, her face appeared almost ethereal, while underneath the table, where no one could see, her left leg was missing, lost two years ago to the ravage of the very un-ethereal disease of diabetes. Don stood as Lauren approached.

"Hey. Gorgeous night, isn't it? We've already got menus and drinks." Don made a raised-hand gesture toward the waiter. They always arrived early, wherever they went, so that Ellen could get positioned before crowds arrived. Lauren leaned over to kiss Ellen's cheek while William ordered bourbon for both of them, but before they could even settle with their menus, his cellphone buzzed in his coat pocket. It was his sister Marie in Shreveport, who rarely called, so he answered.

"Will, I've got some bad news. Are you where you can talk?"

"No," he said, in puzzled concern. "Just a minute." He muted the phone. "Lauren, this is Marie. Something's up. I'll be back in a minute. Y'all excuse me, please," he said to the others. "I don't know what's going on."

"Do you want me to come with you?" Lauren asked, her face reflecting some concern.

"No—back in a minute." He weaved through the tables back out to the sidewalk and unmuted the phone. "What's wrong, Marie?"

"Oh, Will!" He could hear his sister choking back a sob. "Buddy's dead!"

"Oh, no, Marie," he breathed into the phone. "What happened?"

The sob broke from his sister's throat and made her voice very high-pitched so that it was not easy to understand what she was saying. Will strained to hear. He could make out: "… scaffold, ledge, eight floors," and ending with something about "instantaneous, praise God." His brother-in-law Buddy Delacroix was a construction worker.

"Oh, Marie, God, honey, I'm so sorry," he murmured into the phone, aware that Lauren had approached from behind. "It's Buddy. Fell from a scaffold on the job," he whispered to her, holding up a finger from the phone to silence her as she started to make sounds of shock and sympathy. "Marie… honey, listen." His sister had dissolved completely into sobs. "Honey, listen. We're on our way. We'll leave in the morning, all right? Unless you want us to leave right now." Lauren was nodding.

His sister apparently gained enough self-control to tell him not to come, the children were with her already, and they would be bringing his brother-in-law's body to New Orleans for the funeral and burial. Either she or one of his nephews would call him tomorrow with details.

"Let me speak to her, Will," Lauren whispered. "You go back and tell Don and Ellen what's happened."

"Okay," he said. "Do you think we should go home?"

"I don't know why," she answered. "There's nothing we can do about anything tonight." Then she was speaking to Marie, asking for details, expressing sorrow and concern.

William returned to the Penfields and told them what had happened.

"Oh, Will," said Ellen softly. "I'm so sorry. Were you close?"

"Oh, I don't know," he said. "I'm close to Marie, yes. She's eight years younger than I am. We're the only two—Mother always called Marie my father's little afterthought. She was a change-of-life baby, and therefore adored by all of us."

"Do you want to go home now?" asked Don.

"No, there's really nothing to be done tonight. I'll leave the phone on, of course, in case one of my nephews calls, or Marie needs to call back. But we might as well have dinner. We have to eat." He took a rather large swallow of his bourbon, frowning. "Might not be such good dinner companions, though," he said with an apologetic smile, thankful for the jolt the bourbon gave him, and still in some doubt about whether it was really appropriate to remain.

Lauren came back to the table and sat down. "I called Elise to let her know about her Uncle Buddy. She'll come home for the funeral. We have to let her know when it is as soon as we can so she can make some arrangements at work." She became more aware of the Penfields and explained, "Elise wasn't close to Buddy or Marie. They had six children who could have been almost siblings for Elise, but Leon, the oldest of the four boys, made fun of her lip scar one time, and after that, she stayed away from all of them. Too bad, really. I always thought it was a real loss for her."

"Yes," Ellen agreed. "His parents should have made him apologize, don't you think?

"Oh, they did," said William, "but the damage was done. The apology wasn't sincere, since it was obviously forced, and I think for Elise, that just made it worse. Anyway, they'd already moved to Shreveport by that time, and we seldom saw them. But Marie still thinks of me as her big brother—which I am, of course, and glad to be, for that matter, even though we haven't seen them in a couple of years now." He gave them what details he knew of Buddy's death, wondering how much life insurance was involved, wondering whether his nephews would be helpful to Marie—the two girls, his nieces, were still teenagers.

They ordered dinner and continued the evening, though something of a pall had been cast over the occasion. William suspected from time to time that, before his sister's phone call, Don had planned to discuss something with him but had to change his mind afterwards. The suspicion grew as the evening wore on and he made up his mind to speak to Don tomorrow morning to find out if he was right—what did Don want to tell him? Had the decision to close the History Department been confirmed? He thought that must be the case, and Don had simply put off telling him in light of the sad news from his sister.

*

That night, with a bottle of Rémy Martin on the table between them, he and Lauren sat on the patio and talked about the coming funeral, calls that would have to be made to William's aunts and his cousins, where everyone would sleep when they arrived. They tried to estimate the numbers: There would be Elise and her three children, Marie, her two teenage daughters and four grown sons, their wives and children—and there was no way to estimate those from the Delacroix side of the family, Buddy's relatives, who would come from out of town and need a place to stay.

Lauren heaved a deep sigh: "Marie is in no state to make any sort of plans, Will, and I don't know about the boys—maybe Leon, but the others? No—I don't think so. Let's face it. This is on us."

"Wait a minute," he said. "You're forgetting the Delacroixs. After all, he's their son, and that's a big family, spread out all over the state. I don't know them, but surely, they're going to step up to the plate."

"Yeah, maybe, but I think we have to be prepared to take on some of this—for Marie's sake." William was silent, wondering what would have to be done, who would do it. Lauren stood up.

"I'm going to bed. Are you coming?"

He said he'd be up in a little while.

Lauren said, "Well, look. I don't have anything on for tomorrow, and you have to go to work, so I'll make the calls, okay? And you won't have to worry about it. I'll call you and let you know what develops." She picked up the bottle of cognac to take inside with her, leaned down and kissed his forehead. "Don't stay up too late."

"Right. I'll be up in a few minutes."

He drained the rest of his glass and sat there, feet outstretched in front of him, and thought about Buddy Delacroix. There was a time when he'd have liked to beat him unconscious for taking his sister, for breaking his mother's heart by eloping with Marie, but more—for being a very good-looking young Cajun kid and seducing his sister with his happy-go-lucky charm. Years later, all that changed. His sister was happy, always pregnant and apparently pleased about it. They were Catholic, very Catholic, and there was always a baptism to go to, or a First Communion—something. The Cauley family had been nominal Catholics; it was part of their culture, but for the Delacroixs, it was part of their lives—there was a difference. They referred to dates by their feast-day names or holy-day names. He had a momentary flash memory of Marie, dandling one of her many children on her knees and saying to Buddy, "You remember, honey, it was on St. Monica's day..." And Buddy, uneducated, was a hard worker. He'd supported his large family well, doing specialized carpentry on construction jobs around the state. William and his mother got over their disappointment in their plans for their beloved pretty Marie, for her cotillion, for a large Cathedral wedding—and all that they'd wanted for her. It was hard to argue with her obvious happiness staring them in the face. And William, much older than his sister and aware of the corruption that seeped pervasively through the upper-class New Orleans society to which his family belonged, was glad that his sister had escaped it by falling in love with a hard-working, fiddle-playing boy from the bayous.

But that wasn't what he thought about sitting in the dark and holding an empty glass. He thought about Johnny Marco. When William was nine years old, Johnny Marco, his classmate at St. Vincent's, suddenly died. The boy had gone fishing with his father and came back very sick. He was rushed to the hospital and less than twenty-four hours later, he was dead from meningitis. William thought about that hot sultry summer morning when his mother told him that Johnny was dead. He wasn't close to Johnny, but Johnny was part of the universe he knew. And he was dead. It was as if the world altered itself forever. Time stopped. He'd never known anyone who died; death had never been a real thing, just something that happened sometimes in movies. Everything was different after that. The world was different; it had become mortal.

After that, he thought, *we just play pretend, to ourselves and to each other, and we get very angry if anyone stops the pretend game.*

Later, he knew others who died—his father, who died when he was a teenager in a small plane crash over the Gulf. He just left one day and never returned. And his mother; even though she lived for years after his father died, she never really returned from her grief. She closed the house on St. Charles, and bought a small cottage on the Gulf in Bay St. Louis, went to Mass every day, attended only the family events that required her presence, occasions when she played the pretend game, though not very well. *We all just play pretend after that, we grow up, we leave childhood, the time when we are all immortal. It's gone forever. And it's an unwritten law among us, we must live as though it were not true, we must pretend.*

He didn't hear the shattering of his empty glass as it fell from his hand to the brick floor.

Chapter Six

It's Not Time That Passes

That was all he remembered, Johnny Marco and then nothing. Lauren was talking to him, half-whispering, with a sad-sweet smile, then lowering her burnished cloud of hair over his hand. There were tubes and plastic straps on his arms, his hand, and something over his nose and mouth. Her hair blurred and returned, then blurred again. A woman in lavender scrubs bent over him, "How are you feeling, Dr. Cauley?" Without pausing for an answer, she touched instruments, looked at readings on screens above his head and to the side of his bed. "Had yourself a little spell there, didn't you?" She patted his forearm. "Welcome back!" She adjusted the drip from a plastic bag at the side of the bed and murmured, "But you're a little early yet, honey."

Lauren's head lay next to his hand on the side of the bed, and he touched her hair with his fingertips. She raised her head, then slid her hand to his fingertips and held them. He faded into a dream as the woman in lavender left. He sat on a bench by the river at sunset, the right time of day to sit watching the Mississippi. A narrow, black, broken line of distant trees separated the coral sunset from the glittering, multi-colored tips reflected on the softly chopping dark waters. The bright colors were the joys of his life that glittered on the water. What were those joys? Charlemagne, bourbon, his cluttered office on the campus, the old brick of his house on Prytania, his herb garden. And the family home on St. Charles, locked up now, with the china and crystal wrapped and stored in the attic. *Beauty lives on, tucked away in attics, cherished, kept safe from hurricanes and rising floods, glittering down on the muddy waters passing, always passing, below.* It was his last thought before he went under the waters.

Coming back up was slow, full of false starts, and full of the memory of another dream he couldn't remember having. A young and very white hand, graceful and lovely, grasped his own as he sat on the bench by the river. He couldn't know who she was, but she had long blonde hair and somehow he knew her—just not her name. Her name didn't matter; she might have had a thousand names. She took his hand and held it, smiling at him. And he said to her, "I love you. I love you because you're so brilliant and pure. You don't know that you need my love, do you? You have no idea. But it's all right. I don't want you to know. How like a child you are, adored, happy, knowing I will always love you, knowing you are safe… but you are so fragile… so fragile."

He could remember that dream vaguely when he woke. And there was more, but he couldn't remember it now. Elise's face was bending over his. She'd cut her hair—he didn't like it so short. Such a waste, lovely long and shiny black hair, thrown away, disregarded beauty sacrificed to mere fashion… She was speaking… "Daddy" several times; "pacemaker" once… He stared at her. She was a big woman, bigger than her mother. A thin faint scar above her upper lip distorted the bow of her full lips, giving her an earthiness like her mother's. She had his Creole coloring, but she was her mother's daughter. A lovely and desirable woman. And she had her mother's pragmatism. "Arrhythmia…," she was saying. He didn't want to listen to her, only to see her, but he couldn't. Being awake was tiring. He went under the waters again.

*

"I know he got this from Daddy." Marie was talking.

Lauren had always been careful not to patronize her uneducated sister-in-law. "No, Marie. Mike Cauley died when his plane crashed into the Gulf."

"But it was a heart attack made him crash the plane, Lauren. He was too good of a pilot to just crash for no reason. Had to be a heart attack." Marie could not be faulted for her ignorance on the subject of her father. She was barely six when he died, and all her knowledge of her father came from William. At fourteen, he'd assumed a paternal role and allowed his little sister to believe what she liked about her Irish father, who loved to fly when he was drunk.

"Will didn't have a heart attack, honey. He has arrhythmia, which means the rhythm of his heartbeat is off. He'll be fine," Lauren said gently.

Marie was sitting in a blue vinyl chair near the wall; her eldest, Leon, stood behind her chair, leaning against the wall, arms folded. She teared up and whined, "Well, I know he wouldn't have wanted to miss Buddy's funeral if he could help it."

Lauren was quick: "No, of course not, honey. He'll go home in a day or so, but it's going to be a little while before he can handle stress."

William could feel Lauren thinking, *A Cajun funeral in Courtebleau Bayou is the last thing on earth he needs*. Aloud, she said, "And I hope you're going to forgive me, Marie, but I'm going to have to stay home with him."

Marie broke down, and Leon's hands went to his mother's shoulders. "Of course, Lauren. No question about that." Her hand went over to Lauren's forearm and grasped it where it rested on the arm of her own chair. "Lord, no. You take care of him, Lauren. Take care. Our time here together is so short. You stay by Will."

They didn't know he was awake, that he could hear them. He wanted to see Elise again, but he dared not ask for her—he didn't want Marie stirred up again, or give Lauren more to cope with. He closed the narrow slits of his eyes and went under again, hearing Marie: "I still can't help but think he got it from Daddy."

*

He had felt a cold stillness in his chest before, and whenever it happened, he closed his eyes and waited for it to pass. It wasn't a heart attack, he knew that, just an odd sensation and he'd always ignored it. The first time he remembered it was long ago—thirty years or more—in a memory that remained a mystery to him. He'd awakened in a strange place and found a woman lying next to him, her hair like a long black satin river across a white pillow. Lying on his side, his head resting on his hands, folded under his face, he gazed at her profile as she slept on her back in that cold room on the edge of the Quarter. The gas heater stood quiet in front of an old sealed fireplace, like a dead sentinel who'd been meant to guard them as they made love, and had died an unnoticed death in the night. Gray morning fog came through the broken shutters, and he lay there, watching their warm breath rise and join in the cold air. And then he turned on his back and lay with his face upwards, like hers, toward the high ceiling, the pale blue chipping paint covering beaded boards high above their heads.

That was the first time he'd felt that cold stillness. She was so still, so beautiful—the most beautiful woman he'd ever seen. She looked like those sculpted images on the sarcophagi of saints and queens in the crypts of medieval churches he'd visited in France. Were it not for that shallow breath, he would have believed her to be dead, like the bones that lay beneath those sarcophagi, so slow was her breathing. He struggled to make his breathing match hers, to watch their breaths join and mingle. It had seemed to him over the years that it was their mingled breath that became the cold stillness in his chest. It returned to him at unexpected moments, and he didn't know why.

At some point in the past, he'd decided that the woman must have been a prostitute, that it must have been the night of his bachelor party, and that he must have been too drunk to remember any details. That decision had worked itself into fact for him. What remained a mystery, however, was why the memory was so indelible, so fixed, and why it seemed to make his heart stop. Memories, he knew, were historical records. If he had this memory, it had to be a record of something, sometime, somewhere.

Once, he'd decided to ask Charlie: "Do you remember the night of my bachelor party?"

"Hell of a lot better than you do, I bet!" Charlie laughed.

"Well, where was that house, that brothel, you took me to?"

"*Brothel?*" Charlie was genuinely shocked. "My God, Will, you think I'd take you to a cathouse in your condition?"

It was the closest he'd ever come, before or since, to that state that alcoholics refer to as a "blackout," a period of which one has no memory, not even a faint image or sensation. He could remember arriving at the house only vaguely. Its total darkness was relieved only by a single dim electric light above the heavy ancient wooden door, which opened directly off the sidewalk. Charlie took him there, the necessary conclusion, he said, to any decent bachelor party, a house, he said, of the noblest repute in New Orleans. He could remember the door opening—then nothing, nothing until a morning when cold fog came through shutters as he lay next to perfect beauty and watched its shallow breath in a stillness like stone.

The lavender scrubs were moving around him again, along with some green ones. He was being lifted and moved to a gurney. Someone's arm was next to his right side, wheeling a stand on which the plastic bag was swinging, and the gurney was moving, fast—too fast. "Slow down," he murmured, "you're going too fast." Someone patted his shoulder. "It's okay, Dr. Cauley, it's okay. No surgery yet. We're just going to do one more test. Dr. Snyder will talk to you this afternoon." He drifted off then, by choice more than by medication, feeling both relieved and humiliated by what seemed an anti-climax—wasn't he supposed to die? It was embarrassing to be alive still.

*

At three o'clock that afternoon he was sitting up in bed eating a ham sandwich and talking to Lauren about how little they knew about arrhythmia, about their mutual approval of Elise's decision to leave the children at home in Savannah, about yet another major repair needed on the Volvo—and agreed it was time to get rid of it—and about Buddy's upcoming funeral.

"What I need your honest opinion on is this: Do you think I can get enough mileage out of this arrhythmia to skip the funeral?"

Lauren smirked. "Shame on you, Will Cauley. You know, it would serve you right if you did have a heart attack." She licked mayonnaise from her fingertips. "But I know what you mean. It's obvious Marie doesn't need your support; she appears to be very well buttressed. And, although I know you liked Buddy well enough, y'all were never close. In fact, you were planets apart. Elise can represent the Cauleys—though she doesn't understand a word of Cajun French, and you know that will be the vernacular at the wake."

"Well, to be honest, I really don't feel up to it."

"Really?"

"Really." He dreaded the thought of a Cajun funeral: The bayou mosquitoes, the over-spiced food, the too-loud music, the wailing and the drinking. Just the thought of attending a Cajun funeral, even as a detached observer, made him tired. But Marie was his sister, after all. "I don't know. I'll see how I feel tomorrow."

Elise's head came around the door. "You awake?"

"Sure, baby, come on in."

"Good grief. You're eating."

"Right. I'm hungry. It's okay. The doctor says I'm going to live—for a while, anyway. No pacemaker—not yet. I'm going to take some pills, and I'm going to avoid some stress for a while, that's all."

Lauren spoke up. "Which brings up the subject of Buddy's

funeral—"

"Oh, no, you don't. I know what you're going to say." Her black eyes shot daggers at Lauren. "I came out of respect for Aunt Marie, but if you think, Mom, that you're going to get away with claiming you have to stay home with Daddy, and make me go to Courtebleau Bayou alone with those people—you know I don't understand a word of what they're saying to each other half the time. Sure they speak English to me, but I know they're talking about me in Cajun."

William understood. "No, baby girl. We won't do that to you. If we don't both go with you, your mom will."

"Thanks a lot, Will." Lauren gently thumped his shoulder. "But he's right, honey. I don't know that the stress would be good for your father, but you and I will go together. And we don't have to stay all day. The Delacroixs will understand that I want to get back to the city and see about Will."

William teased her: "So now who's getting mileage out of this arrhythmia?"

"You know, my dear. I could have just left you there. You passed out, you know, probably oxygen-deprived, so you might have been brain-damaged if it hadn't been for me. I think maybe next time I'll just leave you there."

Lauren and Elise left together. William was a little sad about Elise's remarks. He knew her prejudice wasn't directed at Cajuns generally, only the Delacroixs. It made him think about how one mocking remark by a thoughtless child, could cause such long-range harm. One remark made so many years ago had created a permanent estrangement between Elise and her cousins. She could never trust them again. How fragile a thing is trust, he thought, how sensitive we all are, and how cruel—most of all, when we don't even know we're being cruel, don't even know the damage we've caused. It was very likely that the Delacroix children had simply grown up thinking their cousin Elise was a snob, which wasn't true. *And if I can see for myself within my own family the consequences of one offense, what did that mean for history, for all of history? The Hundred Years War between France and England, and all the thousands of innocent lives that were lost, could have begun over an equally small offence. What difference did it all make?*

He'd spent his whole life researching, reading, thinking, writing, analyzing—to what purpose? He'd believed—all his life, he'd believed—that if the world only knew the truth about its past, about itself... But what difference did it make? He was very tired, so tired he felt that he would never recover from the fatigue that now pervaded his whole being. He wasn't certain, he hoped it wasn't so, but there was a fear close to panic that loomed like the muddy waters of his dream. He didn't name it because he wanted with all his heart for it not to be so, and if he named it, he'd have to acknowledge it. What he needed was rest. The world would look different tomorrow.

And then suddenly there was nothing. William Cauley died. It lasted only a few seconds, and it lasted for years. For that time, however long it was, he was not among what the world calls "the living." Where he was remained a mystery even years later. It may have been the mention of the bayou funeral that revived the memory that accompanied him as he left the living, or it may have been the memory that revived him, or it may have been both:

His father had bought a fishing camp on a bayou where there were more alligators and snakes than humans, and when Will was very young, he was allowed to go with his father and a couple of his father's friends to the camp, where very little fishing and a great deal of drinking went on. His mother, wiser than her husband knew then, was aware of what happened at the camp and stopped Will from going with him after a few weekend trips.

While he was at the camp, he found ways to amuse himself while his father drank and pretended to fish. He wore snake-proof boots and wandered up and down the bank, taking an occasional side-trip into the swampy inland woods. It was on the bank he met Ben Joe.

Ben Joe did not have a last name, just the name given him by his long-dead father who had loved only one thing—his banjo, which he'd played in his church and on his front porch. The banjo still stood next to the fireplace in Ben Joe's cabin, a one-room clapboard construction with a front porch and a detached kitchen in the back, built according to the old ways. There was no way to imagine how old it was; it was built of cypress and might last forever. Ben had never played the banjo, never even tried. His instrument was a cane pole and his church was the riverbank.

He had never held a job for more than a day or two, since he was illiterate and had no social security card. Likely, he'd never been counted on anybody's census. His skin was smoky-black, deep and opaque as an eggplant, without a drop of coffee in it, much less the café au lait common to New Orleans Creoles. Ben was not Caribbean, but descended from African slaves. He was one of a few in that bayou along the River Road in Ascension Parish whose forebears were freed by care-taking sugarcane plantation owners. When the War came, they simply chose to stay home, to stay where they were, on the land owned by their former masters, whose own houses had been looted and burned by Yankee invaders.

Ben's mother had died giving him birth, and his father died while he was still a boy. By the time William met him, Ben was an old man. His age, as for most Africans, was hard to determine, and it was doubtful Ben had any idea himself. He had lived his life on the riverbank, a can of worms set on the ground by his side, and propped between his knees, a fishing pole. There was always a string of catfish softly lapping in the brown water below his bare feet.

With as much manhood as his seven-year-old voice could muster, Will asked, "Mr. Ben Joe, do you just like to sit here and watch the river passing?"

He addressed Will as "Boy." It was not a sign of disrespect; he saw Will as a white boy, and all white people were addressed by their age and gender: Boy, Girl, Lady, and Mister. He did not clutter his mind with white people's names. "Ain't the river be passing, Boy, it's you."

The river isn't passing. I am passing. He smelled the dank earth of his grave. Of the riverbank. Of death. He did not know which it was.

Ben's church fascinated Will. It was not the voodoo-inflected black Catholicism of some of the other bayous, nor was it the white Protestant bayou churches, where people talked in tongues and handled snakes. The music was the expression of an animist Christ strange to Will, in moaning voices, some kind of flute-like sound, a drum, and oddly—a banjo. It was actually a kind of blues, though not the brassy blues produced and exported by New Orleans. It had a deep slow pace.

No, I am not dead. The river and I are both alive, but only for now, only for this moment. What is it then that is passing? Time... Time... It is time that's passing... time that's dying. Dead history... He struggled, slapping at the always-moving, indifferent waters, trying with all his strength to reach the bank. Pure white hands and slender arms held him up. When he left them behind him, they receded through misty Gothic arches, and he landed breathless, panting, on the muddy bank. They had saved him.

*

"Sorry. I don't remember you," he said to the red and silver cloud, gathered and fastened with some kind of dull green cloth.

"Silly boy." She smiled down at him. "How do you feel?"

He was supposed to know her. It was required of him, and so he stirred his memory. Yes, he knew her; he just didn't know her name. "I'm sorry. What is your name?" He was being polite; he didn't really want to know.

The cloud lowered over his face, kissed his forehead. "It's Lauren, honey. I'm your wife."

"Yes, of course." He wanted to remain in that delicious privacy of anonymity that anesthesia gives. No names, please; faces are intrusive, accepted if necessary, but no names. Please remove name tags. He himself had wisely chosen to remain anonymous.

"Dr. Cauley." A lavender intrusion was speaking,. "Dr. Cauley, you can come back now."

I prefer not to.

"Will, honey, they want you to wake up now."

No, thank you, Lauren wife. You have beautiful hair, you know. I suppose everyone tells you that? He didn't know if he spoke aloud or not, but as if in answer to his question, he saw the face of Paul Cunningham—not the gray-haired man at the market, but a young Paul, with wild raven hair and Wagnerian intensity, conducting with a magic wand an orchestra of red and silver cloud, which waved and flowed in perfect obedience, as if it were an extension of the wand.

Did you love him, Lauren? But he didn't want her to answer. He didn't really want to know. And he didn't want to intrude. A mist-covered Gothic arch beckoned to him and he wanted to follow; he did not want to stay and listen to her music. He turned away from her. *Goodbye, Lauren wife.* He felt no pain. All he felt was a blissful lassitude.

But she was concerned. He could tell. He should come back. With a heavy and unwilling hand, he opened the door to her, to everything he didn't want to see, to know.

"Hi," he said. "So I'm okay, am I?"

Lauren chucked softly. "Everything went well, honey. You're okay."

"Do I miss Buddy's funeral?"

"Yes, you lucky man. I knew you didn't want to go, but I didn't know you'd go to such lengths to avoid it."

He smiled. "Going to take a nap now, okay?"

Lavender spoke, "It's okay, Mrs. Cauley. It may take a little while, but he's going to be just fine."

"Okay." She patted his arm and leaned back in her chair. And he was free to leave her.

Chapter Seven

Time to Go Home Now

Elise sat with one leg tucked under her and her elbows on the table, licking sugar from her fingertips. She'd gone to the bakery and picked up some pastries instead of cooking breakfast. She and William sat on the patio under the wisteria arbor, sipping coffee.

"Do they have chicory coffee in Savannah?" William asked.

"If they do, I haven't found it," Elise answered. "There's one brand in the grocery store that claims to have chicory, but it's not the same."

"Wonder what they drink in Statesboro when they want coffee," he mused.

"Oh, Dad, stop that. Yes, it's a different culture—but you're not going to Outer Mongolia, you know." She tried to tease him about leaving the city. She knew he was having a hard time with the prospect of leaving, and she wanted him to take it less seriously. "I'm so proud of you," she said softly.

He looked at her with admiration mixed with affection. How did she get so wise? It had to be Lauren's influence, not his. "Tell me about this—what's his name? Owen?"

"Well, there's nothing to tell, really." She looked at him with a little mischief. "Don't force me to be indelicate here, please." Her eyes twinkled.

"Oh." he said with raised brows. "I see." How like Lauren she was—so down to earth, practical, and unromantic. Owen was a bed partner. Nothing more. There was nothing to tell. He had hoped for more. He wanted her to be happy, to have love in her life.

"Dad, I know what you want for me. But, actually, you see—I've had that. And it can't be repeated. Yes, there will be other sunrises but it will never be the same experience as seeing the first one. You have to just know that, and don't go looking for it, because it's not there and you'll just be disappointed—or worse."

William looked at her with narrowed eyes over the rim of his coffee cup. She was saying something important to her, and he wanted to be sure he understood it.

"Mack and I both knew we were crazy lucky. Some people go their whole lives and never know another person the way we knew each other. And in spite of his death, that means I'll never be alone again. He'll always be with me."

"But, see, honey, that's what worries me. As long as you feel that way, as long as he is 'with' you, you'll stay closed off from happiness. You have to let him go."

"No, no. It isn't like that. I know you mean well, I know what you want for me. What you don't know is that I have something better, something even better than that. And I will always have it. I can only lose it by losing the memory of it. While I live, he lives too." She patted his forearm where it lay across the table, as though reaching for her.

"Can you…" he started and stopped, unsure of himself. "Can you try to explain what you mean by that?"

There was an awkward pause before she answered; the awkwardness was not in the length of the pause but in the fact of it. It would have been the easiest and most natural response simply to say that what she'd had with her husband was like what William had with Lauren. Her pause revealed to William that she knew it wasn't the same at all. Her answer was slow, groping, like someone trying to explain vision to one who's been blind since birth.

"Well . . . . Okay. It's like . . . ." She sighed. "I can't explain—I'll just tell you this: When I saw Mack for the first time, he was with somebody else at a restaurant, a girl I knew from work. But he looked at me and I knew he saw me naked."

"What? Oh, you mean it was erotic?"

"No, no, no. More than that. Or different. I mean, I knew he saw the wart on my back, he saw the cellulite on my thighs, and he saw—he looked straight at it—the scar on my lip. I knew that he saw all this." She made a circular gesture around her face and spiraling down toward her body. "And that he—he claimed it all. It was his. I was his."

"You mean you knew all that the moment you met him?"

"Yeah. Yeah, I did. I knew we would be married. He was in uniform, so I knew he was a Marine. And I always knew, right from the start, that he might be horribly wounded or even killed someday. But I wanted whatever time I could get, whether that was three years or thirty. That was true for both of us. Neither one of us ever gave a damn about time, about how short it might be—worrying about time was a waste of time." She made a little self-mocking shrug.

William smiled at her, surprised, and pleased for her. "Honey, I never would have believed you could be so romantic."

She laughed. "Romantic! Oh, heavens, Daddy. There was nothing romantic about it. That was just the way it was, that's all."

They sat in companionable silence for a while, each of them looking out toward the garden, and each of them having thoughts that might have surprised the other. Finally, Elise said she was going to the study and tear her mother away from the computer. "I've got to get on the road. My sitter's bill is going to be astronomical. I've been gone over a week!" She brushed sugar from her hands and took her coffee cup inside with her.

William sat and thought about his daughter's declaration that she was not romantic. No, maybe not, and yet—the love she'd had with her husband sounded like the stuff of romance novels. Except that it was real, not fiction. And something more significant: Was it actually "love?" She hadn't even used the word. He realized that he'd never believed in that kind of—feeling. He'd never experienced it, not the way she described it, as something transcending death.

Elise came back through the doorway carrying a suitcase, with Lauren carrying her totebag for her. "Well, come on bionic man, stand up and hug me goodbye." She set the bag down and held out her arms.

Will stood and hugged her as long and hard as his wounded shoulder would allow. She was over-cautious: "Dad, be careful! We don't want to disturb your machinery."

He had loved having her there without the children. He was fond of his grandchildren, but they were exhausting, and it had been good to have Elise to himself again.

"Now tell me, Elise," Lauren's voice was firm, demanding. "Tell me you're *not* going to drive all the way through."

"No, Mom, I'm not. I'm going to stop halfway—just don't know where yet, somewhere across the Georgia line. I'll call you tonight. And if you get worried, just call me. Okay?"

They walked to Elise's Bronco slowly, Elise murmuring something to him about keeping her informed, "Dad, now call when you get back from the doctor's tomorrow. Tell me every word he says. Promise?"

"I promise, baby girl. Now don't worry. I'm going back to the office on Wednesday. He knows that, and he approves. He's already said so."

Lauren added her assurance, "Honey, he's really doing very well. Don't worry. If he starts being a problem, I'll let you know. Kiss the boys for me." The car door closed and William felt his heart lurch when she backed out of the driveway. He and Lauren walked back to the front of the house and waved farewell.

William knew there would be conversation now that Elise was gone. While she was there, no mention was made about Georgia, about moving, about his work—nothing that might cause him any discomfort or concern. He knew that both his wife and his daughter were pampering him emotionally as well as physically. That would have to end.

"Well," he said to Lauren over his shoulder as they filed down the hall toward the kitchen, "now that we're alone, what do you want to do? Make passionate love? Or talk about moving to Georgia?" He was ready. He knew his unwillingness to talk about moving had caused him more stress than confronting the inevitable.

"I don't think we should make any kind of plans at all until you see the doctor tomorrow."

"You know that all he's going to do is check the pacemaker, maybe make an adjustment or something. He knows we're planning a move, and he's already okayed it, as long as I don't do any heavy lifting or something like that."

"You should avoid stress."

"Not talking about something can cause stress too, you know."

They had reached the kitchen and Lauren started to make some decaf while Will settled in at the counter with his newspapers. "Lauren, I want regular coffee, please. You know it's all right."

She continued measuring the decaf into the pot. "You've already had at least a couple of cups with Elise. We're drinking decaf. When's the last time you had Tylenol?"

"When I first got up. I could do with a couple more."

She put two tablets on the counter with a small glass of water. "Okay," she said, "we'll talk about the future—immediate, mid-range, or long-range?"

"Well, the immediate is already pretty much planned out, don't you think? I can't drive for another two or three weeks, maybe longer, so you're going to have to take me in to the office Wednesday. We'll see what Snyder says tomorrow about working, but I know he's going to say it's all right—at least half-days, and of course, there's a lot I can just bring home."

"Will, you ought to be working on your book, not worrying about the History Department."

"I shouldn't have to remind you that I still get a paycheck, and while I do, I work for the university."

She handed him a mug and leaned across the counter to kiss his cheek. "So loyal."

"Lauren, I'm not being fired. The university has a right to my loyalty."

"I love you, Will Cauley."

She was patronizing him, talking to him like an affectionate mother speaks to a child. He did not resent her tone; it just made him feel so far away from her. Resentment would have been better, more intimate than this sad distance.

*

The following day, William listened in amazement to his doctor's instructions on how to use his cellphone to transmit his heart rate to the doctor, who could actually control his rate remotely. The entire process astonished him. He didn't mind being a "bionic" man, as Elise had called him; the procedure fascinated him. Medical technology itself now fascinated him. He'd often complained that the benefits of technology were overrated, especially in the area of education, but its actual scientific uses in the medical field—of which he'd been a beneficiary—were wonderful. He had a lengthy conversation with Elise that night, during which she told him very interesting things about the use of technology in speech therapy.

He felt like a new man, not so much physically as mentally. He was making discoveries that had gone unnoticed before because they were not relevant to his life. Now it was all very important and he felt as though he'd been somehow remiss in not learning things outside his own field of expertise.

He thought about this change. When he was an undergraduate, the Cold War was still raging. Science seemed focused on the development of weaponry with ever-increasing capacity to destroy—the atom bomb, the hydrogen bomb, the neutron bomb. His generation had grown up with the certainty that rivaling political theories would eventually destroy the world. Did that account for his interest in history, for his preference to look backward instead of forward? No, he decided, he would have been interested in history anyway—because it was narrative, and narrative was the way his intellect functioned, following various threads, strands, seeing how they wove together to create a wholeness of events, persons, and changes, how they created a kind of story of mankind, as it were. And this reflection put technology and all its glitter in its proper place. The new development in science was just one of those strands that fit inside history. It did not displace it; it was only part of it.

He and Lauren watched a television show that night in which technology was praised for the development of cabbages and cauliflowers the size of car tires. The same biotechnology that had made his pacemaker would feed the world's hungry, claimed the narrator, who was certain that technology would solve all the problems of the world. Lauren was impressed, but William felt that he could detect in the giant cauliflower only a new kind of bomb. He thought about how his colleague Bettie Somers and her theory of history would record the development of giant vegetables—in positive or negative terms? Neither. In totally disinterested terms, of course. For Bettie, even the Holocaust had no causes, no effects. Everything that happened was taken digitally; all events were isolated. There was no story, for story implies a *point* , and points were not allowed in her theory. Wherever a point was made, or even suggested, there lurked the possibility of forbidden moral judgment. It was a theory that permitted no analogical reasoning, no connection between one event and another—which might have implied underlying relationship. History was recorded without chronology—lest cause or effect be implied. It was chaotic; more, it asserted that all reality was chaos.

Maybe she was right. Maybe Auschwitz was just something that happened, maybe we should be morally indifferent, make no judgment; maybe the discovery of America was the moral equivalent of Auschwitz. No matter; it was all chaos anyway.

"Lauren, do you think a cabbage can be a bomb?"

"Go to bed, Will Cauley. I know where you're going with that question, and the answer is the same it's always been: it all depends on the morality of the developer. Go to bed."

He went to bed, knowing that giant vegetables would not be in the hands of people like his wife. They never were. The unwitting midwives who assisted the birth of any horror were always the first victims of that horror.

*

On Wednesday, Lauren drove him to the office. He'd have to get used to depending on her for transportation since the doctor had said he couldn't drive for another three weeks. She left him there, agreeing to come back for lunch with him and Don in the faculty cafeteria.

"Oh, Dr. Cauley!" The department secretary heaved her two hundred pounds up from her chair with the lightness of a butterfly. "Oh, welcome back! I've been praying for you every day. I'm sooo happy to see you! How *are* you?" She rushed to hug him, stopped by his cautioning gesture pointing to his left shoulder. "Oh, yes. Right." She awkwardly attempted a hug of his right shoulder.

His desk was frighteningly tidy. "Charlotte! Where is everything?"

"Oh, I gave your students' papers to Dr. Samuels to grade. And the other stuff I just farmed out. But the enrollment figures for summer are in your inbox." He glanced at the printout—maybe twenty or thirty names, hardly enough for one instructor.

For the next hour or more, colleagues dropped in, welcomed him back, asked how he felt. He thought he should just put a sign on the door: *Thank you. I'm fine. Yes, it's good to be back.* Then Don called. "Hey, Will. Welcome back. You okay?"

"Yes, the doctor says half-days are fine. I expected to take work home today but I'm confronted by my superfluity. Charlotte farmed out nearly everything. I am, it seems, pretty much unnecessary."

"Well, look. I know we're going to meet Lauren in the cafeteria in half an hour. Can you come upstairs for a private talk first?"

"Right. So—this is it?"

"Yeah, afraid so."

William entered Don's office and found him not behind his desk but sitting in one of the wing-back chairs in the little sitting area at one end of his office. He thought this was good judgment on Don's part. Bad news was best delivered in a more personal, less official setting. He had to smile.

"Okay," he said, "lay it on me. I know what it is—give me details."

Don did not trouble with preamble, or with any attempt at

polite small talk. "Okay. You stay—of course—and Somers and Harmon. All the full professors. But the other two stay with the understanding that they share Humanities' courseload—otherwise, they're invited to adjunct with English."

"Wow. That's pretty drastic."

"No, not really. It's no worse than we—than I—expected."

"Me, either. It's just that when it actually comes down, it seems that way. Like any suspicion of something bad. You know it's coming, but it still arrives like a sledgehammer. You're never prepared."

"Yeah."

Both men sat in silent companionable grief, Don leaning forward with his elbows resting on his knees, his tie hanging down between them; Will, with his ankle crossed over his knee and his arms on the arms of the chair. Both stared down at the large glass-topped table in front of them as though they were peering through it, waiting for something to appear. They sighed almost simultaneously.

"Well," said Will finally. "I'm leaving. That opens a space for one—maybe Josh. He's got a family, you know."

"Another space, actually. Bettie's leaving. Taking a position at Tulane. Turns out they've been negotiating for two or three months already."

"She saw it coming, I guess. Nothing much gets past Bettie. So you've already talked to her."

"Yes. I wanted to give everybody as much notice as possible. I was going to tell you that night at dinner, but you got news about your brother-in-law and then you got sick. I told Bettie the next day. Didn't bat an eyelash. She made one phone call and that was that."

"So there are no real casualties here."

Don looked up at him. He knew Will's sorrow and shared it. "No casualties in personnel. Only History."

"Come on, Don. It's not that nobody gives a damn about history any more. The fact is nobody gives a damn about anything any more that can't be *used* somehow. That's not a question, or a theory, it's just the way it is."

"Well, it's a different philosophy…"

"*Philosophy*? What the hell is that? Nobody knows. There's no such thing as philosophy—only agendas."

Don raised his eyes to Will: "We're all irrelevant now—unless we can make ourselves useful somehow. You've given up, though, haven't you."

"Yeah. It's time." Will stood to leave. "I'll see you in the cafeteria."

*

Lauren took the news as though it were mere office gossip. She asked a few questions about details, the fate of the rest of the History faculty, and said she was glad Will had already decided to leave. "So nobody is really out of a job, right?" she asked Don. For Lauren, that was all that mattered.

"No, Will and Bettie will be gone and that means the remaining two will stay full-time—just on the Humanities faculty."

"Then there's no real tragedy here, is there."

Just then Joanna walked into the cafeteria with Bob Henckels, a young English instructor. Will saw them in his peripheral vision; there was an air between them that connoted intimacy. Henckels had a hovering kind of posture around her shoulders. He smiled inwardly.

"Okay, my love," said Lauren. "Time to go home now."

And he was indeed ready for his prescribed afternoon nap.

He didn't sleep, however, until he'd done an internet search on Bob Henckels: Recent Ph.D., his dissertation was on Melville, joined UNO English faculty two years ago, and he was 28. It looked promising—enough so that William slept soundly until Lauren called him to dinner. Joanna was safe.

Chapter Eight

Where Past and Future Meet

Lauren came through the back door and closed it rather too hard behind her.

"Will, you need a new car. That thing is ancient. It won't start—again."

"Must be the battery. Call the garage."

"You just got a new battery, not even six months ago. I know it's got a warranty, but I also know that the car is not immortal, no matter how many times you charge its battery. You've got to get a new car. And *don't* get a Volvo. Your last one was just the same. Volvos have maintenance problems. Get something more reliable."

"When I can drive again, we'll go get a car. Meanwhile, thanks for starting it up for me, or trying to. Are you sure you held the key in the ignition long enough? Give me the key, let me try it."

She slapped the key into his palm. "Go for it. I'm telling you—it won't start."

Will tried the ignition. Dead. Yes, it was time for a new car. The thought occurred to him—would Statesboro Georgia have a Volvo dealer? Probably not. Certainly not. He couldn't get service there. He should get a Bronco or something like Elise had. Maybe he should get a pickup truck. He sat behind the wheel and sighed. He sighed a lot lately. He looked around at the interior of his dead car, so familiar after twelve years of driving it every day, driving to shop, to Savannah for visits and Mack's funeral, to Bay St. Louis to visit his mother, to the university and to History every day. Suddenly, he was crying, not softly, but like a child. It was just a car, he told himself, there was no rational reason for this, but he felt grief-stricken as he had felt when his mother died. He put his head against the steering wheel and turned the key again—several times. The car would not start. He popped the lid of the storage console and grabbed a handful of tissues, wiped his eyes and blew his nose. Then he went back to the kitchen.

"We'll get a new car, Lauren. I'm going upstairs and take a nap now."

"Okay, honey. I'll take the Subaru and go get the beer."

It was Saturday and the poker game would go on as planned,

though Will would have to go easy on the beer. And Marie was coming tomorrow after Mass. He was tired just thinking about that. She'd called yesterday and talked to Lauren. His sister was done visiting all the Delacroixs in Courtebleau and wanted to visit him before heading back to Shreveport. Lauren reported the news and said, "Lord, Will, she wanted to bring Leon and his wife and their kids with her. I told her not to, that would be too much stress, so she's just bringing her daughters."

Marie's daughters were teenagers, and that might be as much as he could deal with. Actually, he felt fine, and knew he was just being inhospitable and using his surgery as an excuse. And when he thought about it, yes, he really did want to spend a little time with his sister. He was just being difficult.

He lay stretched out on the bed with his right forearm covering his eyes. Maybe depression was part of his medical condition, and he should ask the doctor about it. No—the last thing he wanted was some kind of anti-depressant drug. He reached for the phone and pressed Glenn Arville's number. Glenn had done odd work around the house on St. Charles, and he'd kept the gardens there for many years. His wife Sarah had done housework for his mother. After his mother closed the house, they converted the carriage house behind the big house into a very comfortable home for Glenn and Sarah. They lived there now and took care of the property.

"Hey, Glenn. How's it going? This is Will Cauley."

"Hey, Will. We're fine. Been meaning to call you, see how you doing with that heart thing. And I wanted to tell you the paint on the inside of the back porch is starting to peel. You want me to take care of it, or do you want to hire it out?"

"Well, I tell you what. You know Marie's husband died, didn't you?"

"Yes, I heard about that. I'm real sorry. Is she okay?"

"Yes, she's fine. But she's coming over from Courtebleau Bayou to visit tomorrow before she goes back to Shreveport. I thought we'd ride over to the house together. Will that be all right with y'all?"

"Sure. Come on. About what time? I'll go turn on the air for you."

"She's going to Mass first, so it won't be till after lunch. I'll call you first, all right?"

"Be looking forward to it."

And then he slept—as he was supposed to do. He didn't wake for two hours and woke feeling foggy; he'd slept much longer than he meant to. He decided it must have been the crying jag in the car. On his way to the bathroom, he hollered over the landing rail, "Lauren, are you back?"

"Yes, Will. I was wondering if you were going to sleep all afternoon. I'm about to heat some of that leftover Irish stew. Can you eat pretty soon?"

"Yes, I'm starving," he yelled back. "Let's have drinks first. I'll be down when I wash up."

When he came downstairs in his bare feet, khaki shorts and fresh tee shirt, Lauren handed him a drink. "Let's go outside. Might as well enjoy the weather while we can. It's getting hotter every day now." She closed the door behind them. Once, several years ago, a bird had flown into the house through the open French doors with tragic results. They'd remembered ever since to close both doors.

"So—what kind of car should I get? There won't be a Volvo dealer in Statesboro for service." He hated to part with his car, and hated even more to buy anything besides a Volvo—he'd always driven Volvos.

"I don't know, get whatever you want. Freddie called, by the way. He wants to come a little early to discuss something or other with you."

"What does he want to talk about?" Freddie, one of the four poker players, was the Cauley family lawyer.

"He didn't say, but I bet it has to do with Marie's trust fund, don't you?"

"Oh, yeah. I hadn't thought about that. Good thing he's coming before she gets here tomorrow. I'll have to explain things to her and Freddie will have to explain things to me first."

"She's all right, isn't she, Will?"

"Of course she is, but she needs to know that. It may be better if Freddie talks to her himself, considering she's known him all her life as 'Uncle Freddie.' She trusts him."

"Yes. By the way, there's no Subaru dealer in Statesboro either. I'll have to go out of town for service, too. Why don't you think about some kind of Ford or Chevy? I saw a huge Ford place there."

"Let's not talk about it."

"I thought you wanted to talk about it. Will, why don't you go in the study and see if you can get some work done on your book? We've got almost half an hour before dinner. I haven't even made the salad yet."

"Okay," he said, sighing, and then made no move to do so. They sat in silence until finally he sighed again, then rose slowly and took his empty glass inside to the kitchen. He went down the hall to his study, sat down at his desk, stared at his closed laptop, and exercised his left shoulder as he'd been instructed. He didn't open the computer. He examined a couple of the open volumes on his desk, sorted the other books he'd left there, and finally opened the laptop to his outline and read it—again. He told himself he was reviewing it, revising it, adjusting it, fine-tuning it. But he struck not a single letter on the keyboard. Finally he closed it and went back into the kitchen, passing the seldom-used dining room on the way.

"Why don't we eat in the dining room, Lauren?" The room looked so abandoned; he was thinking that soon it would be truly abandoned.

"Will, we don't have time for that. Freddie's going to be here at six-thirty. Set the table in the breakfast room, please—or even better, set up the counter."

Feeling like a little boy obeying his mother, he put out the placemats, napkins, and flatware on the counter.

*

Dinner was barely over when the doorbell rang and Freddie arrived carrying a briefcase, which looked somewhat incongruous with his polo shirt and khakis. Lauren gave him a beer in the living room while she and Will cleared up the dishes. Then she brought in decaf for herself and Will and they settled in to look at papers Freddie had spread on the large square coffee table. He'd brought more than they expected.

He put on his large horn-rimmed glasses and smoothed his immaculately trimmed gray hair. "Look, y'all. I've made some copies of your present situation, but I'm leaving some other stuff with you to look at later."

Lauren sat back in her chair and sipped her coffee as she skipped over the first pages to see the bottom line of the financial report. "Well, obviously we're in great shape, Freddie, but we need to find out about Marie. What is this other stuff?"

"Of course, you're in great shape. Mike Cauley was a fool about a lot of things, but never about money. But you're leaving the city. You're going to have to make some real estate decisions."

Will felt a little chill. "I think it's a little early for that, isn't it? Shouldn't we wait to see if we're going to leave—" He felt Lauren's eyes fasten on his face, but he didn't look at her "—permanently?"

"Okay, so give me some parameters to talk about. I know you're not going to rent anything out."

"No, definitely not."

"Well, do you plan to sell anything at all?"

"No."

"Will, we need to talk about this." Lauren's remark was quick, gentle but unhesitating.

"Okay," said Freddie. "That's what I mean. I'm just going to leave this with you to think about, but sometime before you leave the city, you should make some kind of at least tentative decisions. Your mother sold Mike's fishing camp after his death, but her cottage on the Gulf is still sitting empty—like the St. Charles house. Do you want the townhouse to sit empty too?"

"I don't know," Will replied, and he could hear Lauren's sigh. "But we've already talked about the Bay St. Louis property." He glanced at Lauren and she nodded. "We're just going to go ahead and sign that over to Elise. She has taken the boys there from time to time and she would have got it in our will anyway. We can just sign it over."

Lauren nodded. "The boys love it there, and Elise has always liked the cottage. It would be nice, I think, for her to call it her own without waiting for us to die. We never use it."

"Okay—so have you thought of selling St. Charles?" He glanced up at William over his glasses as though he knew the answer but needed to hear it. The question was only a formality but it should be asked. "It's eating taxes like crazy and there's the expense of keeping it up—and, of course, the Arville expense."

"It stays," said Will without pause, expecting no disagreement from Lauren and getting none. It was the family home and it would stay as long as they could keep it.

"Right," said Freddie, "but what about Marie?"

"She doesn't want that house, Freddie. You know that."

"No, I'm sure she doesn't. But that brings us now to her. Look at the report. And, by the way, did Buddy have life insurance?"

Lauren spoke up: "I asked Leon about that. He said Buddy had a hundred thousand, but you know that won't last long."

"Tell her, if she wants to invest it, just let me know. Meanwhile, it should be obvious from the report that none of you would ever have to work if you didn't want to. Marie has never worked, has she?"

"Not a day in her life," Will answered. "And I don't see her suddenly becoming some kind of career woman. And she does still have the girls at home. Her sons are married and working. Actually, Freddie, I think what we need to decide—by tomorrow, if possible—is how much she should get from the trust from here on out. Buddy wouldn't let her take anything from the trust. Mother made the down payment on their house as a wedding present, and it was hard just to get him to agree to that much. Of course, there's been the occasional emergency, but he's gone now, and as far as I know, she has no income at all."

They were quiet for a while. Then Freddie spoke: "Will, you're the administrator. You decide. But tell her to let me know if she wants to invest any of that hundred grand. I can handle that for her."

"Okay. I don't know if she's still got a mortgage on the house in Shreveport. That would make a big difference. And if she does, how much it is, and what's the balance. You know, I'll bet she doesn't even know. And I don't know if Buddy left any debts. He died so suddenly."

Lauren stood up. "You're going to have to have a serious talk with her tomorrow, Will. I'm going upstairs. You guys can set up the game while you're talking, can't you? It's almost time for Charlie and Hans."

They stood also, Freddie stacking the papers and handing them to Lauren, who took them with her to the study. Freddie said, "You ought to make a list of questions for Marie now, Will."

"Right," he said, sitting back down, and taking the yellow pad and pen Freddie handed him. "Okay—mortgage, payment, balance, debts—what else? I think she should need about five thousand clear every month. What do you think?"

"Sounds good to me, but ask her. Where's she going to Mass tomorrow? I might see her if she goes to the eleven o'clock at St.

Maria Goretti's."

"No idea. She just said to expect her at lunchtime."

*

Around noon on Sunday, Lauren came into the study carrying her cellphone. "It's Marie. She's outside Immaculate Conception. Talk to her." She handed the phone to Will.

"Hey, Marie. So you're downtown?"

The phone was on speaker. "Yes. Listen Will, the girls are wanting fried oyster po' boys. If y'all haven't made any lunch plans, we could stop at Johnny's and pick some up, if that's okay?"

Lauren nodded, and Will continued. "That sounds pretty good. You're closer to the house than you are to us. I called Glenn yesterday and told him we'd come over this afternoon. Let me see if I can get him, and I'll call you back. We could eat the sandwiches there."

"That's a great idea. I'll head on over to Johnny's while you're calling him."

Will punched Glenn's phone number and made arrangements. Glenn would open the house, turn on the air, and have Sarah make them some iced tea. Since the Arvilles had not yet had lunch, Marie was to bring sandwiches for them also. Will called his sister back. They were on their way to Johnny's.

"Marie, you're not talking on the phone while you're driving, are you?"

"No, Will, Dorothea's driving."

"Oh, my God. Yes, well I guess she's old enough now, isn't she. Good grief. She was just fifteen when I saw her last. So—you're going to get po' boys for Glenn and Sarah, too, okay? They also want oyster and so do we. So that's seven sandwiches. Sarah's making the tea."

Lauren took her phone back and told Marie goodbye. Then she asked Will, "We're not going to take all those papers with us, are we?"

"No," he said. "I've got my list of questions for her—I just hope she can answer them. Leon has handled everything for her, I think, and he's not with her."

"No, but we can call him if we need to. Marie said he and Richard were staying over at the bayou a few days to do some fishing. He could come over here easy enough, if he had to."

"You know, this might be a bit of an experience for them, seeing the house. They haven't been there since Mother died. I remember Dorothea saying she wanted to have her wedding reception there some day."

"I remember that. She loved the house."

He and Lauren had made some notes in addition to Freddie's suggested questions, primarily in consideration of the children. None of the boys had expressed any interest in higher education after they graduated high school, so that had not been an issue. Leon started a towing service and automotive body shop, Richard had gone to work for him, James said he would go to tech school for plumbing after he'd worked as a plumber's helper one summer, and he didn't know what Edward wanted to do when he finished school. He also had no idea about the girls, who were fifteen and seventeen now. There was a lot to talk about.

*

They pulled into the narrow drive. Marie's Toyota was already there when they arrived, and they found her and the girls in the back garden with the Arvilles, looking at Sarah's vegetable garden. In February, Glenn had called William and asked permission to plant the garden, a small plot about twenty feet square, but it looked as though it was thriving, with tomatoes and peppers already in full fruit. Sarah had set up iced tea on the black wrought iron table.

Marie wore a black dress, managing somehow to look both dowdy and comely at the same time, a mysterious gift he had never seen in women outside the American South. Her daughters could not have looked more different, both from their mother and from each other. Dorothea looked very grown up, even smart, in a silver gray pantsuit, while her younger sister Alyssa wore tight denim leggings and a gold ring encircling one end of her left eyebrow. There were hugs and how-are-you's, remarks about how the girls had grown, questions and automated responses from William about the status of his recovery.

Glenn said, "I turned on the air for y'all, but you probably want to eat out here, don't you?"

Everyone agreed they would indeed rather eat outside since the weather was so fine. Sarah poured tea for everyone. Marie talked about Buddy's funeral, reporting the details of his death to Glenn and Sarah with only a slight tremor in her voice; she talked about the bayou and the Delacroix clan, making comments to William about various members, few of whom he could remember.

Lauren turned everyone's attention to the girls, asking them about school. Marie said, "Oh, Will, I haven't even had a chance to tell you—Dorothea's got a scholarship!"

"What? Really? What kind of scholarship? Where?"

Dorothea smiled: "You remember the last time you and Aunt Lauren came to Shreveport? I played the piano for you—and you said you thought I was really good."

"Yes, I do remember. So you kept up with the lessons? It's a music scholarship, right?"

Her smile became wide and happy. "Yes. I'll start at LSU in the fall."

"Baton Rouge. You know, Lauren and I went to grad school there. Still know a few people. I'll alert them my prodigy niece is coming. This is great news, Dodie. Are you excited?"

"Yes, I am. But I'm especially glad Daddy got to know about it. I got the letter about a week before he—before he fell." She looked wistful. "He was happier about it than I was."

Marie took her daughter's hand and held it, then turned to William. "Will, is the piano still in the house? Dodie could play for y'all."

Glenn said, "It is, Marie. But nobody's touched it in years. I'm pretty sure it would need tuning."

"Yes, I know it would, Mama, if nobody's played it."

Will had an idea. "But you could go in and check it out, honey. There's something I need to talk to your mother about. Glenn, why don't you and Sarah take the girls through the house while we talk to Marie about family stuff?"

Marie settled in her chair. "I know you want to talk about money, Will. I guess that's good."

"Yes, honey. Now is where past and future meet." It didn't take long. Leon was going to file a claim on Buddy's life insurance when they returned to Shreveport, and Marie would contact Freddie about how to invest it. There were no debts except a couple of credit card balances that could be easily handled. There was a mortgage, but the balance was only ten thousand or so. Marie objected to the five thousand trust fund allowance.

"Will, that's more than Buddy made. I don't think we'll need more than my husband provided for us."

"Okay, Marie. I understand. Let's get the girls taken care of now. What about Alyssa's plans? She wants to go to cosmetology school? How's that going to be paid for?"

"Well, we hadn't got that far. I guess it would be okay to pay for that from the trust fund. I think it's a year-long course, and after that, of course she'll get a job."

"Okay, now Dodie. Is this a full four-year scholarship at LSU? I doubt that, honey."

"No, no, it's not. It's just one year. We were just so happy for her we didn't talk about anything beyond that, Will. I think we were just hoping that if she didn't get tired of it, something else might turn up, and if it didn't, we'd just find a way to pay for the rest of it."

"So, you don't know how serious she is about her music?"

"Well, to tell you the truth, Will, she loves it." Marie paused, trying to explain to herself her daughter's love for music even as she spoke of it. "I don't really know where she gets it from, except her daddy was always crazy about the violin. He played Cajun music, you know."

"Yes, I remember."

"Dodie can play that too, and of course, she can play jazz—but she likes all that classical stuff, concertos and that kind of thing. She's had recitals, and everybody thinks she's very good."

"I can hear her," Lauren said, commenting on the sounds of chords that came through the open door. "Will, we need to get that piano tuned."

"Well, here's what I think we should do for now. Tell me if you agree, Marie. First, let's pay off the mortgage and the credit cards, so you won't have that to worry about. Then, why don't you set up an account for Alyssa's cosmetology school. Find out what it costs and we'll put the money in the account to cover it. And then we're going to set up an allowance from the trust at four thousand. Let me or Freddie know if you need it increased. Does that sound okay? We'll wait to see how much Dodie really wants to study music before we make any plans there."

Marie nodded, commenting that since there would be no mortgage payment, she thought the allowance would be more than enough.

Just then the girls came back outside with Glenn and Sarah, and Lauren told Glenn to get the piano tuned. "Dodie, honey, you've got to come back and play for us when it's tuned, okay?"

"Sure, Aunt Lauren. I'd love to come back and play in this house. It's so beautiful! But it's so empty. There's furniture, and there's the piano, but where's all Grandmother's beautiful things? I remember pictures and linens and figurines—and all her china and crystal."

"It's in the attic, Dodie. Safe from burglars and hurricanes," answered Will. "It may sound strange to you, but when your grandmother was your age, her mother often had big dinner parties. That's why the dining room is so big."

Lauren added, "Would you believe it? She had sterling for sixteen place settings. There must be thousands of dollars just in silver in the attic. Such a waste!"

"Yes," said William. "Such a waste."

Chapter Nine

Time Passed

"*Boudin.*"

"No way, Babe."

"*Boudin.* And not only that, but *boudin noir.*"

Lauren stopped walking and turned to face him, her hands on her hips. "Will, if you think for one minute I'm going to let you eat stinking hog guts, let alone with that grotesque boiled hog blood in it, you've lost your flipping mind. I mean it, Will. It's not going to happen."

They had almost reached Benny's, a tiny shop in an alley that sold the objectionable sausage. They'd parked the Subaru a block away; Lauren, determined to walk more in order to lose weight, and William, following his doctor's suggestion for mild exercise. The alley ran parallel to Canal Street where Maison Blanche was located. Lauren wanted to buy clothes a size smaller than she wore in the belief that the new clothes would inspire her to lose weight.

Will was doubtful about her plan. "Don't you think you ought to wait and see if you're going to be able to lose the weight?" he'd suggested. "Or maybe just buy a few things, inexpensive, to sort of test the feasibility of your plan."

Lauren was impatient with his lack of understanding. "Will, you miss the whole point. I wear a twelve. If I buy some really lovely things to wear in Georgia—yes, expensive things—in size ten, I'll *have* to lose weight. I'm giving myself incentive. Don't you get it?"

"If you say so."

As they moved up the alley toward the rear of the department store, they met a police horse, his muzzle snuffling along the pavement in a semi-circular pattern. A dismounted policeman leaned against the side of a building, one booted ankle crossed over the other. He held a piece of greasy white paper to his mouth

Lauren demanded, "You are not giving that poor horse *boudin* to eat, are you?"

"Lauren, don't be silly," Will said. "Horses don't eat meat." Then he looked at the policeman. "You didn't give him *boudin*, did you?"

The policeman laughed, his mouth full of sausage and bread. "No, no. He's just jealous of mine."

"I know how he feels," Will said, enjoying Lauren's outrage.

But they had arrived at Benny's open doorway, cut diagonally on the corner of an old wooden shotgun house. The entire room wasn't more than twenty feet square. A single high ceiling fan, black with years of grease-laden air, clacked overhead as a few customers stood in line at a makeshift table-top counter to buy a blood sausage served up from a blackened griddle behind the counter by a large black man in a tee-shirt covered with a greasy apron. The odor of red peppered spice and hot grease thickened the air. A green plastic basket held pre-cut squares of white paper on the counter, along with bottles of hot sauce and several chrome containers of white paper napkins. Slices of baguette bread were stacked on a large platter, and a refrigerated case held bottles of beer and coke beside the counter. The sizzling noise from the griddle drowned the noise of customers' chatter and the whirring, clacking of the overhead fan.

Lauren tugged at William's shirt. "No, you don't, mister. Tell you what. You pass by this grease pot and we'll stop at Anthony's on the way home, and get Andouille and red beans—and air-conditioning! How's that?"

"It's a deal."

She muttered something about just hooking him up to an IV and pumping straight cholesterol in his veins, and he laughed as he responded with chiding remarks about which of them had to go on a diet—and not only that, but had to be coerced into a diet by buying clothes too small. "I mean, that's really kind of pitiful, don't you think?"

She slapped his arm and said, "Just shut up and keep walking." They had reached the corner of the side street next to the department store entrance and Will stopped.

"Listen, I'm going on over to Immaculate Conception for a while. Just come by there and pick me up when you're done, okay?"

"You promise you won't go back to Benny's?"

"I solemnly swear. I will go wait in the church and meditate on Andouille and red beans."

"Good boy. I won't be long." She disappeared through the glass doors of the department store.

The drunk was there. William was glad to see him stretched

out on the pew as he sat down on the opposite pew across the aisle. As always, the nave was dark; the only lights were those down on the altar, the ornate reredos behind it, and the gold tabernacle. Golden spires ascended from the screen and the tabernacle, where a single candle in a red glass chimney was always burning. The dim ambience calmed and sobered him. He'd had no intention of eating the sausage at Benny's; he simply enjoyed evoking Lauren's maternal, corrective outrage. But the point was that he never ate boudin. Lauren knew that. And he knew she knew that. It was just a little dance they did, like so many others. He could not remember any romantic speeches either of them had ever made—no "love talk," but often this teasing, this bantering exchange. Love-making, their time in bed together, had always been like this, full of play and laughter, and sitting there in the silence, he knew this to be true and lasting love. He allowed himself to feel his blessedness. And then he allowed himself to not think at all, not plan, analyze, consider, or even remember. Just be. Not at all unlike his companion on the opposite pew, for whom there was no past or future, no present. There was no time there. No memory.

After an hour or more, Lauren tiptoed behind him and whispered, "Are you ready for lunch?" He roused himself and followed her outside into the bright sunlight and street noise. "So, do you want to go to Anthony's?" she asked.

"Sure," he answered. "I could do with some red beans and rice. I'll forego the Andouille, I think. But you are going to let me have a beer, aren't you? I'm not driving, you know."

"You're a good man."

On the way, they passed Wainwright's storage. The new rows of individual storage units, in some kind of bright blue metal, were almost completed. Lauren remarked that the sight made her taste gall. "Why do you think somebody would waste such valuable real estate, for heaven's sake."

"I don't know. Doesn't matter. Another hurricane will wipe it out anyway."

"Well, that's cheerfully optimistic of you, Will."

"You know, ever since I can remember, there were hurricane warnings. We're below sea level and we sit on the Gulf with a giant lake behind us and the Mississippi right there—the fact that we hadn't been hit before Katrina was a miracle. People just never believed it would really happen. New Orleans is exempt from that kind of thing, you know."

"That's how come so many people were killed. They didn't even interrupt their dinner to listen to mandatory evacuations. That's New Orleans. I'm just glad we were in Shreveport. I don't know if we'd have listened either, Will."

"Probably not. We're just as stupid as everybody else."

There was a moment of silence then as bad memories surfaced. Then William said, "You know, I almost said just now, Let's not think about it. But that's what we do, isn't it. Katrina is already forgotten. Because we just don't want to think about it. We never do." The subject was rousing unexpected anger in him; he didn't know why it bothered him. "Katrina is part of history now, and future generations will wonder why in the world we didn't listen."

"No, they won't. They know New Orleanians. This city will never change. It will always be that way."

"But didn't we just establish, just a minute ago, that, contrary to everyone's opinion, obviously we *can* be destroyed. And see? Already, almost in the same breath, we're saying we'll never change; we'll always be the same. Is that the definition of doom, I wonder."

They pulled into Anthony's up by the lake, with its small white crushed shell parking lot still full of cars at one-thirty. Lauren didn't respond to William's comment. Instead she said, "I'm going to have a stuffed artichoke. Anthony's does them better than just about anybody—I think because they always use fresh crab." William pulled open the glass door, stickered over with credit card logos, and they were met by the sounds and smells of a crowded dining room full of braised, broiled, or fried seafood, pungent red beans and Andouille sausage, and customers engaged in the serious business of enjoying lunch. Katrina was forgotten.

They pulled out wooden chairs, scraping them across the tiled floor, and sat down at a littered table recently vacated. William thought he saw, from the corner of his eye, long sleek blonde hair sitting by the window at the side of the dining room. He tried to keep his peripheral vision focused there as a waitress hurried past and handed them printed menus encased in clear plastic with a black border. "Be with y'all in a minute," she said over her shoulder. He stared at the menu and kept his attention on the side of the room where the blonde hair swayed on a young woman rising from the table. Not Joanna. He should have known; Joanna didn't like New Orleans cuisine.

But he was disappointed. Why, he asked himself, why would he experience a feeling of disappointment when he did not, in fact, want to see her? It came to him that he only wanted to know that she was still there, that she continued to *be,* there, in the world.

"I'm not all that hungry," he said, looking at the menu. Just going to have a spinach salad, I think, and some bread."

"Right, Will. Make me feel guilty, okay? You know I want a stuffed artichoke."

"Okay. So how many calories do you think it has?"

"Bastard."

His phone signaled a text from Don: *Call me. Now.*

He did. "What's wrong?" he asked when Don answered.

"I'm at Charity Hospital, Will. They're admitting Ellen. Blood sugar is all over the map. I couldn't get her to wake up this morning, so I called an ambulance."

"Oh, my God, Don. What are they telling you?"

"Nothing yet. She's awake now, but they're admitting her anyway. Look. Do me a favor. I can't get Margie on the phone. Keep trying for me, will you? There's a meeting I was supposed to get to this afternoon and I'm not going to make it. It's about the realignment for next fall. Get Margie to postpone it, okay? She'll know who to call."

"Right. I'll get back to you and keep you informed. Let me know if there's anything else we can do, okay?"

"Sure. Thanks, Will."

He told Lauren the news. "Look, let's not order, all right? Take me to the campus and drop me off. Then you could go to the hospital, if you want to."

"Right. Poor Don." They rose to leave just as their waitress arrived at their table. "Sorry," said Lauren. "Something just came up, and we can't stay. We'll come back later."

As she backed out of the parking space, Lauren said again, "Poor Don. This isn't the first crisis, and it won't be the last—at least, I hope it's not the last. She's never going to get better, you know."

"No, I know. He's been here before. He didn't sound alarmed, but of course, he is very worried."

"I'll call you when I get to the hospital and let you know how she is—and how he is, too."

*

William took the elevator up to Don's office where he saw through the open door several people in the conference room, already there in anticipation of the meeting. Some of them he recognized, but not all, so he took his message straight to Margie before speaking to those he knew.

Margie rose from her desk and spoke to the group, "Excuse me, folks, Dean Penfield has had an emergency at Charity and can't make it this afternoon." She turned to the assistant dean, Gladys Riker, and asked whether she'd like to try to chair the meeting in the dean's absence.

"No, I don't see the point." Gladys turned to the others: "Do you all agree? We couldn't commit to anything decisive without Don anyway." Heads nodded in agreement. "Is this about Ellen?"

Will spoke up, "Yes, he just called and asked if I'd get a message to you. It's about his wife Ellen—I think everybody knows she's severely diabetic—and they decided to admit her. My wife has gone to the hospital. She'll call me later and I'll let Margie know how things are."

Everyone left, agreeing to wait to hear from Margie and murmuring sympathetic remarks for the Penfields. Will followed and asked John Thibodaux, the chancellor's assistant, whether there was an agenda for the meeting, and if so, could he have a copy.

"Sure," John replied and handed him three stapled sheets, "but I think you already know about all the changes. By the way, I couldn't believe you're leaving, Will, but I guess you knew what you were doing—must have seen the writing on the wall, huh?"

"Not quite, but something like that."

The department secretary expressed surprise when William walked into the office. He explained his unexpected presence and said he wouldn't be staying long. He had settled on three full days a week instead of the five half-days originally suggested by his doctor. Since Lauren was still driving him to work, this schedule was much easier for her; it also allowed him to meet his afternoon classes instead of having to turn them over to someone else. Today was not one of those three full days, however.

He sat at his desk and looked at the meeting agenda John had given him. It was sad, painfully sad—and again, shocking, the more so because the shock was so irrational. John was right; yes, he did know the closing of the department was coming. Why then was he surprised to see that it was actually happening, all of it as bad as he imagined but never quite believed. And the Humanities Department, expecting to absorb history faculty, would not have the increased budget they might have expected. Instead, the floor space, the actual floor space now occupied by the History Department would become a "writing center," with banks of word processors and staffed by one graduate assistant, and not an English graduate assistant, but one from I.T. And because of the center, there would be no more graduate teaching assistantships for English. Class size for Freshman Composition would necessarily increase, along with the teaching load. The only beneficiaries of this change would be I.T., and of course, computer companies. He was glad to see, however, that the History Department secretary would receive a lateral transfer to Humanities. William wanted to make sure he told her that; he knew she was concerned about her job with the dismantling of History.

The dismantling of history.

Indeed. Yes, that was really happening. No euphemism needed now, not any more. No point now in talking budget, enrollment, or changing cultural norms, societal needs, or any of that nonsense. The dismantling of history.

Last night's news reported the demand for the removal of more statues of historical figures, now considered offensive to some ethnic or racial groups, and some because the newly dishonored figure had not supported women's suffrage. Anachronism, the assumption that historical figures should embrace modern beliefs, was such an egregious error in logic—but that error is not recognized when history itself is not recognized. Logic itself had been re-defined anyway. It was now utilitarianism by another name.

And intra-faculty bulletins had for some time now constantly updated language, course descriptions and other printed instructor materials, formerly considered a matter of the instructor's discretion and now a matter of self-protection by the university. Academic freedom had all but disappeared.

Language was simply a useful tool to meet the needs of the moment's agenda, having no relationship to the truth. For there can be no reverence for truth if truth does not exist. Bettie Somers was right: There is no such thing as history, and there never was, if truth exists only in the eye of the beholder.

Education, as it had been understood for a thousand years; education, which had given birth to unbelievable achievement in science, art, music, to all that is good in human life, was not dying—it was being killed. It was being literally, deliberately, killed, by a thousand cuts, every day now. He felt nauseous, thinking about John's comment: "…the writing on the wall…" as though his resignation was due to an awareness of the political times. It wasn't—but so what? It didn't matter. Nothing mattered.

Time passed. He sat staring at the academic robe he kept hanging on the back of his office door, the regalia denoting Liberal Arts and History. Like a costume now. Like the Mardi Gras costumes of nuns' habits, no longer worn by nuns—were there still any nuns? The Church had originated education, universities, the whole concept of academia, of higher learning. Whatever happened to the Church? Drunks slept there now. Rats and plagues took over the slums of Rome.

The phone rang. Lauren. Ellen was stable but the hospital determined that she needed observation for twenty-four hours. Don was coming over for dinner. She was going to cook some red beans and rice. He told Lauren that he didn't feel like working this afternoon, after all, and please come get him in about an hour. He knew he should call Margie and let her know that all was well and Don would be in tomorrow morning, but first he called his own department secretary in and told her she'd be transferred to Humanities in the fall. She was visibly relieved. He could see that she clearly wanted to say something then, something conciliatory about the demise of the History Department and his own departure. But he didn't feel up to it; he interrupted her struggle for words and asked her if she would call Margie upstairs and relay Don's message, and please close his door on her way out.

More time passed. He glanced at photos on his bookshelf: a photo of himself with Lauren on their twentieth anniversary, a photo of Elise, Mack, and the kids. Why did people put family photos in their offices? It was tacky. It was artificial sentiment, which demeaned love and made it false. They did it because they were supposed to. A matter of image. All-important image. Image was what mattered when there is no truth.

Did the Roman infatuation with the image of Rome kill any

authentic fealty and devotion to the city? Kill an entire civilization? Yes. Hypocrisy remains when real love dies. It's all that remains, and so easily destroyed by a single blow of anything authentic. Even if that authenticity was axes and bloodlust, it was real.

He glanced again at the academic robe hanging on the back of his door, and he saw a shroud. He left the office without saying goodbye to Charlotte; he saw her look up from her desk in surprise.

Wednesday. Three-fifteen. Joanna would be gone now. Her little cubicle office would become a storage room now.

He was tired of thinking. Everything in him felt broken by a heavy weariness of grief he felt no longer able to bear. Her door was closed. He stood in the hallway opposite the door and whispered, "I will always love you. You will never be unloved while I live." Fatigue and despair almost paralyzed him, but he managed to turn and leave. He would wrap her in white paper and keep her safe in the attic. He felt weak and faint and leaned against the wall by the elevator until he could feel some strength returning to his legs. Then he took the elevator down to the parking lot to wait for Lauren.

Chapter Ten

That Time Had Passed

William and Lauren sat at the counter in the Camellia Grill on Carrollton Avenue, eating pecan waffles in resigned silence. The shouting of the waiters and the clatter of dishes made attempts at conversation pointless, a situation for which William was grateful—because they were going car-shopping.

They had decided to eat breakfast at the Camellia because it was uptown, and they planned to stop by the house before heading to Metairie to the dealerships that Lauren thought they should check out. Glenn had called yesterday to tell them the piano was tuned, and—as far as he could tell, he said—it sounded great. Anyway, Sarah had tried it out, playing the only thing she knew by heart, "Just a Closer Walk With Thee," and it sounded really good to both of them. Lauren said, Well, it's a Steinway Grand, and anything is going to sound good if it's tuned. Neither he nor Lauren could play, so they were looking forward to hearing Sarah. Especially William. He could remember Sarah singing that bluesy hymn while she cleaned house. She had a good blues voice, strong—and loud. She didn't stop even when she ran the vacuum cleaner, just increased her volume. It went up all three floors to his room.

They paid the check and left, taking coffee with them. William drove. Officially, he wasn't supposed to drive until tomorrow, but Lauren said she wanted to be with him on his first time back behind the wheel.

"You know," he said, "this is ridiculous. I'm not going to get a car today, get the title, tag, insurance, and all that on a Sunday, and have it ready to drive tomorrow just so you can take the Subaru back to Statesboro."

"Well, we know that, Will. What we're doing this morning is simply shopping. I can put off going back till you've made up your mind, done the deal, and got the car."

"But you said you had to go back next week."

"And that's enough time—if you don't lollygag and spend all day whining."

"I think we should just go on over to Slidell and find a nice beat-up old pickup. It should be right at home in MacDonald's parking lot in Statesboro."

"Will, do try not to be such a petulant snob."

Glenn was in the backyard waiting for them when they arrived. "Hey y'all," he said. "Sarah's in the house, trying to find some sheet music. I told her 'Closer Walk' would be fine. You just want to hear the piano, not get a concert. So the old Volvo finally died, huh?"

"Be respectful, Glenn. He's still in deep mourning."

"It was a good car," said William, as the three of them went up the back steps together.

"When it wasn't in the shop," she countered. "Glenn, the porch looks great. So did you decide to paint it yourself?"

"Yes. Hired somebody, but it was too much trouble getting him to go back over places, so I just did it myself. Besides, hired guys use cheap paint, you know."

They could hear Sarah rolling over chords inside. "Y'all come on in," she called through the dining room. "It sounds wonderful. I just wish I could play something good for you."

They stood around the piano while she played the old hymn. She played the chords heavy, in the jazz way, like cloudy skies and rolling thunder, while the plaintive lyrics expressed a spiritual longing. Glenn's head was slowly nodding, Lauren was swaying, and when the song ended, Will said, "I don't know whether it's the piano or Sarah, I just know it sounds fine to me!"

They headed back outside. Glenn walked with them to the car, his hands in his back pockets. "I've been meaning to ask you what you're going to do about the house. I mean, I know Lauren's planning on going to Georgia for her new job, but you're going with her, aren't you?"

Will was surprised. He could tell that Glenn was concerned, worried even, about how the move might affect him and Sarah. "Yes, I am. Glenn, but don't worry about the house. You don't have to worry about your place here. I thought you knew that. This house will always be the Cauley house. As long as it's here, y'all have a home here—if you want it. I thought you knew that." For the first time, he realized that his going to Georgia himself might be open to question. It came as a mild shock.

Glenn made a nervous gesture wiping his fingers across his mouth. "Oh, yeah, we did know that. But it just seemed like—well, if you're leaving… Sarah thought I better ask you."

Lauren was watching him. He could feel it. "No. On this we are in perfect agreement. This house will always be in the family. And as long as it is, you have a home."

"Marie—is she maybe thinking about coming back now?"

"What? No. Her home is Shreveport with her kids and grandkids. She won't come back here. But Georgia's not so far away. Lauren and I will be back from time to time, maybe even bring Elise and the kids sometime. And we'd stay here, right here."

"That would be great, having kids around again. You got to let us know ahead of time, though, so we could get the house ready."

"Sure."

As they headed out on St. Charles Avenue driving to Metairie, Will thought he could feel a little more tension in the car. "Did I say anything to Glenn about the house that bothered you?"

"No, it just brought the subject up again, that's all." She was quiet then for some time. Only when they got to I-610 did she continue: "It's just that, you know, honey, we've got a condo in Barbados, and the one in Ashville that Dad left me. Barbados stays rented, but not Ashville; we don't rent that out. But Freddie didn't mention either one of them. The only reason he mentioned St. Charles is that it's here—in the city—and he knew we'd say no, not for sale, even when he asked. But he asked about the townhouse. Now why is that? Because we *live* there, Will. That's why he had to ask what we want to do with it. It's our address—it's *your* address—and yes, I'm still bothered by why you want to hang onto it. And I have to ask you—why do you not want to let it go?"

When he didn't answer right away, she said, "I think you don't want to go, Will."

He still did not answer, so she went on: "Well, I mean, I know the city is your home—our home—but it's not going anywhere. It will still be here. And you're not cutting ties, not as long as the family home stays. And as you said to Glenn, we can come back anytime. The difference is that the townhouse is your address. And I have to ask—*what is your problem?*"

He reached his right hand out to her knee. He'd been very selfish; he hadn't realized how his reluctance to talk about selling might be making her feel. He made a firm resolve not to do that again. "Honey, I'm sorry if I haven't been clear about the one most important fact: Where you go, I go. Don't even think of leaving me behind." He patted her knee. She didn't answer, but he noticed that she turned her head to the passenger window.

*

It was the third car dealer. Ghastly places, Will thought—all car dealers, with those silly pennants waving, the unctious salesmen—why were car salesmen always so repulsive? They weren't really. He just didn't want to buy one of those tank-like SUVs. He didn't want a Ford, a Chevy, a Dodge; he wanted his old Volvo.

Lauren was exasperated. "What do you *want*, Will Cauley? You've got to drive *something*!" They had just returned from another test drive in some kind of Toyota with the improbable name of "Highlander."

"Do all cars nowadays have to be tanks? You climb into them. They tell you that it's safer, but even a car-idiot like me knows that height is definitely not a safety feature in cars. Why do people want these things?"

"I don't know. But I do know this. I've had enough, my beloved. Get somebody else to go car-shopping with you. It's three o'clock, we didn't have lunch, and I want to go home."

"Right. Tell you what. I'll get Hansi to come with me. I'll tell him to wear his fuschia tee-shirt and bring Cecily. I bet the salesmen would eat it up. What do you think?"

She had to laugh. "Call him. See what he says. You know, it would be fun, wouldn't it. Hansi in his ear-rings and with his fluffy mutt—driving his Land Rover! What a hoot. Call him, Will."

"It's too late today. I'm dying for a drink. Let's go home. And anyhow, I don't think he'd be a lot of help in deal-making. For that, I need Charlie. I haven't got a clue how to make a deal. Every guy we've talked to out here fairly salivated when we drove up. They know a patsy when they see one."

"*Patsy*? Good grief, you're such an old fogey, aren't you? *Sucker* is the word, I think."

It was the kind of frustrating defeat that brings laughter over the hopelessness of an endeavor. They drove home in good spirits, despite the failure of the mission. Just as they pulled in next to the corpse of the Volvo in the carport, Lauren brought up the house on St. Charles again.

"You know, it's in our will that the next of kin gets the house.

That would be Marie, but what would she do with it, Will? She'd sell it, wouldn't she? Some investor would buy it from her and turn it into yet another New Orleans B and B."

"Yeah, I've been thinking about that myself."

"Could we leave it to Elise instead?"

"Yes, we could. But then she's stuck with it. She doesn't want it." He paused, picturing Elise wanting to "do the right thing" by her grandmother's house and keeping it like the burden it would be.

"We need to think about it, Will, before too long. We're both in our fifties now."

When they got inside, Will phoned Charlie while Lauren made their drinks. He told Lauren as they settled on the patio that Charlie would pick him up at ten on Monday morning and take him to buy a car.

"Thank God! Now don't come home without one, okay?"

"Okay."

*

Late that night, William woke to find that Lauren was not in bed. He went downstairs and found her sitting in the dark in the living room, curled up on the sofa and hugging a pillow.

"Lauren? What's the matter? Why aren't you in bed?" He turned on a lamp and sat down on the sofa, taking her feet and holding them in his lap.

She sighed. "Oh, it's okay, Babe. I couldn't sleep, just came down here to think, so I wouldn't toss and turn and wake you."

"Well, I'll tell you what—I'll sleep down here with you, but it will be kind of tight with two of us on the sofa." He rubbed her feet and felt concern. This was not normal behavior for Lauren, who always slept like the dead under any circumstances.

She tossed the pillow at him and chuckled. "Come on, let's go back to bed." She rose and took his hand and led him back upstairs to bed. He held her while she slept, but he didn't sleep.

No mention was made about the incident the next morning. Charlie arrived and had coffee with them in the kitchen. As they were leaving, Lauren admonished him, "Charlie, do not bring this man back to me without a car. If you let him, he will drag his feet—and you—all day long and buy nothing."

"Yes, ma'am!"

When they got in Charlie's Mercedes, William said, "Well, this will be short work, Charlie. I know what I'm going to do. We've got two stops to make and that's it."

"What are we going to do?"

"Let's go to the Volvo dealer. Head out on West Napoleon to Bergeron's. If they don't have what I want, they'll get it, and then we'll go to Hertz."

"Right."

Within an hour, he'd ordered a new S90 in white at Bergeron's. The dealer would go to the house and pick up his old car, now undriveable, with a tow truck. The new car would be there in a week; meanwhile, he'd drive the Camry from Hertz. When they left Hertz, he took Charlie to brunch at Commander's Palace and indulged him in bourbon milk punch.

"Charlie, if we sell the townhouse, how much do you think we'd get?"

"I don't know. If I sell it for you, you'd get a lot more—no commission. Are you going to do it?

"I'll let you know."

"I'll do some scouting and give you a call."

*

He went to the office and sorted out students' papers. He'd gotten behind. He had to meet his class in half an hour and felt guilty about not having their papers ready to return. He'd never been slack on returning papers before. Final exams were Friday, and students were understandably nervous about their grades. He made a note to tell students that their papers would be available from the secretary tomorrow morning. He'd stay up tonight and get them finished and drive over early tomorrow to deliver them.

He thought he should call Lauren and tell her about the car, but he could tell her later. Instead, he called Marie. "Hello, dear, how are you?"

"Oh, Will, it's harder than I thought it would be. I couldn't deal with Buddy's clothes, so Marcine and Richard came over and handled that for me. But now, I got—well, I've got the other things, things that were—that were ours, you know? And nobody can help me with that. Dorothea's keeping the violin."

"I know, or anyway, I can imagine. Just do it. Do it, honey, and just don't think about it."

"Oh, I know. You're right. If you think about it, it will kill you."

"So don't."

"You know, that's exactly what Our Lady told me."

"Well, I wanted to tell you we got the Steinway tuned, and it sounds really good. Do you think Dorothea could come and show us how good?"

"Oh, that's a wonderful idea, Will. She'd love that. Her last class is Wednesday and graduation's on Friday night. She could go down this weekend."

"Do you want to come with her?"

"You know, this would be a good time for her to drive herself down. I know she'd do anything just to see that house again. And more than that, she'd *love* to play that piano. She's never taken a road trip by herself. It would be an adventure for her, she'd feel very grown up. Supposed to start her summer job next week. This would be a real treat for her."

It was like Marie to always think of her children. "But, Marie, I think you could use a break from what you're doing. Come with her, okay? We'd love to have you."

"Thanks, honey. I think I'll do that. I could finish this next week—or maybe even never. I don't know... Attics are good places, you know?"

"Yes, I do. I'll tell Lauren about it when I get home. She was going back to Statesboro this week, but I don't think she has to. I'll ask her."

*

Lauren came out to meet him when he pulled into the drive. "You bought a Camry?" Her glasses were on her forehead; she must have been working.

He got out and kissed her cheek. "Well, no. It's a rental."

"Will! I knew it, I knew it." She threw up her hands.

"You underestimate me. I bought a car. It will be here in a week."

"Let me guess. You bought a Volvo."

"Yes, my dear, I did. An S90—white, of course—"

"Of course."

"Lauren, I've owned three Volvos, all white, yes. They've been good cars for me. I like Volvos. Period."

"How much?"

"Well, Charlie did the dealing. It's thirty-five."

"I don't know whether that's good or not, to tell you the truth."

"Well, it's about five or six off the list price."

"Okay. Are they coming to get ol' Bessie here?"

"Yes. Probably tomorrow."

"Well, I have to ask—what about service?"

"So what? So I have to go to Savannah sometimes, so what? Good opportunity to see Elise and the kids. Besides, as you said, there's probably no Subaru dealer there, either. Maybe we can arrange simultaneous service days and go to Savannah together."

They walked back into the house together. "You're thinking, William Cauley. You're thinking. Want to go out to eat, celebrate, maybe?"

"Can't." He lifted his briefcase. "Papers. It's a real have-to. All evening."

"Well, I've been working all day and I don't feel like cooking. We'll call Major's, okay? Get a nice big fat pizza with anchovies and the works. We've got beer."

"It's a deal."

When they reached the kitchen, Lauren was already calling Major's. William made drinks.

"Listen, honey," he began. He knew she wouldn't like the idea, at least, not at first. Just like she didn't really like the idea of the Volvo. "I called Marie."

"Oh yeah. I should've done that already."

"Well, she is having a hard time."

"Yeah, I imagine she is. The children can only help so much."

"Right. So I asked her and Dodie to come down this Saturday. Have Dodie play on the Steinway."

She turned and looked at him. "Will, I was going to Statesboro tomorrow morning. I can't go and be back by Saturday." She stepped back from him. The gesture gave him a sinking feeling for a moment, a reflex that said he'd done something he shouldn't. But he knew that was not so.

"Lauren, what were you planning to do there?"

She threw up her hands. "I've got forms to be completed. A

lot of them! And I need to get textbook orders in, and I need to get my office set up—"

"You can fill out forms next week. You can order textbooks from here, and you've got all summer to set up your office."

"—and I was going to start looking for a place for us to live."

There it was. There was an almost undetectable emphasis on the word *us*. That was her real purpose, he knew. He crossed the kitchen and wrapped his arms around her neck, pulling her face to his shoulder and holding her close.

The room became quiet. She turned on the news, set places for them on the counter. He took his drink and his briefcase into the study. The room was dim, but he didn't turn on the lamp, just collapsed into his chair behind the desk and swung his briefcase on top of it, but he didn't open it. Instead, he leaned his head back and rubbed the bridge of his nose, allowing sadness to enter him. Grading papers had become an increasingly depressing task in recent years, as it became ever more difficult to find coherent thought in his students' papers. When he could get past the proliferation of grammatical errors, all he could find was the obvious evidence of students' desire to write what they thought he wanted to read. Worse than the absence of study, of thought, was the presence of naively overt attempts at manipulation, a blithe unawareness of their own deceitfulness. Most depressing of all—when he thought about it—was the ease, it seemed, with which most students now turned themselves over to a protocol of academic prostitution, trying to please him in order to get a grade. He dreaded it. He didn't open the case, didn't turn on the lamp, but remained in the growing dark, his head resting on the chair behind him. He'd had little sleep the night before. In less than a minute, he was asleep.

He was back in the river, the dark river, red in places, green in places, but always brown, muddy brown. It was moving fast. There was the flowing silken hair, and long, slender white arms reached to him, slender fingers moved to his face, lifting it from the water when his head went under, again and again. He fought the hands as he grasped at the water, trying, as before, to save himself. Then, suddenly, as he gasped for air, he knew that he could not save himself. That time had passed. When he stopped fighting, he realized with a shock that what he must do was to save the arms that were trying to save him. The arches moved forward then instead of receding, covering him. His head went under again, but the hands lifted his face out of the water and he kept it up this time by searching for a place, a place out of the river, as the hands held his face.

Lauren was leaning over him, kissing his forehead. "Pizza's here, Babe. My, my, Dr. Cauley," she patted the unopened case. "You just work so hard, don't you?"

He sat upright and blinked. "Yes. Yes, I do. But not hard enough. I'll be there in a minute."

Lauren left. He reached into his case and retrieved Angela Martinez's essay. *Right, Angela. Let's see if you've experienced an epiphany of some kind.* It was drivel, as always, predictable clichéd academic phrases, a complete absence, not just of intelligence, but of integrity. Nothing new here. And then he decided: Angela Martinez would not pass. That was unfortunate, but it wasn't the end of the world. He could hear Don murmuring what he knew he'd hear, "Will, cut the girl some slack here…" Bullshit. It was that slack that had killed Angela Martinez' mind. He couldn't change academic politics, he couldn't undo decades of damage. But he had a last chance now to do what he knew should be done. It was too late for Angela, too late for any of them, but he would do his tiny impotent part now to save her mind. He wrote an "F" on the paper along with the comment: "You must read a text before you can comment on it."

Lauren came back to the doorway. "Will, the pizza's going to get cold."

"Go ahead without me. I'm going to finish this."

It took very little time, actually. By the time he finished, the highest grade was "C-" and only two essays achieved it.

Chapter Eleven

A Moment Removed from Time

The next morning William delivered the essays to the secretary and told her to expect "perhaps some reaction" when students picked up their papers. "Sorry I won't be here to help you manage it. I've got a call to make and then I may be out to lunch for a pretty good while. If it gets a little rough, tell them to see the dean."

She took the papers, tapped them on her desk to align the edges and put a large clamp on them. She looked up at him above her glasses. "Dr. Cauley, what have you done?" Then she thumbed the papers to see the grades. "Oh, my God. All hell's going to break."

"That's too bad." He went in his office and pulled a file drawer open. For some reason, he'd saved copies of some papers graded twenty years ago. He pulled a few A, B, and C essays and left them on his desk. On his way down to the parking lot, he called Paul Cunningham and left a voice mail. He didn't go home but sat in his rented Camry for a while. *That's not fair*, he thought. *It's not their fault. So whose fault is it, then. Mine. Everybody's. Education has been murdered. Whose fault? Everybody's.*

His phone rang. Paul.

"Hey, Paul. How are you? Or should I say 'Father' maybe?"

"'Paul' is just fine, Will. I'm good. What on earth is up? Haven't talked to you guys in—what, a couple of years, at least."

"We're okay. Listen, you know how we're always saying we should do lunch? Well, Paul, let's do lunch. Today. Can you?"

There was a silence, just a second too long to be natural. "Yeah. Yeah, actually I can, Will. It'll be good to see you. Where do you want to meet?"

"How about Marconi's?" It was a tavern where they'd met as students.

"Hey, yeah, why not? Let's make it early, if that's okay. I've got a one o'clock class. Is eleven okay?"

"See you then."

He drove to the Quarter—he hadn't been down there in ages. He had never enjoyed it—always called it an adult theme park. It was, of course, covered with tourists, and he'd never been comfortable around large numbers of people. Most of the stories about the Quarter, stories that littered old movies, cheap novels, and countless sexual fantasies were tripe. The authentic tales of the Quarter, those that gave birth to people to like Louis Armstrong, customs like jazz funerals or voodoo rituals—all that legendary stuff—ended around the 1930s. Since then, authenticity had steadily waned, and nothing was left now except something like a B-movie set, but it was a movie set that was profitable. Even the cuisine now, done to death on TV cook shows with chefs faking an accent. There was a time when even street vendors in New Orleans made better food than the best restaurants in other cities. Not so, now, but it was still good. That would probably always be true. New Orleans did not, at heart, care that much about its own place in American culture, mostly because they didn't care much about anything except that which pleased them—and not at all about that which pleased others. That would never change. It was both their vice and their virtue.

He walked until it started raining. He made it back to the car before getting drenched, and then sat there in the car, watching tourists run into doorways, laughing, holding totebags over their heads. Umbrellas are not what one thinks of carrying on Bourbon Street.

His family—his mother's family—had arrived here in 1780. Françoise, an indigenous daughter of Martinique had married a French planter after bearing him six children and moved with him to New Orleans. He was wealthy, and they'd become part of New Orleans French colonial aristocracy, which never cared much about a morality more English than French. His father's family, the Cauleys, began in Savannah, arriving as refugees from the Irish Famine. His hard-drinking and hard-working father had the drive and the will to make a successful drill in the Gulf, and then to court and win the beautiful Madeleine Dubois, his mother.

He wasn't like his father, who was really very much like Buddy Delacroix—whom his sister had had the wisdom of heart to love. William remembered his father with both love and affection, though not with admiration. It is possible to love and not to understand, and he'd never understood his father. William believed that only his mother had understood Michael Cauley. She never called him "Mike," as everyone else did, but always "Michael." And she never recovered from her grief when he died.

His daughter Elise had also known that kind of love. But he had not. He never had, never would. But—yes, he thought, Elise was right. He thought it would be "enough" even if it was brief. Enough for a lifetime.

He sat in the Camry, watching tourists run and squeal like children in the rain. The colors of the city ran down the windshield, like washing paint off a whore. For him, it would always be home—and it would always be the place where death comes on a sultry summer morning and wakes us from the sleep of our childhood.

*

Paul sat at a table in the middle of the long narrow dining room of Marconi's. He was wearing a clerical collar. He wished he could tell Lauren he'd seen Paul in his collar.

"Hey, old man, how you doing?" He smiled and walked toward Paul, extending his hand. Paul grinned, rose and grasped his hand, pulling William toward him and clapping him on the back.

"How are you? God, it's good to see you, Will. How many times have we said we'd do this and didn't?"

"Yeah, I know. I guess it's one of those things you have to do when you think of it, and not make some vague future promise."

"Well, you know all the great philosophers say there is no future or past—there's only now." Paul seemed genuinely glad to see him. The waiter brought menus; they both ordered beer. It was good to see him—why had he not kept this friendship? But then he suddenly realized: It had somehow been left to Paul—it had been Paul who'd let it atrophy. Why?

"Where is everybody now, do you know?" he asked. "Oh, you did know Jason's gone, didn't you? Killed in Israel during one of those short wars over there."

"Yeah, yeah, I heard about that. Well, Jocelyn left for the Peace Corps, you know, and I never heard from her again."

William raised his bottle: "And only we remain—"

"—to tell the tale," Paul finished it.

Lunch was good. They both had muffelattas, an olive salad, and beer. They laughed and reminisced. William wished they'd remained friends.

"Paul, do you remember the dead Romans?"

Paul paused in the middle of raising his bottle to his lips. "I do.

And you do too, I guess. It was a numinous moment."

"A what?"

"Well, that's one term for it. It was a moment removed from time."

William frowned. "Yeah. That's exactly what it was. And this was too, this moment right now, the memory of it."

"Funny how that works, isn't it?"

William took a deep breath. "I want to ask you something."

Paul lowered his head a little, looking down at his plate and twirling his bottle of beer with his left hand. "I know you do. Let me spare you: You want to ask me about Lauren."

William felt himself blush. "Well, yes. Yes I do. Will you talk about it? If not, that's okay."

Paul looked at him, smiling, with understanding and with an obvious affection he made no attempt to hide. "You guys are okay?" Will nodded quickly, and Paul continued, "Well, there's not much to tell, or maybe too much to tell. She's the only woman I ever loved. And I loved her as much as any man ever loved a woman. With a passion that consumed me, blinded me, and nearly killed me." The smile never left his face.

"My God." What his friend said was stunning enough, but what made William's heart almost stop was the openness with which he said it. No timidity, no embarrassment—and no regret.

That was why they hadn't maintained the friendship. That was why Paul had allowed it to wither away.

"Paul—"

Paul said, "Look, Will, what I just told you is truth. And truth exists outside any control of ours, any attempts at alteration or interpretation. It's not a matter for subjective opinion. It's sovereign. Now, here's the 'how I see it' part: She left me. You know that, likely. And she did exactly the right thing. Right for her—and for me. In fact, I think she did it more for me than for herself. I wouldn't be surprised, anyway. Amazing woman, Lauren."

"Yes. Yes she is." William felt stunned.

"Well, it's been great to see you again, but I've got to go meet my one o'clock." He smiled and stood to leave.

"Oh. Sure. Good to see you, Paul."

Paul patted his shoulder as he walked past him toward the door.

He should go back to the office now. Actually, he should

probably just go straight up to Don's office where he suspected several students had already lodged complaints. He should prepare to defend his grades. He should face the music. He would. But not yet. He sat there alone in Marconi's long after the lunch crowd left, drinking beer, remembering. There had never been any sign from Lauren. Of course, he didn't even start dating her until after the affair with Paul was over. And then he left her for Europe. And Paul went in seminary. Lauren wrote to him—letters, most of which he never answered, except with an occasional guilty postcard. Lots of letters, interest in his travels, campus gossip, New Orleans news, how the Saints were doing… The relationship would not have survived but for her tenacity. He was distracted by churches and crypts and museums, by girls, by food, music, by everything, but most of all, by Charlemagne. He felt no remorse about that. He didn't feel somehow unworthy, particularly, of her—was it devotion? Or maybe simply her determination.

Paul did not look like a man suffering. Sure, it was thirty years ago, but there was no trace of unhappiness in his face. He was a happy man. How was that? "Amazing woman," he'd said. William tried to find a cause, something that would account for Paul's obvious contentment, the complete absence of bitterness or jealousy. On the contrary, his happiness at seeing Will was genuine.

Finally, he became self-conscious sitting there alone, drinking beer, fingering the little Perrier bottle with its white carnation, or staring into space. He paid his check and left.

*

He was glad the drunk was there. Sleeping as always. Finding a drink is hard work, and a man needs his rest. He decided to try it out. He retrieved one of the kneeling pillows from the end of the pew, put it under his head and stretched out on the hard wooden pew, surprisingly comfortable, lying on his back like the drunk and looking up at the distant dark ceiling of the Gothic arched nave overhead, where he saw—without surprise—starlight.

He drove back to the campus. The secretary spoke as soon as he pushed open the glass door of the department office. "Dean Penfield says come up to his office as soon as you come in."

"Right," he said, and walked past her into his office, picked up the handful of old student papers from his desk and walked out again. She watched him go as though she were watching the progress of some unexpected insect, some creature not supposed to be there, waiting to see what it would do.

Don's door was open. "Come in, Will, and close the door. Have a seat."

"No thanks. I can't stay long."

"Okay. Have it your way. What in the world..."

"Yes, I know. You've had complaints from my 4410 class. You'll probably get some more."

Don started to speak, but William stopped him. "Listen, Don, I already know everything you want to say. I understand. You have to. But here's the point from where I stand: I don't. I don't have to."

"Will, I can't—I can't let this stand."

"I know. It's okay. Do what you have to. Here are a few examples of what A, B, and C papers from 4410 should look like. They're handwritten—sorry about that—students didn't have ready access to computers then. But you can still read them; they're in blue or black ink. I don't really want to discuss it. Change the grades of the complainers if you have to. It won't change the truth. I know you have to do what you have to do."

He didn't wait for Don to speak but turned to go. "By the way, I was talking to Harmon last week, and we agree that a 'farewell' party would not be welcome. We don't want a wake. The same goes for a retirement party for me, please. But listen, Lauren and I would love it if we could make it to dinner with you and Ellen again, okay? Good luck with—all that." He made a gesture to the students' papers on Don's desk. "See you later."

When he arrived home, Lauren wasn't there. He saw frozen okra gumbo thawing in the fridge when he got a bottle of water. He grabbed a handful of salted peanuts from the cabinet above the stove where poker snacks were kept, and that reminded him that he'd have to cancel the game for Saturday. He called Hans first and left a message, then he called Freddie, who answered.

"Listen, Freddie. I can't make poker on Saturday because Marie and Dorothea are coming overnight. We had the Steinway tuned at the house, and Dodie's going to come and play for us."

"Oh, hey, I'd like to be there for that. Can I come?"

"Sure. We'd love to have you."

Then he called Charlie. "Hey, what's up, Will."

"We got company coming Saturday—Marie and her daughter—so poker's canceled, Charlemagne."

"What?"

"Poker's canceled."

"I mean what you called me."

"Charlemagne. It means Charles the Great, and you are the Charlemagne of our time."

"Go to hell, Will."

William laughed. A real laugh, as he'd laughed with Paul at lunch.

"Well," said Charlie, "did you know that Clyde Thomas is going to be at the Maple Leaf Sunday afternoon?"

"You're kidding. I haven't heard that trumpet in a long time. Too long. Are you going?"

"Yeah," said Charlie. "I love old Clyde. You know he's an old man now, but he's still playing."

"I bet Lauren would like to hear him too. Let's go early. You know it'll be crowded."

"Right. I'll see you there. I've got a call waiting. I have to go."

William took his water and peanuts down the hall to his study, sat down and opened his laptop. He first looked at the outline, then opened a new blank document and typed "Chapter One." He leaned back in his chair, kicked off his shoes, and ate his peanuts. Then he double-spaced twice and wrote "On the second day of April in what was probably the year 747, a male child was born who would become the first Holy Roman Emperor..."

*

The back door slammed and Lauren came into the study. She leaned down and kissed his cheek as he clicked on Save Document, and closed the laptop. "Been shopping," she announced.

He stood and followed her into the kitchen where he saw several shopping bags on the counter. "Uh huh," he said.

"Well, Will, I have to have *something* to wear. I'm not going to get rid of the size ten things. I'm not giving up. But I have to have *something* to wear."

She sounded so pitiful that William, standing behind her, rubbed her neck with his hand as he leaned around her and lifted the edge of one of the bags to peek inside. "I know, Babe, I know."

He kissed her cheek. "I love every ton. Let me see what you got."

She elbowed him in the diaphragm. "You know, you're just so supportive, aren't you. How could I ever lose an ounce without your unflagging support!" Her phone rang inside her handbag on the counter, and she answered. "Elise! Hey, honey. Is everything okay? Your dad's here, let me put you on speaker."

Elise's voice came through, too loud since Lauren maxed the volume. "I don't believe you guys. I'm holding here in my hand a quit-claim deed to Grandmother's cottage. I just received it by registered mail from Uncle Freddie. He says in the letter that y'all signed it over to me!"

"Yes," said Lauren. "You knew you were going to get it in our will anyway, honey, and we just decided to go ahead and give it to you now. Something you wouldn't have to deal with when we die."

"Oh, Mom, that is so sweet and thoughtful." There was a slight pause. "You know how wonderful my parents are, don't you? I mean, I could tell you if you don't know."

Lauren was smiling one of her sweet smiles, rare and wonderful to behold, William thought, glad they were rare. Such smiles are hard to fake and he was glad he'd been present for this one. He spoke to Elise: "Freddie moved right out on this. We didn't expect him to move so fast. We were going to tell you about it first, but I guess it's better this way—makes it a nice surprise."

"A nice surprise indeed!" answered Elise. "I was just going to plan a trip to the cottage for July—Savannah gets as unbearable as New Orleans in July—and now I'll plan a trip to *my* cottage! Thank you guys so much! I've got to go. Joey is about to flush something down the toilet. Bye! I love you."

"Bye, honey." Lauren turned to William. "Know what, Will? I think we done good."

"I believe we did," he answered her with a hug. "Show me what you got, and then let's eat some gumbo and drink some bourbon."

Chapter Twelve

Keeping Time

Dorothea Delacroix sat on the pale green brocaded piano bench just in front of the bay window. Glenn had arranged chairs for Sarah, Freddie, and Marie, and he'd brought the Louis XVI loveseat in from the parlor for William and Lauren. The long lace panels covering the window gave a soft, dappled afternoon light at her back. She ran her small bare feet lightly over the brass pedals. William thought she looked so young and diminutive, like a child. A thick dark blonde braid moved gently across her narrow shoulders as she arched her back, stretched her arms out and flexed her fingers.

"Okay," she said, "I'm going to start a piece and let's see who guesses it first." She seemed perfectly at ease with an audience, William thought, in surprise, until he realized she'd played for audiences before, including auditions.

On the second note, Freddie spoke, "Clair de Lune!"

She laughed. "Right! Good for you, Uncle Freddie!"

It was lovely. No one moved while she played. An air of gentleness and delicacy made movement undesirable. It was restful, quiet, wistful and tender, and probably exactly what Debussy intended when he wrote the sounds of moonlight. When she finished the piece, everyone leaned back a little and sighed. No one spoke.

Then she said, "I'm going to play this piece for my father." And she played the largo movement from Dvorak's New World Symphony. Lauren's head fell to William's shoulder, her hand resting on his thigh. Marie left the room, her heaving shoulders an indication of impending sobs. Glenn leaned against the wall, arms folded and ankles crossed, looking down at the floor. Sarah sat in the chair next to him, hands clasped tightly together, swaying gently as she silently mouthed the spiritual lyrics: *Goin' home... goin' home, I'm a-goin' home...*

William looked to the ceiling above the bay window, his eyes traveling down the twelve feet of white lace behind Dorothea's head. He was a child sitting on the polished wood floor. These same curtains moved then, in the days before air-conditioning. On those gentle summer afternoons when the windows were opened to the garden, and the warm breeze wafted them gently into the room. His niece sat on the bench in shorts and tee-shirt, like a child, so astonishingly petite, her bare feet gliding expertly over the pedals, moving forward and back as she played. Her thin small arms embraced the keyboard of the massive instrument in unconscious mastery. Curling tendrils framed her face—like morning mist rising over the bayou; and like lacy filigree moss swaying in the breeze, the tall lace curtains framed her body as she moved, her small fingers telling an ancient tale.

William made a decision in that moment. This piano belonged to Dorothea, and among all the members of the family, only Dorothea loved this house. When she finished, there was silence. Then Freddie broke out, "Bravo!" as everyone clapped and smiled and congratulated her: "Dodie, that was wonderful!" Marie beamed. Dodie stood and made a small curtsy.

William thought it might be appropriate to consult Lauren, but he knew she'd agree: "Dodie, honey. Give that limited scholarship back to LSU." He walked over to the great carved mahogany pocket doors to the dining room, slid them back, and stood there. "This is a *big* dining room, plenty big for a bed-sitter, I think, but if you want more room, you can have it. I think the kitchen, music room, and dining room is enough, if you think so. Glenn can put a bathroom over there in the butler's pantry—it's already plumbed..." He didn't finish because Dodie was jumping and squealing so loud he couldn't. He glanced at Lauren, who was smiling and nodding at him.

Marie had her hands crossed over her ample bosom. "Oh, Will, oh Will..."

The idea was a hit. He continued, "You could go to Tulane or Loyola, without any financial accounting to some student aid office... And we—Lauren and I—have a dear friend in music at Loyola. He's in baroque, brass as I remember—trumpet—but he'd look after you like you were his own, I know." He glanced at Lauren; she was smiling.

Marie was ecstatic. "No strange city, no dormitory, no worrying about—about anything!" Dorothea finally stopped jumping to run to him and grab him around the waist. "I'd get to live here—*here*!"

"Yes, honey. Here, in Grandmother's house—if you want to.

And you'd have Glenn and Sarah to look after you."

Everybody meandered outside to the backyard. Glenn and Sarah remained inside, returning furniture to its proper place, setting the security system and locking up. Dodie and Marie sat in the backseat of the Camry. They would spend the night with William and Lauren and head back to Shreveport after early Sunday Mass. William and Lauren, their arms around each other's waists, walked with Freddie to his Lexus, which was blocking the Camry in the narrow driveway.

Freddie said, "I think you just did a good thing, Will Cauley, a right thing."

"Well, not yet, but eventually, I think we'll probably be naming a designee for the DuBois-Cauley house in our will."

*

Around eleven on Sunday morning, as they sat at the breakfast table with the Sunday *Times-Picayune* spread everywhere, Lauren announced that she needed a little nap. She, Marie, and Dodie had stayed up late drawing up plans for transforming the butler's pantry into a bathroom, decorating the bed-sitting room, and creating a study niche for Dodie's desk, and her computer—the house would have to be wired for technology now. The chatter had become too much for William, and he had gone to bed early. He left Dodie at the computer, poring over the music programs at Loyola and Tulane. When he went to bed, she'd pretty much decided on Loyola. He thought he should give Paul a call next week when Lauren returned to Statesboro.

"I'll never make it at the Maple Leaf this afternoon if I don't have a nap, Will."

"Are you packed?"

"Well, yes, pretty much. I don't know how much to pack because I don't know how long I'll be staying." She paused at the doorway.

He looked at her, knowing she wanted some hint about looking for a place to live. "Think four days, or a week, maybe? Would that be enough time?"

"Yeah," she said, turning away. He had to talk to Charlie first, so he wasn't ready to be more specific. That would come in time. *Time.* That imaginary thing we invented to give ourselves—what?

The illusion that we control things?

His sister and niece had risen at six-thirty to be able to go to the seven-thirty Mass at Immaculate Conception, planning to stop for breakfast on their way back home. They'd left a note for him on the counter: Goodbye from Marie with still more much-repeated thanks; Dodie added a long string of X's and O's. He felt good about having followed his spontaneous inspiration, something not planned, something that simply announced itself. He'd merely given it voice. It was right that the house should have life again, young life; someone in the family would live in the family home, someone who loved it. Yes, it was right. He could perceive a faint realization, not yet arrived. Rather like light behind a dark horizon—not dawn, but a promise that it would come.

*

The Maple Leaf was almost full already. William and Lauren found Charlie standing at the bar talking to a couple who were seated there. His arm hung around the neck of an attractive brunette; with his other hand, he lifted his bottle of beer as they came through the door and motioned toward the left, toward the adjoining tavern room and a small table he'd staked out just inside the wide doorway. The room held a low, small podium at one end, well lighted. Drums were already there at the back, and several chairs were placed, some with instruments standing next to them—a trombone standing on the floor, a guitar leaning against a chair, and a trumpet case with "Clyde Thomas" stamped in gold on its cover.

Charlie just had time to introduce his companion as Louise, a real estate broker, when the place filled immediately, standing room only in the adjoining bar. A young man in tee-shirt and jeans came to the microphone as the musicians took their places and started to wipe down instruments, adjust mouthpieces, and take their seats.

"Hello, everybody, and welcome to the Maple Leaf! I don't know how we got this lucky to get such a fine group here this afternoon, but let me introduce them to you…" He took each instrument and musician in turn, from back to front, drums first, then keyboard, guitar, trombone, clarinet, and last, just as an old black man with gray fringe around a shiny bald head, round shoulders, and thick glasses came out from the bar, "…and just back from his latest European tour, folks, welcome Clyde Thomas home to New Orleans!"

There was applause, cheers, and whistles, as the band got down to work immediately without waiting for quiet. The drummer put everything in motion, and the band started off with "I'm Confessin'."

By the time the band took a break after "Potato Head Blues," the bar was so crowded it became uncomfortable even to sit. William said they should either go outside so they could breathe or just leave. Outside, Lauren was dancing down the street toward their cars.

"I don't even know if there's such a thing as a jazz band without a trumpet," oozed Charlie's brunette.

"I'm very partial to the trombone myself," Charlie answered.

Lauren said, "You know, back in my distant youth, it seemed like girls always went for either the trumpet or the drums. Not the instrument, but the player, you know?"

"So which did you go for?" asked William.

She didn't pause. "Oh, the drums. Yes, definitely the drums. I mean, the trumpet sort of reaches out and grabs you, says 'you *will* pay attention' and you do! It's the shiny brass that splits the air and takes absolute charge of everybody in the room. But there's the drummer at the back or off to the side, keeping everybody together, keeping the rhythm going—just by keeping time. The drummer was always my man."

William turned to his wife and kissed her cheek.

*

The next morning he kissed her goodbye as she loaded the Subaru and got in the car to leave for Georgia, with promises to call when she got down the road, when she crossed state lines, and when she got there and checked back in at the Holiday Inn. "I think they believe I'm going to live there," she joked.

"No, Babe. We're going to live somewhere together—somewhere permanent."

"Permanent? What, not a rental?"

"Not unless that's what you want."

"Will, do you mean that?"

"I mean that."

She got back out of the car and hugged him. "I love you," she said.

"I know. I love you, too," he whispered into her hair.

As soon as she drove off, Will called Charlie. "Charlie, sell this place."

"Hey, it's sold. I was just waiting for your go-ahead."

"What do you mean it's sold? Who's buying it?"

"I am."

"*What?*"

"I need it. Where are we going to play poker? I got Louise to appraise it a few weeks ago when you guys started talking about moving."

"What did she say?"

"Market value, two seventy-five. And you're getting a real bargain because I won't even ask for inspection, none of that crap. I'll pay closing—and I won't even take a commission!" He laughed, clearly enjoying William's shock.

"I just don't know why you want a three-two on Prytania. This is a family neighborhood."

"Will, we don't categorize people like that in New Orleans. You know that. Fact is, this condo, nearly half a million as it is, only has one guest room, and it's usually occupied, one way or another. And sometimes I have people from out of town I'd like to put up, you know? And hotels are expensive! Besides, I don't want poker here, Freddie's wife won't let him have it there, and can you imagine poker at Hansi's place in the Quarter? No way. And the last and biggest reason—I can write it off. It's a good deal for me."

"Y'all are going to keep on playing poker here?" The idea was bizarre.

"Yeah, why not? If you come to town, you can join us."

"Oh, my God."

"Yeah, look, Will, I'm real happy about this and I bet Lauren would be, too. I'll get the paperwork together today and we can meet tonight at Patty's, okay?"

"Oh, my God."

"See you at five? I got a client at six."

"Yeah, okay." He was still in shock. He'd just sold the townhouse.

*

He went to pick up his car. One of the Bergeron employees drove it when he went to the Hertz place to drop off the Camry. He got in his new Volvo and started the engine. It felt so good. Quiet, just so quiet. The Bergeron employee showed him all sorts of electronic stuff he had to discover, programmed his phone for him. However Statesboro turned out, he would enjoy the drive there. But for now, he drove to the campus, stopped by campus police and picked up a visitor's parking permit. The clerk said, "Don't you want a permanent sticker, Dr. Cauley?"

"No, I'm not coming back."

He went to the office, unsurprised to see boxes behind the secretary's desk. "Well," he said, "does the dean want to see me?"

She said, "No, he doesn't. I think he doesn't see much point, Dr. Cauley. You really don't give a blank now, do you?" She seemed not to know whether to laugh or worry.

"Well, no, I guess I don't."

"But I think, I really do think, you ought to have some kind of farewell, Dr. Cauley."

He thought for a minute. "I'd like the history faculty, their families, and you, Charlotte, to come over for a barbecue before we leave."

"That would be lovely, Dr. Cauley. I'll let everybody know. When?"

"Not long, maybe in a week or so. When my wife gets back. She's in Statesboro now looking for a house for us."

He went into his office and closed the door. His academic robe swung gently on the back of the door as it closed. He went back out to the secretary: "Charlotte, can I have one of those smaller boxes?" He just didn't feel like attending graduation this year. Nothing personal; he just didn't feel like it. He took down the robe and regalia, folded it loosely and put it in the box, packed his hanging diplomas and his framed pictures, and a few personal items from his desk. He was done. He sat down at his desk and opened his laptop: "Chapter Two…" His phone rang.

"Hi, honey," Lauren chirped. "I'm heading into Mobile now. How are you? You pick up the car yet?"

"That's a little quick, Lauren. You've got all the time in the world, you know. And yes, I've got the car—got to learn how to operate all the electronic gadgets."

"That will be fun, and Will, I haven't broken seventy at any point."

"Okay. By the way, the townhouse is sold. Charlie bought it."

There was silence. Then: "*What?*"

"Yeah, that's exactly what I said. And so, my love, we need a place to live." He didn't want a long conversation now, here, at the office; he'd rather talk later after she arrived. "Listen, I've got to go. I'm meeting Charlie at five to get a check. I'll talk to you tonight."

She was hesitant to reply—shocked, he thought.

"Okay, Will." Her voice was uncertain. "Are you all right, honey?"

"I'm fine, Lauren. You've got a checkbook with you, don't you?"

"Yes."

"Go buy us a home. And I'm just fine. I love you. Talk to you tonight."

"Will, don't you even want to see it first?"

"No. Surprise me. Take pictures. You can give me all the details when you get back. I can't think of anybody whose judgment I trust more. Now, go for it, Babe. I want to try to get some work done now, okay?" He didn't want to talk now. Conversation now would just be more reassurances. Lauren could do this on her own. Whatever she bought, he'd hate Statesboro, Georgia, but not as much as he loved his wife. And Savannah wasn't far. He'd gone online and looked at the beautiful St. John the Baptist Cathedral there—no tall buildings to block the stained glass windows. Anyway, if his outline was accurate, *Charlemagne* would be at least five hundred pages when he finished the final draft.

*

He left the campus at lunch, went home and walked through every room of the house. It wasn't the house, no—the house was just a house. What was it? He got back in the car and drove to Immaculate Conception. He sat there in the semi-darkness, letting time pass in peace.

Five o'clock. Patty's was busy, but William managed to get one of the small tables along the wall. He was on his second drink by the time Charlie arrived. He came in, waved to the bartender and pointed to William and to himself, sat down and placed a check for twenty-five thousand dollars on the table, along with a form for William to sign.

"Earnest money. This says I've got forty-eight hours to change my mind. But I won't. You might, though."

"No, I won't." William signed the form without reading it, folded the check and put it in his pocket.

"You'll be back, Will Cauley. Even if you go through with this, I wouldn't be surprised if you tried to buy the house back. You can't leave this city."

Drinks arrived. This would be William's third. "Just shut up and drink, Charlie. I'm leaving New Orleans."

They were quiet for a moment. Charlie was watching William, as though he were waiting for him to tear up the check. Finally, he said, "Hell of a city. Do you remember Katrina, Will? They didn't show everything on the news—the bodies from the crypts getting flooded out—too much like a horror movie, I guess. They just showed live people getting rescued from rooftops. Stuff like that. What people want to see. Nobody wanted to see all the shooting and robbing, and they certainly didn't want to see the crypts broke open and dead bodies getting swept away by the flood. Scare people to death, that would have. But we came back, by God, we came back," he said, almost too loudly. "And you'll come back, too."

He paused, and then did something very unusual for Charlie: he became pensive, frowning. "Why do you suppose it didn't really scare us, Will? It did, but it didn't—I mean, not really, not like it should have. Katrina was terrifying, wasn't it? So why weren't we terrified?"

Will looked at him. It was a real question. And it was the one nobody asked. How ironic that it should be Charlie who asked it. He had to smile.

"Why weren't we scared? Well, yes, all that horror. But the thing is, you *knew*, all the time, you knew you'd just re-build, re-construct, duplicate and replicate, and have it all back again. All of it. And of course, that's what the media and the politicians and the celebrities—all the people who talk, and tell us in their talk, what we're all supposed to say. The thing is, though, all that talk was really true, just not true because of what it implied about us. Yes, we *would* build it all again, but the reason we would do that is not that we're so resilient, undefeatable, heroic, or any of that crap. No. We would build it all again because we don't know what else to do. It's all we know, the stuff we make—it's all we know."

Charlie looked puzzled, so William continued, "This city is full of charm, everything cultivated so much that even cultivation itself is cultivated. It delights us, and delighting ourselves is what we know better than anybody. We even go so far as to stain it, sleaze it over, and rough it up deliberately, just to add to it, just so we can add nonchalance to the charm.

"It's the *making* of that charm that so addicts us. The food, the houses, the music, Mardi Gras trinkets and toys—our self-made bonds and bondages are all the things we make to delight ourselves, to evoke lust or sentiment—it's just jazz, but we love it. So, when it's all destroyed, of course we're all right. Because we *know* we'll just make it all up again.

"But—put an ocean like the Pacific in front us, or mountains like the Rockies, maybe, with nothing of our own making in it, none of our art—and *then* we feel terror, so we stay away from that, stay home, surrounded by our stuff, and keep to ourselves."

Charlie looked at him as though he were a stranger.

"You know, it doesn't take courage to love, Charlie. That's easy. What terrifies us is being loved."

Charlie dismissed him with a look of bored tolerance. "I would say you're full of shit, Will, but I think you're just full of bourbon."

Will laughed. "Yes, I am. And I need to go home before I get any drunker. I want to be there when Lauren calls."

Dena Hunt's first novel, *Treason* (Sophia Institute Press), won the IPPY Gold Medal. Her second, *The Lion's Heart* (Full Quiver Press), won the Catholic Arts and Letters Achievement award. She is the book review editor of *St. Austin Review*. *Jazz & Other Stories* is her third book. She lives in Georgia.

Made in the USA
Columbia, SC
27 September 2021